Where Petals Fall

Melissa Foster

"With vivid prose and a tender heart, Melissa Foster has crafted a psychological and emotional mystery fueled by love in all its forms."

— *Jennie Shortridge, Author of Love Water Memory*

ISBN-13: 978-0-9910468-4-3
ISBN-10: 0991046846

Cover Design: Natasha Brown

WORLD LITERARY PRESS
PRINTED IN THE UNITED STATES OF AMERICA

For Mom

PRAISE FOR MELISSA FOSTER

"Contemporary romance at its hottest. Each Braden sibling left me craving the next. Sensual, sexy, and satisfying, the Braden series is a captivating blend of the dance between lust, love, and life."
—Bestselling author, Keri Nola, Psychotherapist (on The Bradens)

"[LOVERS AT HEART] Foster's tale of stubborn yet persistent love takes us on a heartbreaking and soul-searing journey."
—Reader's Favorite

"Smart, uplifting, and beautifully layered.
I couldn't put it down!"
—National bestselling author, Jane Porter (on Sisters in Love)

"Steamy love scenes, emotionally-charged drama, and a family-driven story, make this the perfect story for any romance reader."
—Midwest Book Review (on Sisters in Bloom)

"HAVE NO SHAME is a powerful testimony to love and the progressive, logical evolution of social consciousness, with an outcome that readers will find engrossing, unexpected, and ultimately eye-opening."
—Midwest Book Review

"TRACES OF KARA is psychological suspense at its best, weaving a tight-knit plot, unrelenting action, and tense moments that don't let up, and ending in a fiery, unpredictable revelation."

—Midwest Book Review

"[MEGAN'S WAY] A wonderful, warm, and thought-provoking story...a deep and moving book that speaks to men as well as women, and I urge you all to put it on your reading list."

—Mensa Bulletin

"[CHASING AMANDA] Secrets make this tale outstanding."

—Hagerstown Magazine

"COME BACK TO ME is a hauntingly beautiful love story set against the backdrop of betrayal in a broken world."

—Bestselling Author Sue Harrison

Chapter One

It was the warmth of Sarah's breath that woke Junie Olson from a sound sleep, a gentle, repetitive wisp flitting against her cheek. A knot tightened in her stomach. Even with her eyes closed, Junie could picture her daughter's cherubic cheeks, her golden ringlets, which couldn't be tamed by even the strongest brush, and her beautiful, albeit vacant, blue eyes. It was those eyes that kept Junie from lifting her lids and meeting her daughter's gaze. She missed her vibrant, effusive four-year-old. Five months of emotional regression interspersed with too many medical tests to count, and Junie still couldn't look at her daughter without feeling like she was watching her drown from a distant shore.

Junie could not resist the pull of her daughter's love. She opened her eyes and lifted her finger to her lips. The gesture was habit, left over from years of Sarah jumping onto the bed in fits of giggles and snuggling in between Junie and her husband, Brian. Had Junie not lifted her finger to her lips, she'd have solicited the same stoic response as Sarah was giving her now. The blank stare, lips parted, tiny fingers twisting the silver ring on her right ring finger. If only she'd speak, say something, anything. Junie would give her right hand to hear her daughter's sweet voice once again.

Junie felt her cheeks flush, ashamed for wishing her daughter to be different, to be normal again. There was no wishing away who Sarah was. In fact, there didn't seem to be any answers, either. Like most moms, Junie had dreamed of a fun-filled youth for her daughter, with too many mother-daughter moments to count. They'd lived that dream for almost four years, and now those dreams were replaced with worry. How could Sarah possibly fit in? Make friends? Could she be socially appropriate? Would she ever pull out of this regression? Sarah didn't have a diagnosis, and that alone had initially pierced Junie's heart. The new psychiatrist was waiting on Junie to complete yet another seven-page questionnaire. Hadn't they been through enough testing? They'd taken Sarah to seven specialists over the past five months—from infectious-disease doctors to internal-medicine experts. Why couldn't they figure this out? Why was Junie having issues completing that last request? She'd tried; she'd stared at the paperwork with a sinking heart, wondering if she truly wanted to know what was behind Sarah's regression—or if she was afraid to know it might be a forever issue.

Junie's eyes trailed down Sarah's nightgown, coming to rest on the telltale wet mark covering her lower half. *Please, God, help her. Help us.* Junie's pulse sped up. The clock glared red on the nightstand: 4:45 a.m. She had fifteen minutes to get the mess cleaned up and settle Sarah back into bed before Brian got up. He had a big court case this week, which meant late nights and early mornings. Junie glanced at her husband, sound asleep next to her, his right arm arced over his head, as if he were sunbathing. She longed to snuggle against him, feel his arm lazily wrap around her and pull her close. She ached for mornings past, when she'd curled against him in the private nook of his body, each breath measured, so as not to wake him and break the moment. It had been five months since he'd woken up in a sleepy haze, his eyes still closed, and sighed the sigh that came from deep within his soul and could mean only, *We are so lucky. I am so happy*. Sarah's regression had caused a fissure between them that swelled with the daily wave of Sarah's silence. It was as if Sarah's silence had been holding hands with their relationship, and as Sarah regressed, it dragged their relationship deeper into an abyss of angst, pitting one against the other. Junie mourned the loss of life without the underlying current of Sarah's regression between them.

Junie was tucking Sarah into her newly changed bed sheets when Brian appeared in the doorway. His thick dark hair stood up in unruly peaks. His wrinkled T-shirt hung loosely around his slim waist. Junie didn't let her eyes drop any further. She didn't know what to do with the sexual desire she felt for him despite the expanding gap between them. She missed their lovemaking, the way they'd sneak into the bedroom together for a passionate quickie while Sarah napped or watched television. Every pull of Sarah's withdrawal took with it a pulse of their passion until there was barely a feather of a beat left. Junie reached out and ran her fingers down Brian's arm, hoping to recapture a spark. That simple touch used to be enough to launch them into a moment of passion, troubles forgotten.

He flinched against her affections.

She pulled away, grimacing inside, fully aware of the extra five pounds she was carrying—and now certain that Brian was just as aware of them as she was.

She felt his angry stare boring into her. Junie bit her lower lip.

"It's fine," Junie whispered. "She just had a hard time sleeping."

Brian's eyes fell to the edge of the wet sheet sticking out of the hamper.

Junie gathered the sheets from the hamper where she'd tossed them and walked toward the laundry room, hoping Sarah would fall back to sleep.

Brian followed on her heels. "Junie, you can't keep babying her. She's doing this for attention."

Sarah's regression had become the elephant in the room. They'd moved from the outskirts of town to a subdivision just before Easter to lessen Brian's commute and to accommodate his later schedule. After he'd won Marco Arzo's case, Brian had become the go-to criminal defense attorney in Tysons Corner, Virginia. Marco Arzo had been accused of murdering three women. The evidence didn't add up, and Brian would have bet his own life on his client's innocence. Two weeks after Marco walked, an anonymous tip brought in the true killers: a husband-and-wife team of psychopaths. Brian was convinced that Sarah's bed-wetting, her silence, and her overall sullen demeanor was her way to get back at them for moving away from her friends at her old school, or for his own crazy schedule, which drew him away from home in the evenings, leaving little to no father-daughter time. It had been almost six months since the move, and he was having none of it. He wouldn't accept that guilt trip from a child. She'd have to learn to adjust, like the rest of them.

Junie threw the urine-soaked sheets into the washing machine and turned to face Brian, arms crossed, shoulders back. "Four-year olds are not that manipulative. There's something wrong." *Why can't you just adore her like you used to? Coddle her a little, accept this as a bump on Parenthood Road instead of thinking she's a spoiled, manipulative child*?

"We've gone through every damned test there is, Junie. Why can't you see it? She changed right after we moved. It's obvious."

Junie shook her head, thinking of the move and how it had changed things for all of them. She was no longer five minutes from Bliss, the bakery she had opened shortly after graduating from college. The new twenty-five-minute commute meant she had even less time to work while Sarah was at preschool. Thinking of Bliss brought her to Shane, her business partner and friend—just about her only friend. Taking care of Sarah and running the bakery left little time to cultivate friends in the new neighborhood. Not that Junie would have done so, at least not easily. She hadn't had many close female friends since grade school. She felt lucky that Brian never raised an eyebrow about her closest friend being both male and her business partner. With Brian's busy schedule, Junie spent more time with Shane than she did with Brian. A wave of gratitude ran through her, chased by her husband's angry stare. "Well, it's not obvious to me. The doctors—the tests—they must have missed something." She turned and closed the washing machine, then switched it on. "An allergy, something." Junie's next thought was that her daughter was acting just like those children you read about who were molested and immediately regressed. She didn't verbalize those thoughts. Sarah's therapist had already gone down that painful line of questioning.

"Whatever. I gotta go to work. I'll be—"

"Late, I know." Junie watched him stomp up the stairs. Her chest ached. She couldn't just stand there and watch her marriage fall apart. She adored Brian. They'd never fought before Sarah's issues began. Junie hurried up the stairs and into the bathroom, where Brian was in the shower. "I'm sorry. Maybe you're right. I'll try not to baby her."

Brian pulled the shower door open, water dripping down his face. "I just want her to get better. Maybe we should move back. The house hasn't sold yet."

Junie shook her head. "No. You might be right. Who knows? I'll try to be tougher and see if that works." *Is it me?* Junie wondered if Brian could be right, if she was too close to Sarah to see something as obvious as a power struggle. Was she just being stubborn, unwilling to believe her daughter was capable of something so manipulative? Something inside her told her that no, she wasn't, and that Brian was wrong, but she couldn't let her marriage crumble without at least giving his idea a shot. She resolved to take a stronger stance with Sarah and hoped that by doing so, she wouldn't be doing more harm than good.

Junie stuffed the grocery bags into the back of the minivan and pushed the lift gate closed. Rain spit from the sky, dampening her sweatshirt. September in Virginia could be fickle. The sky had become as gray as it had been sunny when she'd dropped Sarah at preschool just an hour earlier.

Sarah would be out of class in an hour and a half, giving her just enough time to put away the groceries and change the laundry over. She felt guilty for asking Shane to cover for her today at the bakery, but her family would starve if she didn't make time to get groceries. Brian's late nights and Sarah's added medical and therapy appointments left her little downtime for household errands. Her cell phone rang. Junie dug past the loose receipts that littered her purse and retrieved her phone. "Hi, Mom." She fumbled for her keys.

"Hi, sweetheart. I have to tell you something." Ruth's voice quivered.

Junie sifted through the keys for the right one and

lifted it toward the ignition. Picking up on the quivering of her mother's voice, she selfishly hoped whatever had caused it would be trivial and quick. "Okay."

"Are you sitting down? This is really, really bad. You need to be sitting down."

Junie froze, her hand hanging in midair. The hair on the back of her neck prickled. *Really bad.* "Mom? I'm sitting. What is it?"

"Sweetheart, Daddy…I found Daddy this morning, in the bathroom."

The keys dropped to the floor with a clank. Junie's hands trembled as she listened to her mother. *Lying on the bathroom floor, pants around his ankles. Heart attack.*

Chapter Two

Sarah stared at the television, oblivious to the sobs coming from her mother. How could she tell her daughter that her grandfather was dead? *Dead*. The thought crippled her. For the first time in five months, Junie was actually glad that Sarah was not the vivacious, curious child she'd once been. She'd never have been able to pretend that nothing was wrong. A wave of guilt passed through her. She lowered herself to the couch, burying her face in her hands.

She had to pack. Her legs wouldn't work. How could she pick out clothes and toiletries to bring to her mother's? Her father was dead. Her mother needed her. Sobs started from deep within her, engulfing her shoulders and turning her legs to rubber. She sank into the couch. *Mom*. At least Selma and Mary Margaret, her mother's closest friends and neighbors for the past thirty-plus years, would be there with her. She took comfort in the thought that her mother would not be alone until she got there. Junie had heard how the Getty

Girls (Ruth, Selma, and Mary Margaret) came to be more times than she could count. When Ruth had first moved into the Gettysburg, Pennsylvania, neighborhood, Selma and Mary Margaret, two friendly though nosy neighbors from across the street had rushed over, welcome baskets in hand. The women got along like three peas in a pod, and before the afternoon was over, the three of them had coined the name for their little trio, the Getty Girls: the Three Musketeers, female style. The Getty Girls had stepped in when Junie's mother had her hysterectomy, cooking and cleaning and doting on Ruth, and they'd brought Junie chocolate bars and conspiratorial winks when she'd had her first period at thirteen years old. She was thankful knowing that they'd be there for her mother now.

Junie took a few deep breaths, then walked from the living room into the kitchen, her mind wrapped in a bubble of grief. She grabbed her cell phone and lowered herself into a kitchen chair, then dialed Brian's office phone.

"Hi, Stacy. This is Junie." Her voice cracked as she held back her sobs. "Is Brian in?"

"No, Mrs. Olson. Do you want his voice mail?"

Junie left a message on Brian's voice mail. Then she called his cell phone and left a message there as well. "Brian, something's happened to my father. We have to go—" Tears took over her voice, and she ended the call.

Two hours later, with the minivan packed and ready to

go, she realized that she hadn't called Shane. As she sat down and tried to think about the bakery's commitments for the week, she remembered how it had been Brian who really brought about the circumstances under which Shane and Junie had met. Junie had just graduated from college with a degree in elementary education, intending to teach, like her father, but when she'd walked across that stage and accepted her diploma, she knew her heart wasn't in it. It would be too painful, she feared. Being surrounded by children every day would be a constant reminder of losing her childhood best friend, Ellen. Junie had gone back home to figure out what to do with her life. She'd been sitting on the back porch, wondering if she'd just wasted four years of her life, when Brian appeared across the white picket fence. He'd gone from being Ellen's older, lacrosse-playing, straight-A, promise-of-a-perfect-future brother to the heart-stopping next-door neighbor.

Brian had returned to his father's house begrudgingly, having no other options while he waited for his out-of-state job offer to come through after graduating from law school. He was anxious to leave Gettysburg—and his father's house—and start a new life. Not surprisingly, Ellen was a subject that brought downcast eyes and shortened conversation. Junie tucked away her desire to share how much she missed her friend, not wanting to cause Brian any more pain than he'd already endured. Within ten minutes, Brian had used his newly honed lawyering skills to get her to admit that she didn't even like the idea of teaching.

She'd just wanted to make her father proud. Twenty minutes later, Junie was planning her route to doing what she really loved—baking—and they were planning their first date.

Bliss was born a year and a half later, after Junie finished a culinary arts program, where she'd met Shane Donolly, a bundle of Irish energy and a wicked baker. With similar goals and complementary personalities, they'd opened Bliss, and Shane had become Junie's saving grace. She'd come to rely on him as a friend and as a business partner. Shane might have made the perfect life partner for Junie, if she'd had anything more than a platonic attraction to him. Shane had held down the fort when Sarah was born, and during the worst of Sarah's recent issues, he'd listened, consoled, supported, and allowed Junie to take time off to focus on her family and not worry about their clients. He was every bit of a solid friend Junie could rely on, and she was secretly thankful that she'd never been tempted to see what else might lie between them. She'd lost one best friend. She had no interest in losing another.

She called Shane to explain that she wouldn't be in for a few days, maybe even a week or two.

He gasped when she told him of her father's passing. She could hear him lower himself into a chair, the music in the front of the bakery playing lightly in the background. "Sweetie, I'm so sorry. Don't you worry about a thing. I've got the bakery covered. Do you need me to do anything else? Contact Sarah's school?"

Shane always thought of everything. “How could I have forgotten? Yes, please. Do you mind?” Junie ran through her days, wondering if there was anything else she might have missed. She lived in such a tight little bubble of family and work, there was nothing else that she could think of.

“Drive carefully, and I’m here if you need me—anytime, Junie, day or night. Call me and I’ll be here,” Shane offered.

“I know,” Junie said. She wondered how such a caring and generous man could be single in his midthirties. Someone was surely missing the boat. There was never a wonder in Junie’s mind about her own feelings for Shane. She’d been happy with Brian, for the most part, since the day they’d become a couple. She had no interest in blurring the lines of her own relationship with Shane from friend to love interest—but it didn’t stop her from wondering what the heck was wrong with the other women in his life. He’d shared just enough banter about his casual trysts for Junie to know he wasn’t gay. “There’s a special delivery coming—”

“Wednesday, I know. I got it covered.”

You always do.

“Go. Be with your mom. Hug Sarah and Ruth for me, and, Junie, you know I’ll close the bakery and come to the funeral if you’d like me to.”

Shane was closer to Junie than to his own siblings. He had moved away from his family the first chance he got. He always seemed to know just what to say, and it made her wonder what his family must be like. Shane had described them as cold, and Junie thought that he must be right. How could anyone not embrace Shane's nurturing side? "I know. It's okay. It's a Jewish funeral, so it'll all happen very fast. We have too much going on this week, and there's no time to call in backup." Junie wished, not for the first time, that they had another employee or two to hold down the fort, but other than the two very part-time kitchen helpers—who were great in the kitchen, not great with the customers—it was just her and Shane. Every time they spoke of hiring counter help, they decided that they had developed such a smoothly run business with just the two of them that another person would just be bored much of the time, though now she could really use Shane's shoulder to lean on at the funeral.

Communication with Shane was so easy. They said their goodbyes, and Junie tried Brian's cell phone again, very aware of the tightening of the muscles in her neck as she entered his phone number, a recent, familiar sensation that had accompanied many of their conversations.

Brian answered on the second ring. "Hey, honey."

Junie heard him shifting papers, and her chest tightened with irritation. Hadn't he gotten her messages? "Brian, focus for a second, please," she snapped.

"I am focusing. I'm in the middle of a big case."

Junie burst into tears.

"Junie? What is it?" He stopped shuffling the papers.

"My dad. Didn't you get my messages?" She wiped

her eyes, suddenly upset that Brian hadn't called her back.

"No, sorry. I was out. Things have been crazy. What's going on? Are you all right?"

"My dad, he...died. Mom found him—"

"What? What happened?"

"Heart attack." Junie sobbed. "We have to go. The van's packed. Can you be home soon? Please?"

Brian hesitated, and Junie's pulse raced.

"Brian?" she snapped. She could picture his lips tightening as he ran through his schedule in his mind. She hoped he'd drop everything and be with her, no matter what doing so might upend at his work. Brian's cases were what paid the bills. She'd heard it one too many times. Sometimes she rued his success and the time it stole from their family. She missed simple things, like family dinners and weekends spent lounging around rather than waiting for him to come back from the office, where he went each Saturday morning to catch up on work for a few hours.

"June, I'm so sorry. Look, I'm on a huge case. You and Sarah go, and I'll be there tomorrow, right after my court appearance."

"Seriously?" She paced, biting back her anger. She and Brian had grown up on the same block. Junie had been Brian's younger sister Ellen's best friend until the day she disappeared. Her disappearance had caused a rift in Brian's family, and now, even twenty-four years later, Brian always found a reason to arrive later or cut his visit short when they returned to their parents' houses in their old neighborhood. Brian was once treated like the quintessential golden boy by Peter, his father, and it was as if all that admiration had been washed away with Ellen's disappearance. Junie often wondered what Brian's relationship with his family would have been like if Ellen hadn't disappeared. She pushed that thought away and listened to Brian's heavy sigh through the receiver.

"I can be there tomorrow afternoon, but I can't leave now. I'm interviewing a key witness tomorrow. I'm sorry."

"Really?" She eyed Sarah in the other room. "You always do this. You did this when we visited them last time, at Easter."

"I can't control when I'm on a case." Brian hesitated.

And I can't control when my father dies.

"I've never hidden the fact that I don't like going back there, but I will go, so back off, please."

Junie bit her lower lip. How could she be so stupid? Ellen's disappearance had been such a taboo subject in their marriage that she had almost forgotten about the feelings that going back home must unearth for him. She'd bundled his discomfort into the rift the disappearance had caused and not the event itself. Of course he would relive Ellen's disappearance with every visit. After they hung up, she called Sarah's therapist and made an emergency appointment. There was no way she could handle telling Sarah this news on her own.

Chapter Three

It was ten p.m. when Junie finally pulled down her parents' dark and quiet Gettysburg, Pennsylvania, street. She'd been home many times in the years since she and Brian had moved away, but tonight the street looked different. Junie hadn't paid much attention to the trees that lined the road, now large enough that their branches arced over the street, creating an ominous darkness. The houses were mostly dark, a few kitchen lights left on. Modest, economical cars were parked in each driveway, lawns mowed, recycling bins lined up like the obedient little neighborhood it had always been. She glanced up the hill toward the house where Brian grew up, thinking of Ellen. If she concentrated hard enough, she could feel the grass on her skin, hear hers and Ellen's giggles as they rolled down the hill toward the fence that divided their yards. She'd always felt ripped off by her best friend's disappearance—

she'd been left with an emptiness she'd never been able to fill, though she knew it was a selfish thought.

The back of Brian's father's Mercedes peeked out from behind the bushes at the top of the driveway. She could hear her father, wondering aloud why anyone needed to spend that much on a car. Her heart sank with the reality of the situation that had brought her home. She pictured her mother inside, eyes puffy, staring at her father's favorite recliner. She wondered if she should have left right away and raced to her mother's side right after she'd called. Her throat tightened, and she took several deep breaths.

Her foot would not press down on the gas pedal. She inched down the road like a thief in the night, counting down the small, 1960s split-level houses to her final destination, silently wishing that when she arrived, she would find it had all been some sort of a bad dream.

Four more houses, three, two. Her mother's red front door swung open, and for a split second, Junie stopped breathing. *Dad?* Her father used to somehow know exactly when she'd arrive and meet them in the driveway. She pictured her father, Ralph, coming out of the front door with his eyes wide, as he'd done so many times before. The smile that would have been on his face, the way his eyes lit up when he saw her and then the way they grew even wider when he saw Sarah. She slowed to a stop and watched the Getty Girls file out of her mother's house, relief easing the tightness of her throat; Selma Smith, her short, stout, pear-shaped body bustling across the street, retreating to the safety of her wiry husband, Phil. Junie swallowed the guilt that crept up her spine as she wondered why it was her father that had died instead of Phil.

Mary Margaret Hatcher (whom everyone called "Old Margaret Thatcher" with an accompanying giggle) walked past the car, her chin tucked into her chest, her face pulled tight. Mary Margaret stopped and raised her eyes to meet Junie's. Sadness swelled in Junie's chest, stealing her ability to speak. She lifted her hand to cover her inoperable mouth. She was thankful when Mary Margaret continued walking, lifting her own hand in a hesitant, sad semblance of a wave as Junie's foot slipped from the brake pedal and she rolled slowly past. At six feet tall, Mary Margaret looked like the Statue of Liberty with her face set in that odd, uncomfortable place between *happy to see you* and *this freaking sucks*.

She pulled into her mother's driveway, feeling the absence of her best friend even more after seeing her mother's best friends, and silently prayed for Ellen's return. *Abducted*. The word sounded so vague, like aliens swept her away in the night. But it hadn't been night—it was broad daylight, and Junie believed that whoever "they" were, they'd taken Ellen because she was cute and outgoing, unafraid of the dark, and maybe even just because they'd wanted a little girl of their own. She still held on to that ridiculous childhood hope like a security blanket rather than accepting what statistics knew to be true: It had been too many years. Ellen was probably dead.

Junie thought about her mother's friends and the

way they'd held her shoulders and looked into her eyes after Ellen disappeared. "Don't you worry, Junie. God will bring her back." Truth be told, they were the reason Junie didn't rush out the door the second her mother called and instead had waited for Brian. She'd known her mother was being taken care of. Of course they'd be by her mother's side. It was Junie who felt alone, she realized, as she turned off the ignition. It was Junie who needed doting on. She needed her husband.

It had been a white-knuckle drive north as the sun set and the rain picked up. Junie silently cursed Brian for not driving with her. She'd waited for him to come home, to see if she could convince him to go with them, rather than waiting another day, but when it hit eight thirty, she knew she had to get on the road. She'd let his nine-thirty phone call go to voice mail. She understood his discomfort in coming home, but that didn't quell the ache in her stomach over his not being there when she needed him. She glanced at Sarah, still fast asleep in her car seat. Halfway to her mother's house, Junie had spun around to look at her as they drove past the train station, expecting to hear Sarah's gleeful shout, *Choo-choo!* Sarah had been staring straight ahead, her eyes at half-mast. Her missing excitement magnified Junie's aching heart. She was thankful when Sarah had fallen asleep—an acceptable, expected silence.

Junie opened the door against the wind and dragged her fatigued body from the car. Her fingers ached from clenching the steering wheel; her thighs felt as if they were tied in knots. The wind howled, whipping her blond hair across her cheeks like swift strikes with a thin blade. She hadn't slept through the night since Sarah had started regressing—if Sarah wasn't wetting the bed, she was crawling into their bed in the middle of the night, scared.

Rain pelted Junie's face. She shielded her eyes with her arm and looked up the hill at the old Victorian home where Brian had grown up and where his father, Peter Olson, still lived. The house had looked so beautiful when Junie was a little girl, surrounded by a white picket fence with crawling hydrangeas and a thick nest of trees hiding the gardens in the backyard like a secret. She and Ellen had spent hours playing hide-and-seek among the veritable maze of roses and flowering plants in the rear of the house. Over the course of several years, the wide, gray wooden planks of siding had lost their sheen; the picket fence had been left to age not so gracefully, chipping and peeling like an untended wound.

Junie closed her eyes against the void in her heart that Ellen's disappearance had left. It still bothered her that Ellen could walk to the library—something they'd done many times as kids—and then never be seen again. It was unfair that someone she loved so dearly could be silently swept away, and now, twenty-four years later, it had happened again. She knew what fate had ended her father's life, but it hurt no less, and no more, than when Ellen had disappeared without a trace.

Thunder echoed in the clouds. Junie startled and climbed back into the van, wrapping her shivering arms around her middle, taking one deep breath after another. For as long as she could remember, Junie had been unsettled by the combination of wind and thunder. Rain didn't bother her, but a strong heat storm had always sent her into a panic. She used to be embarrassed by her childish insecurity, but at thirty-one, Junie had no control over the trembling of her limbs or the racing of her heart. She'd accepted long ago that it was just part of who she was.

The door opened slowly, and Ruth moved under the arc of the porch light, a thick brown cardigan sweater wrapped tightly around her small frame. Junie's heart swelled. She'd never again see her father standing next to her mother, arm draped over Ruth's shoulder. Ruth would never again utter the words that Junie heard so often while growing up, *Oh, Ralph,* said with a hint of a smile. How the hell would she handle this and be strong for Ruth when she could barely be strong enough for herself?

Junie gritted her teeth against her anxiety and forced herself to step from the car into the wind again, scoop Sarah from her car seat, and run into the house.

Ruth shut the door behind them. Junie leaned in to her, Sarah heavy in her arms. She kissed Ruth's cheek, one arm wrapped around her, afraid to unwrap herself from their embrace.

"Mom," she whispered, at a loss for any meaningful words. *I'm sorry* was too weak. She had no experience with consoling someone other than her daughter, and a scraped knee was far from the passing of a husband.

Ruth nodded, pointing to the stairs. Junie saw the

tears in Ruth's eyes and allowed her the silence she needed. She carried Sarah upstairs and down the narrow, darkened hallway to her childhood bedroom. She laid Sarah on the twin bed, watching her stir. The sheet lifted and dropped ever so slightly with each breath. Junie could almost forget Sarah's issues while she slept. She looked peaceful, the pinch of life receded. She envisioned her waking up with a beaming smile and an energetic cadence in her high-pitched voice. Maybe seeing her grandmother would do that for her. *Grandpa.* Her hopes deflated.

Junie reached for the curtains, hesitating as light in Peter's den flicked on. Junie watched the familiar sole illumination, thinking of Brian and his strong work ethic, which mirrored his father's. Peter had groomed Brian from the moment he could read, and Brian had sucked up that one-on-one attention as any golden boy would. Junie still found it curious that Brian hadn't joined his father's law firm, choosing instead to move an hour and a half away. Brian had claimed that he'd wanted to make his mark on his own, out from under the wings of his father. Junie couldn't help but think there might be more—Ellen's disappearance had been such a thorn in their relationship, she could only imagine the rift it might have caused within his own family.

As she looked at the light that had been on every night of her childhood, her chest constricted; sharp edges of memories she couldn't reach hung before her like carrots to a horse.

Junie dropped her gaze to Sarah. Perspective was

everything. Sarah was there; she was healthy, reachable, safe. Emotionally regressed, Junie could handle. Couldn't she?

"How is she?"

Junie startled, lifting her eyes to her mother, who she knew was putting on a strong front for her benefit. At five foot two, Ruth had always seemed slight to Junie's five-foot-eight stature, but the pointedness of her shoulders and the way her jeans hung loose around her middle caught Junie's attention. Had she always been so thin? Was it magnified by her father's sudden death? Junie bit back the regret that squeezed her heart. Months had flown by while Junie was taking care of her family's daily lives—preschool, dinners, groceries, not to mention endless medical appointments, teacher conferences, and other time-consuming activities surrounding Sarah's regression. Junie had given little thought to anything outside of her inner circle of Brian and Sarah and the bakery. Even phone calls from her mother had been rushed. *What's up, Mom? I'm making dinner. Running out to get Sarah from school, Mom. Can I call you later?* While she was busy racing from one moment to the next, her father had been slowly dying. His arteries had been silently clogging, wearing down his heart like a ninja, undetected until it was too late. He and Ruth hadn't been gifted the grace of time to say goodbye. Junie bit her lower lip. She hadn't had time to come home again, had she? With Brian working late night after night, and Sarah's issues, life was too chaotic, wasn't it? *Excuses,* her father would have said. *Life doesn't choose our actions; it only presents opportunities.*

Guilt surrounded Junie like a cape. She ached to see her father's serious blue eyes, his short-cropped haircut, which Ruth had deemed his *schoolboy* cut, just one more time. Tears welled in Junie's eyes.

Ruth wrapped her arms around Junie. "You okay?"

Junie nodded. Strong, practical Ruth Nailon. It was just like her mother, Junie thought, to take care of Junie instead of allowing herself to be the one in need. *Why can't I be that strong for Sarah?*

"I saw Selma and Mary Margaret leaving," Junie said, trying not to talk directly about her father's death. It hurt too damn much. It had been Selma and Mary Margaret who'd coordinated the candlelit prayer vigils after Ellen's disappearance. Junie remembered Selma and Mary Margaret sitting at Ruth's kitchen table, talking in hushed tones, consoling each other, and praying for Ellen's return. Selma had spied Junie peeking into the kitchen, and she'd knelt down, held Junie's shoulders, and looked into her eyes: "Don't you worry, Junie. God will bring her back." Junie wished God would bring both Ellen and her father back, but she knew that real life did not work that way.

Ruth pulled back; her trembling hand trailed down Junie's arm to her fingertips. "They've been with me since...the whole day." Ruth squeezed Junie's hand, and Junie could tell she wasn't ready to talk, either. "It's late. Get some sleep and we'll talk in the morning."

Chapter Four

Junie pulled the sheets from Sarah's bed, closing her eyes for a second, wishing her daughter would regain her footing, that whatever was pulling Sarah under would somehow just unhinge and float away, taking the bed-wetting and silence with it into the air like a hot air balloon gone AWOL.

"She's still having trouble?" Ruth asked.

Junie flushed, tucking the clean sheets onto the bed. "Sometimes, not as often," she lied, feeling both embarrassed and protective. Sun streamed in through the window, warming the morning chill, and yet everything felt wrong. The absence of her father's heavy footsteps as he made his way downstairs, careful not to wake Sarah, and the loud *click* of the front door as he'd leave to retrieve the newspaper from the porch. Junie's heart constricted within the walls of her chest.

"Where is she?"

Junie nodded out the window to where Sarah sat beside the sandbox that Ralph, Junie's father, had built for her. She swallowed the plum-sized lump that was lodged in her throat, picked up the urine-soaked sheets, and went down to the laundry room, Ruth at her heels.

"Have they figured anything out?" she asked.

Junie hated talking about Sarah's issues. Talking about them seemed to somehow inflate them. If she didn't talk about her daughter's regression, she could pretend it didn't exist for a few minutes.

"No." She let out an exasperated sigh. Junie hadn't slept a wink. She'd vacillated between wanting to call Brian and talk about her feelings now that she was back home and her father was gone and wanting to curl up in a ball and sob with sadness for her father's death. She'd called Brian when she arrived the evening before, and although he paid complete attention to every word she'd said, she knew he was focused on his case and working as fast as he could so he could come join them. She wouldn't pester him again with her neediness.

She turned on the washer, threw the sheets and detergent in, feeling her mother's presence behind her. She drew in a breath and closed her eyes. *Don't break down. Be strong for* her *this time.* Junie kept her eyes trained on the stairs as they headed to the kitchen, afraid she'd break down in tears if she looked at her mother.

"Are you okay, Mom? Did you…have any inkling that Daddy was sick?" She entered the kitchen and peered outside at Sarah, who was still beside the sandbox, staring up the hill at the Olsons' house, a small stick in her right hand. Junie drew her eyebrows together. Shouldn't she be playing, moving, doing something? Anything?

"I'm as okay as is to be expected, I suppose." Ruth's eyes filled with tears. "We had no idea about his health. He had a physical just a few months ago…" Her voice trailed off, swallowed by tears. Ruth poured a cup of tea and sat down at the small kitchen table. She smoothed the light red tablecloth, wiped her eyes, then set her hands awkwardly in her lap. "It's like…it's like I'm a little lost. I don't know what to do with myself."

Junie sat next to her. This she could relate to. She didn't know what to do with herself around Sarah—or lately, around Brian, either. She covered her mother's hand with her own. "I'm so sorry, Mom. You should be a little lost. You only just lost Daddy." Saying "Daddy" brought a sob. Junie coughed, trying to cover the sound. She took a deep breath before asking what she knew she had to. "Mom, Daddy's…funeral? Is there anything we should do?" Junie remembered Ellen's memorial service. The finality of it came rushing back to her.

Ruth stared down at her lap and shook her head. "We did all that planning years ago." She sighed. "Do you remember when we did it? I thought it was so stupid, so morbid. Who plans their own funerals? But Daddy insisted. He said he didn't want to make you deal with anything more than losing one of us."

Junie pressed her lips into a tight line in an effort to hold back her tears. "I remember." Junie had argued with him at the time, worried that planning a funeral would somehow make their deaths come sooner. Her stomach twisted in knots. She wanted to turn around and find her father behind her, his hand on her shoulder. She wanted to hear his quiet, even voice say, *Good morning, pumpkin.*

"The funeral will be tomorrow at nine," Ruth said. "Selma and Mary Margaret took care of whatever your father hadn't."

"Thank goodness for the Getty Girls." Junie looked down at the table, then fidgeted with her hands in her lap. Not for the first time, Junie felt a pang of jealousy, having spent her high school and college years longing for such close friendships. She'd tried to connect with other women, tried to fill the gap that Ellen had left behind. As young girls, their connections were about silly things like agreeing on whose house they'd sleep at on Friday night and if brownies were better than cupcakes. Ellen liked brownies. Junie liked cupcakes. Frosting mattered. Junie longed for an adult confidante that didn't come with a familial tie, someone who would console when need be, but just as readily give her a good what for if she deserved it. She could not burden her mother with her marital troubles, but she could burden a girlfriend. Wasn't that what they were for? Just when Junie had given up on finding a replacement for Ellen, Brian came into her life. Brian's absence felt as blatant as a missing thumb. Junie transferred her anger to her father's upcoming funeral. "I hate the Jewish rules of death."

"Junie," her mother chided her.

"It just seems so rushed. No wonder Daddy took care of it all." She looked away, then laid her hand atop her mother's. "I'm sorry," she whispered. "I guess we should leave around eight tomorrow morning to get to the funeral home. Brian should be here later tonight." She turned away as a tear slipped down her cheek.

Ruth's chin quivered. She nodded. "It's okay to cry, Junie."

Junie was seven years old again, sitting under the oak tree in the backyard. Her mother came and sat beside her, taking her hand just as she did now and telling her it was okay to cry. Ellen had been missing for two days, and Junie had been waiting for her to reappear. She was sure she would. The adults were wrong; she just knew it. Ellen hadn't been kidnapped by a stranger. During those first two days, Junie's seven-year-old mind believed that Ellen was just hiding somewhere, playing a stupid game. She believed what the Getty Girls had said, that God would bring her back.

"Daddy loved you." Her mother's voice brought her mind back to the present.

Junie nodded. "He loved you, too." Their eyes met, bonded by a sadness that was bigger than them.

"Tell me something happy," Ruth said, wiping her eyes.

"Happy?" What could possibly be happy? Junie drew her eyebrows together, desperately running through her thoughts, grasping for something happy. She came up empty, offering a shrug instead.

"How's Sarah's therapy going? Do you like the new therapist?" Ruth ran her finger along the rim of her cup.

"Yeah." Junie's voice went soft. "She's...different. She's not clinical, like the last one. I like her." Junie had been in such a rush the last few weeks that until then, she hadn't taken the time to think about Theresa, Sarah's therapist. Yes, she liked her very much. Theresa was close to Junie's age and had an easy style and openness about her that drew Junie in. She hadn't pressed Junie to take care of the initial questionnaire that the previous therapist seemed to believe held all of the answers, and Junie suspected it was because Theresa thought she could gain whatever insight into Sarah's issues through her dealing with Sarah and the other medical reports. Maybe she thought the questionnaire was as pointless as Junie did.

"You're always so busy."

Junie knew her mother was trying to keep her mind off of the reality of her father's death, which pressed in on them from every angle of the room. He stared down from the photograph on the small decorative shelf behind Ruth, and even the *Science Illustrated* magazines that lay in a stack on the table were like needles that poked them with each glance.

"Why don't I put these away?" Junie stood to gather the magazines.

"No, please. I like them there."

Junie sat back down. "You're sure? I can put them in the other room, so you don't have to see them."

"I want to see them," she said.

Worry about Sarah and the growing issues with Brian pecked at Junie. "Mom?" She wanted to ask her advice. She looked into Ruth's shadowed eyes, then let her eyes travel down her fragile frame, diminished in the too-large long-sleeve polo shirt she wore, as if losing her husband had meant the withering away of a piece of her strength.

The doorbell rang.

"Never mind," Junie said. "I'll get that."

A young deliveryman stood holding a bouquet of red roses. "Ruth Nailon?" he said with a practiced grin, thrusting the flowers forward.

Junie took a step backward. The hair on the back of her neck prickled. "No. Just leave them on that table, thank you." She pointed to a small café table on the porch.

"Are you sure? They need to be watered."

"Yes, thank you," Junie snipped. Her heartbeat sped up.

"Oh for goodness' sake, Junie." Ruth pushed Junie aside and took the flowers from the baffled young man's hands. "Thank you." She closed the door and followed Junie into the kitchen. "What is it with you and roses?"

Goose bumps climbed up Junie's arms. She tried to rub them away—or maybe she was hiding them from her mother; she couldn't be sure. Ever since Ellen's disappearance Junie'd had an aversion to roses, all colors and types. The very sight of roses made her heart race and sweat form on her brow. Junie's theory was that the rose-induced panic was caused by stolen moments of hiding in the gardens with Ellen. That was their thing, and maybe when Ellen went away, their thing was just too painful for Junie to enjoy. That was the best explanation Junie could come up with, anyway.

Ruth efficiently filled a vase, clipped the ends of the stems, and arranged the red roses in a wide and beautiful fashion. She set them on the kitchen table. "There. That ought to brighten things up a bit."

Junie shot her a stern look and wondered who had sent them. Selma and Mary Margaret knew about the effect roses had on her.

"Really?" Ruth lifted her eyes. "What do you suggest? That I throw them out?"

"That might be a start." Junie opened the side door and walked outside, her mother's voice trailing behind her.

"The rabbi sent them. They're flowers, not demons."

Junie crouched by the sandbox, a green plastic ball in her hands. "Hey, sweetie. Whatcha doin'?"

Sarah dropped her eyes to the damp sand where she'd used the end of the stick to draw a square with a triangle on top—a four-year-old's rendition of a house.

Junie looked up the hill. "Is that Papa Peter's house?"

Sarah didn't respond.

"Grandma's house?"

Sarah pressed her lips together.

Junie smiled. "Oh! Is that our house?"

Sarah's eyes bloomed. She nodded, pushing herself to her feet and walking toward the front yard.

"Whoa, honey." Junie raced after her. "We're not

going home." Junie reached for her arm.

Sarah dashed through the side yard, her little body like a dart in the sun, heading toward the van. Curls bounced against her shoulders and her hands splayed out to her sides as she ran, as if she might grab anything she passed.

Junie ran after her. "Sarah, wait!" She scooped her up into her arms from behind. Sarah's face was a pinched mess of anger. She cried, wriggling her way out of Junie's arms, then banged on the side of the van with her little fist.

What the hell? When Junie had told Sarah about her grandfather's death, she had reacted with little more than silent tears. Had she finally understood what had happened? Junie knelt beside her.

"Honey, I know you're sad about Grandpa." She touched Sarah's slim back. "He's with God now, but he's still here." She laid her hand on Sarah's chest, feeling Sarah's heartbeat pounding against her thin cotton shirt. "Come here." Junie pulled Sarah close, holding her struggling body until she relented, sobbing into her mother's shoulder.

When she finally calmed down, extracting herself from her mother's grasp, Sarah clung to the door handle of the van, refusing to move.

"Come on, Sarah. Let's play ball." Junie tried to entice her toward the backyard. "Wanna get a cookie?" *Just get out of your own head, maybe?* Junie never knew how to get through to the new, troubled Sarah. She had become so introverted that even enticing her with the usual games or goodies sometimes weren't enough to reach her, but Junie didn't know what else to do, so she did the best she could. She reminded herself not to get angry and chastise Sarah. Whatever had caused her to regress was obviously beyond her control, despite what Brian might think.

Sarah hung on the door handle, staring at Junie with a blank expression.

"Okay, you hang there. I'm going to play ball." Junie turned and walked toward the backyard.

It was a standoff, one that had become all too familiar. The will of a four-year-old was enough to break even the strongest of motherly intentions. Junie thought of Brian's comment—*She's doing this for attention*—and remembered her pledge to take a stronger stance with regard to Sarah. It went against every parental vein in her body, but she did not turn back and coddle Sarah and didn't beg Sarah to join her. Junie sat on the back porch and waited. Time crawled by. Every few minutes Junie peered around the side of the house, only to see Sarah standing next to the van, the fingers of her left hand wrapped like a vice around the door handle.

The quiet nearly made Junie unravel. Everything reminded her of her father. Junie had once refused to look at a particular dead bug he'd found, and she'd been just as adamant as Sarah was now. Her father had tried to coax her gently toward him. He'd used science, not bribery of goodies. He'd tried to lure her in with explanations of "neat presentations."

Junie looked quickly at her father's toolshed, then

to the sparse flower garden against the fence that she'd help him define with rocks from the woods. Junie heard a low moan, then realized it was coming from her. She couldn't believe he was gone. Junie looked toward the sky, knowing her father didn't believe in any type of spiritual contact after a person died, and she wished he did.

"I miss you, Daddy," she whispered to the clouds. After forty-five painful minutes, Junie went to the front yard and decided to take a different tack with Sarah. She threw a green plastic ball up into the air, catching it and laughing, drawing Sarah's attention.

"Wanna play?"

Sarah shook her head.

Junie shrugged, continuing to toss the ball.

Sarah watched intently, angry eyes shifting from where Junie stood to Peter's house in the distance behind her.

Junie turned around, expecting to see Peter—he wasn't there. She walked toward Sarah. Sarah clasped the handle tighter. Junie walked past her to the side yard, where Sarah could focus on only her.

Eventually Sarah slunk toward her, spreading her fingers out in front of her. Junie tossed the ball. Sarah caught it against her stomach, then threw it back. "Nice throw!" Junie tossed the ball back again, higher than she'd meant to. She inhaled deeply, soaking up the fresh smell of the damp earth.

Sarah reached high above her head to catch the green plastic ball. Her ring caught the sun, flashing a brief burst of white toward the sky. In that instant, it was the face of Junie's childhood friend Ellen that Junie saw, not Sarah. Ellen's hands reached up toward the sky, her silver ring catching the sun—only Ellen wasn't smiling, like Sarah was. Ellen's lips were contorted into a wide *O*, tears of terror streaming down her cheeks. At that moment, twenty-four years after Ellen's disappearance, Ellen's screams echoed in Junie's head, screams Junie could not remember ever hearing when Ellen was alive.

Sarah tugged at Junie's arm.

Junie was paralyzed; sharp pangs surged through her limbs, as if she'd stepped on shards of glass from a shattered vase that appeared years after the vase had been dropped. Her whole body tingled with anxiety. Why was she suddenly seeing Ellen, and why had Ellen looked so terrified? Even worse, why had Ellen's image replaced her own daughter's? Junie's heart thumped against her rib cage. She fought to catch her breath without alerting Sarah to her trouble. The image left her with a sinking, hollow feeling and a gentle tug at the back of her confused mind.

Sarah stood before her, blond curls blowing in the gentle breeze.

A chill ran down Junie's back. What was happening to her? She took a few deep breaths, then crouched, putting her hands on Sarah's bony shoulders and stared into eyes so blue they rivaled the sky. Junie looked for a hint of Ellen, something that might have spurred the image, but she came away with nothing to root the mistake into reality. Ellen had dark hair and olive skin, while Sarah was fair. Ellen had been as thick as Sarah was slight. *I must be overtired,* Junie thought. Ever since Brian had taken on his latest court case, he'd been working late into the evenings, and Junie had waited up for him each night, sometimes into the early hours of the morning. Even with the way their relationship had become fractured and strained, Junie still felt the need to wait up. More than that, she still had the *desire* to wait up, to have those few moments of adult time with Brian, even if they were now filled with tension. *Not anymore,* she thought. Tonight she'd go to sleep when Sarah did.

Sarah stood with the ball in her hands, staring at the ground, her eyes sad once again.

"Sorry, sugar," Junie managed, brushing Sarah's bangs off of her forehead. "Senior moment." She took Sarah's hand and they walked toward the kitchen door.

Sarah crinkled her nose, a facial expression Junie had come to interpret to mean that she didn't understand something.

"It just means Mama needs some water."

Junie thought back to the afternoon Ellen had disappeared. Junie was eating a chocolate ice cream cone, sitting on a two-foot-tall brick wall that surrounded a garden of purple and white pansies and the greenest ivy she'd ever seen. In the center of the garden was a beautiful maple tree, a tree that her father used to say had grown from sugar seeds. Junie remembered the day because it was a Tuesday, and her father came home from work early every Tuesday—or as her father called it, Treatday. Their ritual was to "sneak" out for ice cream each week, just the two of them.

She remembered that particular day because her father was late, and after waiting for what seemed like forever on the front porch, her mother told her to get in the car, and she took Junie for her ice cream. Her mother had been short-tempered, Junie remembered, because that was as rare of an occurrence as her father not showing up to take her out. It was the only Tuesday afternoon he'd ever missed. Junie was just seven years old, and up until that afternoon, the worst day she'd ever experienced had consisted of being punished for using permanent marker on their kitchen table—she hadn't known the ink would bleed through the paper. She remembered the day Ellen disappeared because she and Ellen had had a skipping race to school that morning. Ellen had won, and Junie said, "I'll beat you tomorrow." The next day came, and Ellen was gone.

Policemen had come to their door and asked her a lot of questions about Ellen's friends at school and if she knew about any adults or children that might not like Ellen. Junie didn't know anyone who didn't like Ellen. They asked her if she knew why Ellen would want to run away, and Junie remembered thinking, *She didn't want to run away.*

Junie didn't go to school on Wednesday. Her mother kept her home. She kept Junie close, so close that Junie felt smothered. She couldn't go to the bathroom without her mother jumping up to follow her.

Later that afternoon, her mother explained to her that the police thought someone had taken Ellen and that they didn't know when, or if, she would return. She said that Junie would be told when Ellen came back, and until then, it wouldn't be a good idea to visit Ellen's house. The next morning, Junie's new routine was born. Her mother took her to school and picked her up after school. Junie spent much of her time indoors, staring out the window at Ellen's house, waiting for her to magically appear.

She had watched as Peter meticulously planted more roses in their already overflowing garden. Roses were Ellen's favorite flower. When she was younger, Junie liked roses. She likened them to the fun she and Ellen had enjoyed around the gardens. That changed after Ellen's disappearance. Junie abhorred them. She watched Brian skulk around the yard, punching himself in the leg, grabbing the sides of his head like an injured animal that couldn't pull away from the fractured limb. Six months later she watched Susan Olson carry suitcases out to her car. She never came back. Eventually they all fell into the pattern of their new lives—lives without Ellen.

Junie pulled her mind back to the present as they climbed the back porch steps. It seemed she was tucking away a lot of emotions lately, and she wondered if an ache could hurt so badly that it could make one's own mind play tricks on them.

Chapter Five

The house was quiet. Junie filled a glass of water for Sarah and one for herself. Sarah waited for Junie to pick up her glass and drink before she moved to do the same. Sarah waited to set her glass down until her mother had done so first. Sarah's idiosyncrasies had appeared slowly over time, until one day they defined who she was. Junie had come to expect these aping actions, while Brian had fought them. *Brian*. Junie withdrew her cell phone from her pocket and dialed his number.

"Junie, I'm heading into a meeting. I'll call you later. Is everything okay?"

Junie bit her lip, then sighed. She fought to keep her voice calm. "Yeah, I just wanted to talk to you about something."

"Can it wait, just till this afternoon?"

Sure. I'll just freak out all day over seeing my dead

friend—your dead sister. "Yeah, sure. Will you still make it tonight?"

"Yes, of course. Leaving right after this. Call you later."

For a brief moment, Junie pictured a beautiful stranger waiting for him, beckoning him. Her hand dropped to her slightly thickened waist, where over the last five months, five unwanted pounds had settled. She furrowed her brow, wondering where such a ludicrous thought came from.

Junie found Ruth sitting on the chair in the living room that Junie's father had deemed "Mom's reading chair." Junie remembered finding her mother in that chair, paperback in hand, each day when she'd arrived home after school, and she'd end the night on the same cozy perch. The dark blue velour was worn and frayed, but Ruth would have no part of replacing the material. Next to her sat her father's empty recliner.

"Can I get you something, Mom?" Junie asked, bypassing her father's chair and lowering herself onto the couch. Her insides quivered. She had to talk to someone about Ellen, and it obviously wasn't going to be Brian.

Ruth lifted her hazel eyes toward her daughter, and there was no mistaking the emotion behind them—lost, as if her father's death had left her mother in a foreign state with no map to find her way. Ruth was strong, capable, someone who took troubled times and whipped them into learning experiences. Junie was not adept at how to handle this side of her mother, which she'd never experienced before. She tucked away her need to talk about Ellen and tried to figure out how to help her mother.

"Mary Margaret and Selma are coming over in a bit. I'm all right. How's Sarah?" Ruth asked.

"Fine. Watching television." Junie looked down, silently scolding herself for not intuitively knowing what to say to help her mother. It was moments like these that made Junie wonder if what Sarah was experiencing was somehow caused by her lack of mothering skills. She'd always felt like she lacked a certain strength that seemed to be present in all mothers, something that allowed them to keep their chin up even in difficult times. Lately Junie had felt her chin leaning on her chest as she floundered to keep afloat. There was only one thing she could do, and that was to ask for help about how to help. *I am so lame.*

"Mom, what can I do? How can I help? I mean...I know that nothing I say will bring Daddy back and nothing I do will make it okay, but I want to help." A lump grew in her throat. She swallowed it down, hoping the tears it incited would remain at bay.

Ruth sat up straighter, placing her hands on the arms of her chair. She looked at Junie for a minute longer than was comfortable.

"Junie"—she placed her hand over Junie's—"we'll get through this." She took a deep breath, then continued. "I'm not sure I'll ever be the same, but we will get through this. Right now I feel like my left arm was cut off and my right one doesn't work quite right, but Mary Margaret assures me that each day will get a little easier."

Junie wiped a warm tear from her cheek.

"It's been seventeen years since she lost Hal, and she's doing okay, right?"

Junie nodded, not knowing the answer. *Seventeen years*. She couldn't think that far down the road. She was just trying to get her arms around a few days without her father. Junie was still dealing with his death as if he were on a mini vacation and would return home at any minute.

"Now." Ruth patted Junie's hand. "We need to focus on that little girl of yours and get her back to her healthy, normal little self."

Junie wanted to ask her mother how the hell she could go from a place of devastation to a place of wanting to help her granddaughter get better within the space of a breath. She wanted to ask her why she was seeing Ellen's face and wanted to crawl into her lap and curl up so the issues with Brian and Sarah didn't seem so overwhelming. She wanted to be completely and utterly selfish, kick her feet and throw herself down on the couch crying because she knew she'd never see her father's face again; she'd never hear him spout out bits of unsought advice that were always just what she needed to hear. Instead, she whispered, "Okay."

Chapter Six

They stood in the bathroom, just two feet from each other, and yet Junie felt miles apart from Brian. The bathroom seemed to be the place they spent most of their time together lately, stolen moments to catch up on their daily plans. Who knew a marriage could be maintained in ten-minute intervals of personal hygiene and sharing of one's day? *Maintained*? Junie wondered. She wasn't sure she was capable of maintaining anything at the moment. Junie watched Brian digest what she'd told him. The image of Ellen had been like a noose, tightening as the day progressed. She needed to tell someone about seeing her, and she couldn't burden her mother with the weight of it. She'd been short-tempered with Sarah, and she wasn't anywhere near the strong shoulder her mother needed. Junie hoped that by talking about what she'd seen, she could dismiss it and deal with her father's death, which she had been pushing aside—another too painful reality boring into her. Brian had barely made it through the door and upstairs at ten after midnight before Junie had unloaded on him.

Brian's jaw hung open, fatigue drawing his eyelids down. "Really, Junie? After I worked all day and drove two hours in bumper-to-bumper traffic, you bring up Ellen?" He looked away, disgusted. "You know it's hard for me to be here. Are you *trying* to make it worse?"

"No, but it was really scary." Junie put the toothpaste cap back on the tube. "Who am I supposed to tell? Mom?"

Brian didn't answer.

"Why would I suddenly see Ellen? I can't ever remember seeing Ellen that scared over anything." She pulled her shoulder-length blond hair back into a ponytail, secured it with an elastic band, and brushed her teeth.

"Things don't just appear out of nowhere. Were you dreaming?"

"No. I was fully awake."

"So you were upset?"

"No. Maybe," Junie answered.

"Overtired?" Brian pushed.

"Maybe." Junie shrugged, wishing he'd stop throwing questions at her.

"Junie, there're a million reasons for this. There's no evidence—"

"Evidence? Stop cross-examining me. I need to have a conversation with you, not be interrogated by you."

There had been a time when Brian's clear-cut route to problem solving had been reassuring; now it had become a defense mechanism for him and hurtful for her.

Brian loosened his tie and sat on the edge of the bathtub. He pulled off his black leather loafers. "Being back here, it brings it all up again." He stood up and removed his trousers and shirt. "The whole thing just has you tied in knots."

"But that's just it. I've been back here a million times. Never once in all these years have I ever had something like that happen." She washed out her toothbrush, tied her robe, and tried to ignore her husband's muscular arms and chest. She dropped her eyes, settling on his carefully placed shoes on the floor. She let out a sigh. Would she ever feel at par with her gorgeous husband? She doubted it. If she didn't now, she never would.

Brian wrapped his arms around her, kissing the top of her head. Her insecurity instantly diminished. "With all that's going on, it's a wonder you have any sanity left. I mean, she was my sister, and being here...Well, you know how I feel about being back here." He pulled her close, then disengaged and walked into the bedroom.

Junie followed. She turned off the bedroom light and climbed into bed next to him, feeling the warmth of his leg against hers. Her instinct was to pull away from him, annoyed by their exchange, his dismissal of her, but she clung to the hope that they would one day emerge victorious from this miserable place in their relationship. "I know. I didn't mean to minimize what you must be going through." She laid her head on his shoulder.

Brian turned away. "I'm not going through anything. Just tired, that's all. This case is busting my balls."

Junie rolled her eyes. The teenage lacrosse lingo had never left him. He could dress up in a suit, play Mr. Attorney with the best of them, but at the end of the day, he was still just a guy. "Sarah will be glad to see you in the morning."

Brian didn't answer.

"She missed you today."

"Really? Did she say that?" he asked in a terse tone.

Junie closed her eyes against her mounting frustration. Sarah's inability to verbalize her feelings had become a barrier between them. She missed the days when they each said exactly what they felt with no thought or worry of how it might be interpreted. How far down would their marriage spiral with Sarah's regression? "No, but I know."

"Mm-hm. Did you fill out that questionnaire yet?" he asked.

The damned questionnaire. It had been only a few weeks since the doctors had said they thought Sarah had deep-rooted emotional issues. Junie was sure there was a medical explanation and that Sarah's issues were more than simply emotional—but she was scared shitless to fill out the forms, just in case. The psychiatrist had given Junie a seven-page questionnaire, which she'd shoved into her glove compartment and ignored ever since. If the psychiatrist wasn't putting much stock into it, why was Brian? Junie knew why. He was a lawyer, and lawyers liked strong cases. Documents led to cases. Sarah was *not* a case.

Brian turned to face her. "Junie, fill out the damned thing. Let's figure this shit out."

"This shit is your daughter, and she's not emotionally disturbed. She has a great life. Something has changed, and it's real, Brian." Same conversation, different night. Junie would never get to sleep now. Why didn't Brian just support her? Why couldn't they find another group of doctors instead of just another therapist?

"She's got issues," Brian said, pointing to his head.

Junie got out of bed, grabbed her robe, and walked out of the bedroom.

Chapter Seven

It was one o'clock in the morning, and the house was silent. Junie padded down the stairs and into the kitchen. She flicked on the light, squinting as her eyes adjusted. The roses were gone. Junie looked around the kitchen and living room, then silently thanked her mother for moving them. Junie placed the teakettle on the stove and lit the flame. She took the last tea bag from the box above the sink and pressed the metal lever on the trash can to throw away the empty container. The roses lay in the trash like forgotten children, beautiful and wrong among the coffee grinds and apple peels. Junie let the lid slam closed and lifted her gaze to the window. Peter's back porch light was on, illuminating his backyard beyond the buffer of trees. Junie thought of Ellen and of the many nights playing flashlight tag and sitting on her back porch talking until one of their moms would call them inside. She wondered what her life might be like if Ellen hadn't gone missing. Would they have remained friends all those years, or would they have grown apart, like Junie and the few other friends from her youth? She couldn't name one childhood friend that she was still in contact with. Was that normal? Would she and Brian have ever gotten together if Ellen hadn't disappeared? Might there have been stolen glances of flirtation between Brian, the coveted older brother, and Junie, the little sister's best friend, as they'd gotten older? A secret midnight tryst with Brian when Junie was home on a college break, she and Ellen catching up over a few too many drinks—Ellen passed out and Brian suddenly appearing in the doorway?

"Yeah, right," Junie said to herself.

When they were younger, Brian had treated Junie like she was nothing more than another little girl running around the house, getting in his way. He'd joked with her and he was cordial, but he also let her know when she annoyed him in a slightly less patient way than he had with Ellen.

Ellen had adored her brother. Junie remembered the way pride illuminated Ellen's dark eyes when Brian called her "squirt." Junie had almost been jealous, back then, wishing she had an older brother to give her a sacred nickname, like Brian had for Ellen, but then again, she'd had a warm and attentive father, something Ellen never had—though Brian sure did.

The teakettle whistled, and Junie quickly turned off the stove and poured herself a cup of tea. Her mother appeared in the doorway. Ruth's hair was disheveled. The faded blue bathrobe that Junie had given her mother years earlier was worn so thin it was see-through in spots. The robe hung open, revealing her mother's flowered nightgown. Ruth's shoulders drooped; her cheeks hung heavily.

"Pour me a cup?" she asked.

"Mom? What are you doing up?"

Ruth looked at her sideways.

"Sorry. I'm sure it's hard to sleep." *I'm so stupid.*

"I'm not used to him not being there. I roll over and the bed seems too big; the room's too quiet." She sat down across from Junie, her hands around the teacup. "I miss the sound of his breathing at night, the way the mattress sank, just a little, next to me." She sipped her tea. "He was always so hot at night, like his body radiated heat. I just miss him."

"I know." Junie didn't know what else to say. Her heart ached for her mother. It ached for herself. "Daddy used to bring me hot chocolate at night when I couldn't sleep." She hadn't thought of that in years, their late-night secret.

"He did?" Ruth asked.

Junie nodded. "He'd come into my bedroom and find me sitting up in bed. Just sitting there." Junie looked away; the edges of her lips rose to a smile. "Come to think of it, I have no idea why I would be awake, or what I was thinking or doing. I wonder if"—she sipped her tea—"after the first few times, I would stay awake waiting for him to come in. You know, like Pavlov's dogs?"

Ruth laughed. "Now you sound like your father."

Ralph Nailon had been a science teacher. Everything in his life was likened to research or science in one way or another. Junie reached across the table and held her mother's hand. "I miss him, too, Mom." Tears welled in her eyes as she thought of her father. He wasn't a verbose man, and he didn't have a commanding presence, like Brian's father did. No, Ralph was more demure; some might even say he was meek, but to Junie, he was smart, careful, and loving in his own quiet way. Junie wiped a tear from her cheek. She closed her eyes, trying to remain strong. The last thing her mother needed was to see her falling apart. Junie glanced outside at the lighted porch on the hill. The images of Ellen screaming flashed before her. Junie dropped her mother's hand.

Ruth lifted her eyes.

"Mom, what do you think happens after we die?" Junie asked.

"I never believed in that life-after-death stuff, but after Daddy…when he—" Ruth looked away and took a deep breath, blowing it out slowly. "I thought, or maybe I just hoped, that I'd feel him right here with me." She looked at the empty chair beside her. "Or, you know, know he was there, but now…" She shook her head, pulling her hand back from Junie's.

"I'm sorry, Mom. I didn't mean to upset you."

Ruth tucked her cropped hair behind her ear, a motion Junie had seen hundreds of times before. When she was young, Junie had tried to mimic that movement, much like Sarah apes her movements—but as she matured, she found that it was not hers to take. "It's okay. It's life, Junie. I still have hope. I may feel him around at some point."

Junie's heartbeat picked up. She needed to hear her mother's take on what she'd seen. As selfish as it was, Junie needed her wisdom. "Something happened today, and I really need to talk to someone about it, but I don't want to upset you." Junie watched her mother draw in a breath and pull her shoulders back.

"I'm okay, honey. What is it?"

She'd seen Ruth draw strength for her so many times that Junie had come to expect it even during such a traumatic time. She knew she was being selfish, burdening her mother with her worry, but who else could she ask? Brian had already dismissed her, and she was asking enough of Shane by leaving him with full responsibility for the bakery. As Junie opened her mouth to speak, she secretly hoped that one day she could show that strength for her own daughter, and somehow, she felt she'd already fallen short of that wish.

"Do you know anything about Ellen's disappearance? I mean, anything that maybe I wouldn't have heard about as a kid?" Junie watched her mother's face soften, the worry in her eyes replaced with empathy.

"Oh, honey. Why didn't I see that Daddy's death would unearth this for you? Of course this would bring Ellen's disappearance rushing back. I'm so sorry."

"It's okay. I don't think it's that. It's just...I saw her

today. I mean, I didn't see her, see her. I saw an image of her, outside, when I was playing with Sarah."

"A memory," Ruth said, plain and simple, as if it explained everything. Her typical pragmatic response.

"That's the thing. I can't ever remember seeing Ellen so frightened. She was terrified, screaming."

"Death does all sorts of things to the living," Ruth said.

Junie's head snapped up. "Death? We don't know if Ellen is dead. You can't know that." The desperation in Junie's voice was palpable. "Don't...don't assume that."

"Oh, Junie, I didn't mean Ellen. I meant your father's death."

"But what if it was something more? What if they missed something all those years ago? What if it's a sign of some sort?"

"Oh, Junie, I really don't think—"

"I know. I know. Neither do I, really, but all I know is that she disappeared. I can't remember the last time we even talked about her. It's almost as if she had never existed at all."

"We talked about her at your wedding. Remember?"

Junie nodded, remembering the passing comment among the excitement. *I wish Ellen could have been here.* She'd been too wrapped up in her own reverie to give Ellen's memory the careful thought it deserved.

"You had such a difficult time with her disappearance. You were so young, just seven, remember. You refused to believe she wasn't coming back and, well, after a while, I guess you realized that maybe she wasn't, and eventually you just went on. We all did. It was a very difficult time for everyone. You might not remember, but Ellen's disappearance changed everything."

"What do you mean?"

"I mean, when a child disappears like that, everyone comes under scrutiny. People say things they don't mean, things they'd never say under different circumstances. Suffice it to say, it's not a time anyone wants to rehash." Ruth got up and put her teacup in the sink.

Junie followed. "Who came under scrutiny?"

Ruth turned to her, letting out a loud sigh. "Junie, I love you, but I'm exhausted. I have to go to bed."

Guilt chased frustration around Junie's body, tightening like a robe around her middle. Another of her mother's pragmatic traits—dismissing her daughter in a gentle, loving way, putting an end to an uncomfortable discussion, and leaving Junie wanting more.

Chapter Eight

Junie woke up at four thirty, too restless to fall back to sleep. She spent the night tossing and turning. Every time she closed her eyes, she saw Ellen's frightened face or heard her father's voice. Her chest tightened, as if a thick blanket of doom were lying over her. She closed her eyes against a wave of sadness and pushed herself from the bed. Brian slept beside her. Junie pulled on her sweatpants and headed for the kitchen, thinking of Ellen.

She pulled cake flour, sugar, and three pans from the cabinet above her mother's refrigerator. She'd learned long ago to keep her mother's shelves stocked with must-have baking items. She'd taken one too many midnight trips to Walmart to grab the necessary supplies to satisfy her sudden urge to bake. At least they carried Wilton products, which made it easier than hunting down supplies. She always packed a few not-so-readily available items, and the rest she kept on hand.

Junie measured the sugar and water, watching it rise to a boil, waiting for the dark amber color to appear. She heated up the whipping cream before removing the boiling sugar mixture from the stove. She never imagined that her father's death would smell so sweet. In fact, she had never imagined her father's death at all. She should be baking funeral cookies or something equally as demure, more appropriate for mourning. She knew that Selma and Mary Margaret would see to Ruth's house being filled with foods for the gathering after the funeral, but Junie *needed* to bake. She also knew that she could no sooner bake a dessert that didn't match her father's love of sweets than she could accept that he was gone and she'd never see him again. A dark chocolate caramel cake seemed the perfect Band-Aid for her pain.

Junie held the warm cream above the caramel, holding the measuring cup at arm's length and turning her head before pouring it in. She cringed as she twisted her wrist, anticipating the hot splatter that would follow. Junie loved making caramel, but she feared the burn that she'd experienced the first time she'd disregarded the advice to turn her face. She reached up and touched the dip in her skin where the splatter had left its mark.

Next, she added the butter and stirred until it was well blended. Her nightmares fell away with each added ingredient. She tucked the bowl into the refrigerator, moving in smooth procession from one task to the next.

She greased the pans, focusing on the spread of the Crisco as the white disappeared into a clear film before her eyes, reminding her of how easily Ellen had disappeared. She wondered if Ellen had been there, would she be up in the middle of the night baking alongside Junie, comforting her? She'd like to think so. Junie boiled water, then poured it over unsweetened cocoa powder in a small bowl, whisking it until it formed smooth chocolate.

She thought of her father, hanging over her shoulder while she baked, waiting for his turn to taste her creation. A lump formed in her throat. She whisked harder, faster, as if she could whisk away her longing to see him one more time. She wiped a tear from her eye with her forearm and set the bowl down, mixing the other ingredients in a separate bowl and wishing she'd splurged on the stand mixer for her mother's house.

Junie beat the butter and sugar, thinking of Brian and the way he'd pushed for an *emotionally unstable* diagnosis for Sarah. How could he do that? She cracked the eggs one at a time, plopping them into the mixture, added a splash of vanilla, and mixed until her arm ached.

Sarah hadn't asked to be different. Why did everyone feel a need to magnify her issues with a quick diagnosis rather than a valid one? Junie lowered herself into a chair, the bowl in her lap. Flour and sugar decorated her sweats. She looked outside. The sun had yet to rise, but the dark of night was lifting. She closed her eyes against the image of Ellen's face. She pushed herself up from the table, setting the bowl on the countertop. What was happening to her? Was this what happened when you lost someone you loved—problems grew so large that you could barely breathe? She had to pull herself together—get the confusion out of her system. How could she face her mother—and her father's funeral—with all that stuff wallowing around in her head? She wished she had someone to talk to. *Damn it, Brian*. If only she were back home and it was a more reasonable time, then at least she could talk to Shane. She debated calling him now, then thought better of it. No need to upset him, too.

Junie eyed a bag of pecans on a shelf. She grabbed the bag, turning it over in her hands, then took a rolling pin from the drawer. She smoothed a clean baking cloth on the counter, spread a thin layer of pecans on the cloth, then pulled the cloth over the top. Junie leaned the weight of her frustrations onto the rolling pin, crushing the pecans with a satisfying *crunch*.

"Yeah, that feels good," she whispered to herself. "You think I'm going nuts just because I see my missing friend? We'll see about that," she said to no one. She pushed and rolled the wooden pin until the pecans were broken into tiny bits.

The morning sun peeked through the window as Junie poured a thin layer of cake batter into the pan, then added a sprinkling of nuts, burying them under another thick layer of batter. She repeated the process with each of the three pans.

An hour and a half later, Junie used a leveling tool to remove the uneven pieces of the cake and layered a thick swathe of caramel across the top of two layers, then assembled the cake, sealing it with a thin layer of rum ganache. By the time she went upstairs, she'd sealed her burdensome thoughts deep inside the cake.

Chapter Nine

Junie changed Sarah's sheets without any emotion whatsoever. She was focused on the event that lay ahead: her father's funeral. How could he be gone? This was it. They were going to bury her father, the man who taught her to ride a bike and secretly brought her hot chocolate. The man who, when Junie spoke of being afraid of sharks at the seashore, rattled off statistics and convinced Junie that she was more likely to get a bee sting than be bitten by a shark, and she still played in the grass, didn't she?

Brian walked by the bedroom, glancing at Junie with a look that translated into, *Again?*

Junie turned her back, unable to deal with his chastising of her mothering skills—not today.

Ruth moved through the house in silent procession. Junie didn't know what to say to ease the tension, so she said nothing. She bathed and fed Sarah and put on the black dress that she knew she would discard after the funeral. She couldn't bear the thought of walking into her closet and seeing the dress, a daily reminder of her father's passing.

When they finally made their way to the car, Sarah insisted on hanging on to her blanket, her thumb planted firmly in her mouth.

Brian reached for the blanket.

"Don't," Junie said from the passenger seat.

"Junie, she's four years old. Come on. She doesn't need it in public."

"Just leave it. It's a hard enough day. Mom doesn't need there to be a tantrum, too."

Brian turned away, grinding his teeth.

The cemetery was only a few miles from the house, but it seemed like a different world altogether. Ten acres of flat, even grass, row after row of headstones, reminders of how often people leave our world. Junie's heart sank, realizing that nothing in life could prepare her for losing her father, just as she hadn't been prepared to lose her best friend.

The parking lot was full of familiar cars. Selma and Phil's blue Toyota Corolla was parked next to Mary Margaret's Subaru Forester in the closest spots. They would have been the first people to arrive.

Junie stepped from the car, staring at the blue canopy with rows of chairs beneath it, the ominous hole in the earth below her father's casket. She eyed the mound of dirt on the ground beside the hole. It seemed unfair, cruel, like a rush to the finish line. *Hurry up, because we have to get on with our lives.* Junie's stomach turned. Couldn't they bring in the dirt later, or cover it? She reached behind her for Sarah's hand.

Selma, Phil, and Mary Margaret were seated in the second row of chairs. They stood as Ruth and Sarah exited the car. Brian rushed to take Sarah's hand.

"I've got her." Brian reached for Sarah again.

Sarah pulled back, wrapping her tiny fingers around her mother's skirt and casting her eyes downward.

Brian's mouth formed a tight line. He bent down, looking Sarah in the eyes. "Come on, honey. Let's give Mommy a break. Hold Daddy's hand."

Sarah hid behind her blanket.

"It's okay," Junie said, reaching for Sarah's hand. She was glad Brian was stepping up to the plate, trying to do the right thing by giving her the chance to support her mother instead of taking care of Sarah. It pained her, knowing how much Sarah's rejection hurt Brian. Why Sarah preferred her over anyone else, she had no idea. Brian was a good father. He adored Sarah. She knew he did, even if that adoration was clouded by the effects of her regression. From the time Sarah was born, Brian had changed her diapers, sung to her, even read to her at all hours of the night when she couldn't sleep. It was only during her regression that Sarah had fallen out of her father's good graces. If only Junie could figure out what had sparked the change—what caused her happy daughter to reject those around her? Sarah's rejection had ignited a negative reaction from Brian. He no longer doted on Sarah. He'd pulled away from their daughter, and Junie knew that it was caused by the way Sarah had pulled away from him. Maybe she would answer the questionnaire, if only to get some answers herself.

"Ruth."

Junie turned at the sound of her father-in-law's voice and watched Peter Olson embrace her mother.

He turned to her. "Junie, I'm so sorry." He pulled Junie close.

Junie had known Peter all her life. Before Ellen had disappeared, their house had been like a second home to Junie; her parents had been a second family. Her memories of Peter included him arriving late in the evening, clad in a suit and carrying a thick briefcase, or holed up nightly in his office, which she could see from her bedroom window. She had vague memories of him talking about Brian's life as if it were a given: *bright future, Ivy league, scholarship, lawyer.* It wasn't until she was older that she became aware of the discrepancy in how Peter hovered over Brian and nearly ignored Ellen.

As a little girl, Junie couldn't understand how Susan—Ellen's mom—could have divorced Peter and left Brian and the East Coast altogether. She wondered if Susan was mad about how Peter treated Ellen, and she wondered how a mother could leave when her daughter was missing, like she was giving up hope for her daughter's return. Susan had moved to Washington State to start a new life, and other than on Junie and

Brian's wedding day, Junie had never seen her mother-in-law again. Now, as an adult, she understood that the painful reminders must have been too much to bear. Junie drew her eyebrows together. Come to think of it, Junie found it weird that no one else had left the area—her parents, Peter, the other neighbors. Wouldn't she have moved, if only to protect her own daughter from a lingering threat?

Brian shook his father's hand. Junie bristled at the cold exchange, wondering where their love had gone. After losing a daughter and sister, you'd think they'd want to hold on to each other at all costs, but for all of their adult life, this odd dichotomy of a relationship had existed—they barely spoke, much less exchanged pleasantries or warmth. They saw each other two or three times each year, and one would think that they could muster a hug now and again. Brian had been the smart, athletic one with so much promise that it gleamed from his father's eyes. The resemblance between Peter and Brian was remarkable—same dark hair and thick eyebrows, same narrow waist and broad shoulders. The coldness between them marred their good looks.

Junie sat before the grave site, her eyes swollen and red, a mound of crumpled tissues in one hand, her mother's hand in the other. She stared at her father's casket, remembering a much different memorial—Ellen's. She pulled her sweater across her chest, locking out the chill of the brisk morning air. This morning was very similar to the morning of Ellen's memorial so many years ago. Junie remembered the lines of cars, parents, and children as far as the eye could see, gathered to say goodbye to Ellen's empty casket.

This wasn't Ellen's memorial, and Junie was no longer a seven-year-old. She was a grown woman, a mother herself, and she couldn't make any more sense of the death of her father than of the disappearance of her young friend. She turned, recognizing faces of students who had been in her father's fifth grade science class and other teachers. Deputy Lyle sat just behind Selma and Phil, their faces drawn, Selma's eyes reddened with sad spidery veins. Mary Margaret sat beside them, in the row behind her mother, bent over, her shoulders quaking. Junie glanced over the attendees. Mrs. Walters, the librarian, dressed in a black polyester pantsuit, stood beside Dr. Rains, a therapist who lived in the neighborhood. Junie was ashamed to remember the childhood taunt, *Dr. Crazy Brains*. Many of the same faces that had been at Ellen's service were there, faces that now boasted crow's-feet instead of the smooth skin of youth.

Junie looked at Sarah kicking her feet, which hung from the chair. Her dark tights made her thin legs look even tinier. Junie wiped fresh tears from her eyes. She hated that Sarah would grow up without her grandfather. Would she even remember him? Would she remember his mini science lessons about how butterflies couldn't fly if their body temperature was less than eighty-six degrees, or how hummingbirds eat every ten minutes? Junie barely remembered Ellen, and she was seven when Ellen had disappeared. *Seven*. Junie ached for all that Ellen missed out on in life and wondered what really happened to her. Adults died. That was accepted as part of life. But a child missing, assumed dead? She swallowed past the sadness that swelled within her. Ellen's disappearance was unfair. Her father's death was unfair, but at least he'd lived a full life.

Junie pictured her father in the casket, his arms crossed, his eyes closed. Ellen's casket had been empty. The funeral had been a memorial service, in honor of Ellen. *Closure for her parents*, her mother had said. Junie remembered the fear of seeing that casket lowered into the ground. Junie squeezed her mother's hand so tight that Ruth let out a gasp. Flashes of Ellen's funeral came rushing back to her, appearing in her mind like a bad rerun. Ellen's mother, kneeling by the casket, her arms draped over the small wooden box, sobs racking her body. Peter stood behind her, arms hanging loosely by his side, a lost look in his tear-filled eyes, and Brian, Junie's Brian, sitting, as Sarah sat now, staring straight ahead, his teeth clenched.

She looked at her husband, his eyes trained on the casket, his jaw set tight. What was he thinking? Was he thinking about all of the things he loved about her father, or was he thinking, as Junie was, about Ellen? A flush rushed up Junie's cheeks, and more memories flooded in. Fourteen-year-old Brian, his hair perfectly combed, wearing a suit so new it had yet to wrinkle. She remembered the pain in her stomach as he pushed himself up from the chair, a disgusted look on his face. Junie saw the look he gave his father, a look of anger and disbelief. He stormed away from the grave site, stomping across the surrounding graves without care, as only a distraught child might do. She'd wondered if he was angry they'd given up on finding Ellen. She had been furious, wanting to plead with Mr. and Mrs. Olson not to give up. She could only imagine how angry Brian had been. *Oh, Brian*. Her heart ached for him. She hoped her father's funeral wasn't causing Brian to relive the same sad memories of the days that changed his family forever.

Chapter Ten

The last of the visitors lingered, taking their time saying goodbye. The freezer was stocked with homemade casseroles and lasagna from well-meaning neighbors; the counter was littered with food that would never be eaten. Junie wiped her hand on a dish towel and went into the den, looking for Sarah. She hadn't seen her since they'd arrived back at the house, when she'd headed for the television. She found Brian hovering over her, his back to Junie, blocking Sarah's face and body from her view. Sarah began to kick her feet; a stifled noise rose from where she lay. Junie's hands grew cold. A shiver ran up her spine, bringing with it a memory she'd long ago forgotten. It was Ellen's feet before her now, Junie's father leaning over her. Junie stood frozen, consumed by the memory. Ellen had spent the night, and Junie awoke to Ellen's empty sleeping bag next to her. She'd gone downstairs, looking for Ellen, and had come upon her father, Ellen's feet kicking, a strangled sound emitting from her best friend's throat. The den had been dark, almost pitch black, save for the moonlight peeking in through the window.

"Stop!" Junie yelled. "Stop it. Stop it!" She pulled on Brian's back, tears slipping down her cheeks.

Brian whipped around. "What the heck, June?"

"Stop it!" she yelled. She swooped Sarah into her arms, cradling her like an infant. Sarah's face was a mask of fear. Junie's body shook and trembled. She looked from Sarah to Brian and back again.

"What the hell? I was finally getting through to her."

Ruth ran into the room. "What's going—"

"Stop," Junie whispered.

"What the hell is wrong with you? I was tickling her."

Junie looked down at her daughter, who now clung to her chest in fear, then up at Ruth, whose mouth hung open in confusion. Junie lowered herself to the couch, rocking Sarah against her.

"What is going on?" Mary Margaret towered over Junie, worry lines deep across her forehead. "Hon, please, you'll upset your mother," she said quietly.

Junie couldn't speak—her voice was trapped beneath the rising memory. She remembered wanting to pound on her father's back. She'd had no idea what he was doing to Ellen, but it felt wrong, very wrong, hidden, in fact. The silence of the guests, their openmouthed gazes, pressed in on her. What was she doing? She looked down at Sarah's closed eyes. Tears tumbled down her cheeks in silent streams.

Mary Margaret sat next to her, her arm around Junie's shoulder, her large hand pulling her close. She must have thought that Junie was having a hard time dealing with her father's death. Junie wished she could tell her the truth, but if she couldn't process what she'd seen, how could anyone else?

"I'm sorry," Junie whispered.

They ate dinner in silence. Brian was still annoyed from Junie's unexplained outburst, and Sarah withdrew even further into her usual introverted behavior. She flinched at loud noises, and she'd clung to Junie all afternoon. Junie pushed the lasagna around on her plate, unable to stomach a single bite of it.

"I'm sorry," she said, her eyes on her plate.

No one responded.

Junie looked up at her mother. Dark circles made her eyes appear slate gray. A pang of guilt rode through Junie. "Mom, I'm really sorry. I don't know what happened."

Brian slammed his fork down on the table so hard, Sarah burst into tears. His face reddened. "Damn it, Junie. All I want is to be part of this family, and as much as you say you want me to reach out to Sar—" He dropped his eyes to Sarah and began again, addressing Junie directly, this time suppressing his anger. "I am trying to reach out, and you are sabotaging my every effort."

Junie shook her head. "I'm not, but..." Sarah clung to her arm. "Can we please talk about this later?"

Brian threw his napkin on the table and excused himself to the den.

"Want to talk about it?" Ruth asked.

Junie took the dish from her mother's hands and began filling the dishwasher. She peered into the dining room, where Sarah sat peacefully playing a game on Junie's laptop.

"I...I'm not sure what happened." How could she tell her mother what she saw? What did it mean? What had her father been doing to Ellen? Why was he with her in the middle of the night? Junie wished she could put the fragments together and figure out something, anything that might help her to understand what was going on. "Mom, how often did Ellen spend the night?"

"Junie, don't you want to talk about today? What's going on? Brian is trying so hard, and you're...I have no idea what you're up to." Ruth wrapped the leftover lasagna and put it in the fridge.

And say what? I think Daddy hurt Ellen? "I'm not *up to* anything," she snapped. "I'm not sure what happened. I think I'm just exhausted, and I'm so sorry. I didn't mean to ruin your, Daddy's...the service." She'd managed to screw up her father's funeral, her family, and God knows if she was responsible for screwing up Sarah, too. *Sarah*. Maybe Brian was right and the therapist was wrong to disregard the questionnaire.

Maybe she should fill out that damned thing, if only to see if the other therapists missed something. If Sarah's issues all came down to some flaw in Junie's parenting, she'd rather know than be ignorant of it.

"Oh, honey, you're overwhelmed. We all are. Daddy's death was so unexpected. Why don't you go lie down? I can finish this," Ruth offered.

Junie set down the dish towel she'd been holding and hugged her mother. "I'm supposed to be taking care of you, Mom. Not the other way around. I'm a big girl. I'm fine."

Chapter Eleven

Sarah had been put to bed, having fallen fast asleep in front of the television. Junie sat at the edge of the bed, fidgeting with her fingers and wondering if she were losing her mind. Brian stormed into the bedroom and closed the door.

"What the hell is going on, Junie?" he asked in an angry whisper.

"I'm sorry. It wasn't you."

"It sure as hell looked like me," he snapped. Brian's face was red. Fury emanated from his entire being, every muscle constricted and strained.

"Oh, Brian." Junie covered her face with her hands. "It was you that I yelled at, because you were there, but it wasn't you I was yelling at. I sound crazy. I know I do." She reached out to him. "I'm sorry."

He pulled away from her. "What the hell is that supposed to mean, I wasn't the one you were yelling at?

I was there, Junie. You yelled at me. All this bullshit about you wanting me to reach out to Sarah, and I finally break through, and you come crashing in." His voice escalated, his words shot like nails piercing Junie's heart.

"I don't know what's happening to me. I walked into the den and, oh God, this is going to sound nuts, but…I saw my dad leaning over Ellen."

"Ellen again? Really, Junie? You're going to blame this on my dead sister?" he spat.

"No. God, no, don't say that. You don't know that she's dead."

"Come on, Junie. It's been more than twenty years."

Junie paced. "Brian, I'm sorry. I'm not blaming Ellen. I don't know what's going on, but when I walked into the den, I swear to you, I saw my dad leaning over Ellen, and Ellen was kicking and making weird, scared noises."

Brian crossed his arms; his nostrils flared, the veins in his forearms visible all the way down to his fisted hands.

"It's…crazy, Junie."

"I know it sounds crazy, but I know what I saw."

"Or you're exhausted and confused." He sat down on the edge of the bed and ran his hand through his hair. "Jesus, Junie."

She sat down beside him.

He set his hand on her thigh. The weight of it comforted her.

"This is why I hate coming back here. It dredges up everything bad."

Junie shrugged and laid her head on his shoulder. She put her hand over his and squeezed. "I had to come."

"We had to come," he corrected her. "But we don't have to stay forever. One more day; then we're out of here."

"I can't leave my mother, not now." She pulled back in anger and sprang to her feet. "How can you even suggest that?"

"Junie, being here is making you crazy. It's putting me on edge."

Junie shook her head. "No, I'm not leaving her. She'd never do that to me. She'd stay no matter how uncomfortable she was."

"I can't stay." Brian stared into her eyes, unwavering. "It's too much, Junie. Every second I'm on this block, all I can think of is what happened to Ellen, how my mom left. I just can't stay." He paced, then said, "Besides, I have so much work to do. I can get it done while you're here."

"Go, then. Leave." Junie crossed her arms and turned away. Tears sprang from her eyes. She couldn't help but be hurt, even if he had good reasons to leave. Junie wiped her eyes and thought about spending a few days apart. Maybe it was better if he wasn't there—it's not like they were comforting each other. She needed to be there for her mother, but she kept doing the wrong things with Brian. It had to be hard for him, being here after losing his sister. She was being selfish again. What was wrong with her? She came back home and immediately turned into a spoiled child. Junie turned back to him, facing his clenched teeth and throbbing muscles in his jaw working overtime. She took a deep breath, swallowing her neediness like a lump of coal, and in a sweet, empathetic tone, said, "It's okay. You go back home. I'll stay for a week or so; then Sarah and I will come home. I know it's hard for you to be here, and we're okay. Really."

Junie could see the relief in the brief closure of Brian's eyes. Part of her wanted him to say he'd stay, wanted him to push his discomfort and work aside and put her and Sarah first, but she knew that, too, was selfish. He had lost his sister, he had a big case looming, and even if he returned tomorrow, he'd already lost a lot of time.

When Junie drifted off to sleep, it was her father's face she saw in her dreams, sitting next to her on the sofa, watching *NOVA*, explaining every scene to be sure she understood the program. She awoke with a pang in her heart—a longing from the emptiness he'd left behind—and a stroke of guilt for thinking that her father could have ever hurt her friend. Junie looked over at Brian and promised herself she'd work harder at helping him connect with Sarah and would be more understanding about his feelings. She didn't like the rift that had swelled between them. She wanted him to be accepted by Sarah, and she sure as hell didn't want to yell at him for warped images she saw in her distraught mind.

Chapter Twelve

Junie sat on the porch, listening to her mother read aloud to Sarah, just inside the living room window. With Brian gone, a layer of tension had lifted. She hated acknowledging the tension that seemed to accompany her marriage these days, but she could not ignore the fraying relationship between her and Brian. She wondered if being home, her father's death, and unearthing memories of Ellen was really the impetus of their recent conflicts, or if there had been something missing before and she'd just been blind to it. Junie began to wonder if she could trust her own judgment, or if it had been clouded, like her ability to qualify her memories as real or fabricated. She'd seen Peter heading toward the backyard and contemplated paying him a short visit. Maybe if she understood more or could remember more around the days and weeks that surrounded Ellen's disappearance, she could gain some sort of perspective to deal with Sarah on a more focused level and have the strength to heal her ailing marriage. She hoped that Peter might be able to shed some light on those missing weeks. She took a deep breath, urging herself not to panic at the sight of the roses, and forced herself through the gate and up the hill.

Her anxiety grew with each step up the steep driveway. The familiarity and the devastation of losing Ellen came back to her as she neared the front yard. The deep porch, the rocking chairs, had each lost their sheen, but they were the same sturdy chairs that had been there when she was growing up. She walked down the stone path that led toward the backyard, each stone perfectly spaced between impeccably edged lawn. She slipped past the towering trees that lined the backyard—they'd been scrappy saplings when she and Ellen had run between them.

Goose bumps traveled up her arms at the sight of the unkempt gardens. The roses were all but hidden by thick, high weeds wrapping around their prickly stems like slim boas. These were not the carefully tended gardens that Peter had so mindfully protected for so many years. For as long as Junie could remember, Peter spent the rare weekends when he was not at work or locked in his den tending to the gardens, knee deep in mulch, clipping dead blooms and pulling weeds. In fact, she realized, when they'd visited during Easter, the gardens had been immaculate. The lawn surrounding the gardens was still beautifully manicured, making the unwieldy gardens look even more like the darkness amid the otherwise light yard.

"Junie?"

Junie spun around, startled.

Deep lines surrounded Peter's squinting eyes like spider legs. Tiny folds of skin formed a deep *Y* between his two brows. As a young girl, June had watched Peter hard at work in his den at all hours, night after night, poring over his law books. Ellen had always said that her father never slept. Junie used to have fantasies about how great it would be to never have to go to bed, to play all night long. As she got older, and when she married Brian and had to live with his late-night meetings and evening preparations for cases, she realized how silly those fantasies were.

"H-hi." Why were her hands trembling? She shoved them into her pockets, suddenly very aware that she had stepped off of the stones and was now standing on the perfect grass. She moved back onto the stones. "Sorry, I, um…I just wanted to see how you were doing."

The bottom edge of his slacks were stained. Junie looked around the backyard, feeling the loss of the gorgeous gardens like harsh, sharp realities marring her fragile memories. Her memories were already held by a fraying thread.

"How's your mom doing?" he asked.

Junie forced her gaze toward the ground, away from the roses. She was fine if she didn't look at them. "She's doing as best she can, I guess. Sad." What was she saying? Peter had experienced that sadness firsthand. "I'm sorry," she offered. "It's all…new."

"Losing someone you love is not easy." Peter looked

at his house. "They say time heals all wounds, but I'm not so sure it does. I think time adds a dimension of fatigue, which just makes it seem like the wound has healed because you get tired of battling the loneliness." He walked toward his gardening shed.

Junie watched him walk away, remembering when she and Ellen had helped Peter and her father build their sheds. *Helped,* Junie thought with a smile. Junie could still feel the weight of her father's tool belt hanging from her waist. She remembered Ellen goading her on to sneak more tools than they were offered. What a thrill it had been to be working by her father's side! While Junie tried to remain serious, so her father would allow her to help with other projects in the future, Ellen had been giggly and bored. Over the course of two days, their fathers had erected two identical aluminum structures, large enough for a workbench and a few garden tools, each given a different name: Peter's a gardening shed and her father's a toolshed. She and Ellen had worked side by side on each shed in the middle of August. Junie smiled to herself, remembering how they "worked" by carrying tools, bending over little remnants of wood that their fathers allowed them to haphazardly bang nails into, and trying to rein in Ellen's goofy antics. They ran circles around their fathers' carefully organized work sites. Humidity had been high that summer, and Ellen and Junie were first in line when Ruth and Susan brought them a continuous supply of icy lemonade. After they'd completed erecting the sheds, the girls were given the ground rules; while Peter's gardening shed was open to anyone, her father's toolshed was declared off limits. *Too many things that could hurt you,* her father had said. He went so far as to put a padlock on the door.

"And Sarah? How is she?"

Hearing her name brought her own issues back to mind. "She's…the same. Not worse, but not better, either." Junie was taken by the concern in Peter's eyes. She wondered if he'd had that same concern for Ellen, or if that awareness came only after her disappearance. She knew he had doted over Brian and hadn't over Ellen, but she wondered if he'd *felt* the same concern, even if not made apparent by his actions. He'd reached out to Sarah since the day she was born, spending time with her even as a tiny baby, when they'd visit Junie's parents. Brian didn't allow for overnight visits at his father's house. The relationship between them was too strained, but Junie always made sure that Peter had time with Sarah, and it surprised her how taken with her he was. He wasn't a go-outside-and-play-ball type of grandfather, but he took Sarah by the hand and walked through the gardens; he read to her and kept fresh cookies and treats on hand when they came into town. Most important, he was mentally present for Sarah. When she was with him, his eyes were on her, and he paid attention to what she was doing, not to his clients' cases, which Junie knew rattled around in his head nonstop. She often wondered if his desire to be there for Sarah had been some sort of reconciliation in his own mind for the way he'd treated Ellen.

"Do the doctors have any ideas?" He opened the

shed, his back to Junie. The smell of fertilizer filled the space between them. He moved gardening tools into a wooden box.

Junie caught sight of the rose clipper. "No, nothing. They're thinking it might be emotional rather than physical." They hadn't seen each other since Sarah's regression had begun, and Junie wondered if Peter and Brian had ever talked to each other about Sarah's regression, or if it was just another issue that would be left to rot between them.

Peter stopped, clipper in his hand. He turned to face her. "And what do you think?" He looked seriously into her eyes.

"I…I don't know what to think."

"Regression," he said. "I had a case once, a little girl had regressed after being sexually abused."

Junie's heart sank. *Don't say it.*

"That's physical, though, not emotional."

He said this so matter-of-factly, so clinically, that it stung. "Yes, physical."

"Well—and I hope I'm wrong—have you considered this? You do have new circumstances. You're in a new area, new teachers, you don't really know the people." He shrugged.

"Peter, how can you say that?" Junie took a step backward. "She's your granddaughter."

"I'm not judging her," he said in what Junie imagined was his best attorney voice. "I'm looking for facts."

"Well, she's not one of your cases. She wasn't

sexually abused. That's already been ruled out." Junie didn't know what was worse, feeling disgusted that her father-in-law would say such a thing, or her growing suspicion that something was off about Peter. He had slipped into attorney mode so quickly, and he'd always kept that side of himself separate when it came to Sarah. Her eyes shot to the wayward gardens. "I think there's some other medical explanation. They did an MRI, but the therapist said they should do it with dye, and I'm going to request that next."

Peter nodded, as if considering the procedure.

"I don't mean to upset you, but I would look at all avenues. Seems strange that she'd suddenly become an emotional wreck without something physical attached."

Shut up. "We're considering everything." *Except emotional manipulation.* Brian's armchair diagnosis weighed heavily on her mind.

Junie turned back toward the roses. "I hope you don't mind me asking, but what happened?" She lifted her chin toward the weeds.

"Oh, that." Peter put the remaining tools into the box, then closed the shed door. "I've just been too busy to tend to them, I guess."

"But you have a lawn service. Couldn't they do it?"

Peter shook his head. "No, they don't do roses."

As much as Junie hated roses, she didn't really want them to shrivel up and die. Peter's garden was a reminder of the times she shared with Ellen. She wanted to say, *You've got more money than God. Find someone who does.* Instead she said, "Oh, well, that's a shame. They were so pretty." She swallowed the lie.

Peter laughed. "Junie, we all know you don't like roses."

She lifted her eyes and threw her hands up. "Caught me." As they walked toward the front yard, the tension in Junie's shoulders eased. She hadn't realized she was clenching her muscles. "Peter," she asked, turning to face him. "Brian won't talk to me about Ellen, never has. Has there ever been any information, any leads?" She cringed, hoping he wouldn't get mad at her for asking.

"No, Junie. I guess there are some things we'll never understand."

Chapter Thirteen

Junie touched the lock on her father's toolshed. She'd spent many afternoons pondering her father's private oasis. She laughed to herself. She used to fantasize about having her own building where she could lock away her private things. Of course, as a child, Junie didn't have *private* things. Her life was an open book. She wondered if perhaps that wasn't normal. Should she have had private things? Secrets worth hiding? Did Ellen have them?

She put her hand against the locked door and closed her eyes, remembering her father coming in and out of the building, each time with a different tool in hand. She opened her eyes as clouds moved slowly across the sky, blocking the sun. The air chilled, darkened. She held the lock in her hand, a memory scratching at the back of her mind. Junie had been standing in her bedroom looking out the window. It was early evening, the sun had set and the moon had not yet appeared in the sky. Movement in the side yard caught her eye. She watched her father lead Ellen to his shed. He reached into his pocket, withdrew a key, and unlocked the shed. He and Ellen went inside. Her father turned, one last glance behind him, then closed the doors of the shed, shutting the rest of the world out and himself and Ellen in.

Had she seen them come out? Had she run down to the shed and banged on the door? When was that? What did it mean? She could not remember ever having been behind the closed door of her father's shed. What were they doing? Had it even happened, or was she seeing some convoluted imagery created from Ellen's disappearance from her life and her father's untimely death? Junie tried to remember, but came up blank. She reached into the recesses of her mind, searching for an answer, her nerves afire. She had to remember something, anything that might explain if what she'd remembered was real.

A tug on the back of Junie's shirt made her jump. She spun around, finding Sarah holding the green plastic ball. Junie's mind was still wrapped around the image of her father and Ellen disappearing into the shed. Her heart raced.

Sarah pushed the ball toward her. Junie grabbed it without thinking. She stared at the ball, wondering if she were losing her mind.

Sarah tugged on her shirt again.

Junie looked down at her daughter. Her silent

daughter. She needed to be present for Sarah, not lost in whatever craziness was going on inside her head. She looked down at the ball and knew she could not pretend the images, or memories, or whatever the hell they were, were not real. She could not play with Sarah. For whatever reason, Ellen had inhabited her mind, and Junie was in no shape to see her screaming face again—memory or fabrication.

Junie tucked the ball under her arm and reached for Sarah's hand. "Come on, sweetie. Let's go create something wonderful."

Sarah stood on a chair, the backs of her hands and the front of her shirt spattered with chocolate.

"What are we making today?" Ruth sidled up to Sarah and hugged her around the waist.

Sarah stared at the bowl.

"Looks yummy," Ruth said, eyeing the remaining chocolate caramel cake that Junie had baked earlier that morning.

Junie whisked the eggs with such vigor that her wrist grew tired. What the hell did her father and Ellen have to do with each other? Why was she arguing with Brian? Why didn't her daughter speak?

"You can't bake this away, Junie," she said quietly. She put her hand on the small of Junie's back.

"I know, Mom. I'm not trying to."

"Sure you're not," Ruth said softly.

Junie whisked the ingredients into a soupy

consistency, unable to concentrate on baking. Her problems were too big for her to wrap her mind around. She opened the cabinet and pulled out the sheet cake pan.

"Uh-oh, this is a big one, huh? Maybe if we eat it all, we'll at least feel better." Ruth laughed.

Sarah stuck her finger in the chocolate and licked the sugary sweetness without ever cracking a grin.

"Oh, the things we teach our daughters." Ruth nudged Junie, nodding her head in Sarah's direction.

Junie set the whisk down and rolled her eyes at Ruth. She took the bowl of chocolate from Sarah. "Let me work with this, sweetie."

Sarah held tight to the bowl, her eyes pleading, then demanding she remain in control of the bowl.

"Sarah, I'll give you the spoon to lick."

Sarah finally relented. She climbed down from the chair and plopped herself down at the table. Junie handed her the chocolate-covered spoon, then folded the eggs into the mixture.

"Mom, do you ever remember Ellen in Dad's shed?"

Ruth shook her head. "What is going on with you, Junie?"

"Do you remember her...doing a project with him, maybe? I don't know, anything like that?"

Ruth leaned against the counter, wiping her hands on a dish towel. She cocked her head. "No, I can't say that I do. What's going on? First you're yelling at poor Brian, and from what he said, you yelled at him because of something about your father and Ellen? What is this nonsense?"

Junie didn't answer. She focused on whipping the batter instead.

"June, maybe this is all too much for you. Should you think about going home, working things out with Brian?" She nodded toward Sarah.

Junie closed her eyes. *What was too much—losing the father I adored or seeing my best friend screaming in fear?* "I'm okay."

"Is Brian still in the den?"

Junie nodded. "Working. He's going back soon."

"You're staying?"

"If you don't mind."

"I have an appointment with Dr. Rains. If you want to go with me, she might be able to help you."

Junie sighed and set the bowl down. Dr. Rains lived around the corner from her mother and had been the brunt of many jokes when Junie was growing up. There was an underlying knowledge that Mary Margaret had seen her. As kids, Junie and her friends never really understood what a therapist did, much less why Mary Margaret Thatcher would visit her weekly. Some kids said Mary Margaret Thatcher was crazy and killed her husband, which Junie knew was just a story made up by bored teenagers. The neighborhood kids used to tease one another. "Watch out," they'd say, "or you'll end up on Dr. Crazy Brains's couch!"

"You're seeing a therapist?" Junie asked.

Ruth nodded. "It's nothing to be ashamed of."

"I know. I'm sorry. I just keep...I don't know what's going on, but Daddy's death has unearthed something. I keep seeing him and Ellen, like there's some connection."

"Oh, Junie, of course there is. They're both gone."

Junie nodded. "Maybe. Maybe that's all it is." She sat down next to Sarah and gently touched her ringlets.

Sarah leaned in to her.

Ruth put her hand on Sarah's shoulder as she walked behind her. "You think Ellen's trying to tell you something. Is that it?" She winked and sat down across the table. "Maybe Sarah's trying to tell you something, and you're just not listening hard enough."

Junie wished it were that simple.

"Tell me something good," Ruth said, smiling at Sarah.

Sarah clenched the wooden spoon in her fist; chocolate covered her lips like lipstick.

"Good?" Junie asked.

"Yes, good. How's your work? How's Sarah's school?"

Sarah looked up.

"Sarah, honey, why don't you go get your Polly Pockets?"

Sarah scooched off of the chair and ran toward the living room.

"Wait," Junie called after her. "Let's wash up first."

Sarah skulked back into the kitchen, washed her hands, let Junie scrub her face and wipe off her shirt. Then she headed toward the stairs.

"Sarah's doing well at school," she lied. "She does fine academically." That part wasn't really a lie, Junie reasoned. Sarah listened and when given a task, she usually completed it. She knew Sarah's teachers made special accommodations for her lack of verbal responses. She pictured Sarah sitting stoically among twenty children who all had their hands raised high. "Pick me! Pick me!"

"How about friends? Does she have any? Do they have any more ideas about what's going on with her? I've been doing research on autism and Asperger's—"

"She doesn't have either." Junie crossed her arms.

"Junie." Ruth shook her head. "There's something going on. This isn't the same little girl who was here at Easter. You're smart; you see the issues."

"Autistic kids do all sorts of things that Sarah doesn't do. I think there's something medical that they're missing, but not autism. You don't just suddenly become autistic. She learns well, without issue. She just...no longer speaks." Junie stood and paced. Why did she have to defend her daughter to her mother, to Sarah's own father?

"And she wets the bed, and I saw her sucking her thumb. She hasn't sucked her thumb in a year and a half. Does she talk to anyone besides you?" Ruth asked.

"Yes," Junie answered, but she couldn't honestly remember the last time Sarah had spoken to anyone else. In fact, she didn't really speak to her any longer, either. She used other visual clues to indicate her thoughts—drawings, facial expressions, eye movements. Her teachers certainly hadn't made any headway. She did play well with other kids, when they'd give her a chance, but the teachers said she often played by herself on the swings at recess.

"Really?" Ruth said, then softened her voice. "Well, that's good. Then maybe we are all overreacting." She stood up and looked in the living room where Sarah was playing. "She's a sweet little thing. I only want a good life for her."

For all of us, Junie thought. She looked outside at the shed again. "There's something wrong, but I have no idea what. She hasn't been abused, so it's got to be something else, and the only thing I can think of is some medical issue that's caused her to regress." Junie threw her hands up in the air. "I don't know, Mom. Do you think I baby her too much? Could it be my fault?"

"Fault? Junie, you're a wonderful mother. Whatever is going on with Sarah, the doctors will figure it out. Fault is something that doesn't matter unless she's been harmed in some way." She peeked at Sarah again. "That little darling does not look harmed."

Junie sat back down and decided to ask Ruth about Ellen. "Mom, you said something to me about people saying things they normally wouldn't after Ellen disappeared. Can you tell me about the investigation? I mean, did they have any suspects?"

Ruth turned her back to Junie, busying herself with washing the utensils that were in the sink. "Oh, Junie, that was so long ago. Let it be."

"I'm sorry. I just…I don't know. I never thought about it much until now, and Daddy's death has brought it all back, and I have these questions. Unanswered questions."

Ruth let out a breath, turned off the water, then faced Junie. She leaned against the sink, her arms crossed. "Go ahead."

Junie saw Ruth's jaw tighten and realized she was being selfish again. "It's okay, Mom. It's nothing. This is the last thing you need. I'm sorry." She'd have to figure out another way to get the answers she needed.

"You'll be home at the end of the week?" Brian put his suitcase in the trunk of the Lexus.

"Maybe, or next weekend at the latest," Junie answered. "Aren't you going to say goodbye to your dad?"

Brian looked away.

Junie looked at Peter's empty driveway. "He'll be sad to have missed you. Maybe you should stop by his office."

Brian kissed her and climbed into his car. "Nah, he'll be busy. I'll call him later. What about Sarah's therapist appointment?"

"She said we could do a Skype visit if necessary, or we can wait until the following week."

Junie watched the muscles in his jaw clench and unclench. The silence between them grew, like a ravine too large to traverse. She hated this new congenial relationship of theirs. There had been a time when Brian wouldn't have left her without first passionately kissing her and hugging her so tight that she could barely breathe.

Junie turned at the sound of the front door. Sarah stood in the doorway, head down, thumb in her mouth. She walked purposefully toward Brian's car and tried to open the door. It was locked. She tried again and again until finally Brian snapped, "Stop it, Sarah."

Sarah didn't stop. Again she tried to get in the car. When the door wouldn't open, she began pounding on it with her fist.

"Sarah!" Junie reached for her arms.

Sarah let out a shriek.

"This is all I need," Brian fumed.

Junie wrestled with Sarah, pulling her away from the side of the car. "We'll see Daddy soon," Junie assured her.

Sarah shook her head from side to side, then pointed to herself, then the car. She obviously wanted to leave.

"We'll leave in a few days. We're staying with Grandma."

Sarah kicked at the air, struggling to be set free.

Brian mouthed the word *questionnaire* to Junie.

Junie held up her palm. "Not now. I'll do it after we get home."

"Right." Brian started the car, his eyes fixed on the hood.

"Call me when you get there," she hollered over Sarah's cries.

"Right," he said, and drove away with a screech of the tires.

Chapter Fourteen

Junie sped down the highway toward the bakery, windows down, letting the wind carry away the scratchy residue of saying goodbye to Brian. She pulled off the interstate and headed toward town. *An hour fifteen, not bad.* The bakery wasn't really a quick *run* from Ruth's house, but her mother knew that, and she didn't seem to mind watching Sarah for a few hours. Besides, Junie needed a sanity check, and Shane was the best source of sanity around.

She breezed into the bakery. The smell of sugar, vanilla, and cinnamon permeated the air so thick she could taste it.

"There she is!" Shane opened his lanky arms, and Junie fell into them. "You okay, sweetie?" He kissed the top of her head.

"I'm good. Thanks for holding down the fort. Mom says hi." Junie tossed her purse on the oak desk and snagged a thick white apron from a hook on the wall. "Mm. Is that what I think it is?"

Shane lifted the right side of his mouth in a mischievous grin, his perfect string of white teeth set off by his shock of spiky red hair. He held up a finger, went deeper into the kitchen, and came back with a beautifully presented white dish with two pieces of thick baklava in the center, chocolate drizzled over the top and across the plate in an elegant design. "When you called to say you were coming by, I figured you needed a little comfort food."

Junie picked up one of the fluffy pastries and took a bite. The warm nuts and cinnamon blended together perfectly, and the phyllo dough fell apart in her fingers. "Heaven. Daddy would have loved this."

She followed Shane through the narrow doorway and into the front of the cozy bakery. There were four round tables near the plate-glass windows that overlooked the street. Junie sat down at the one nearest the corner. She gazed out the window at the sign that Shane had set out on the sidewalk. She loved the draw of the sign, the way it reeled customers in off the busy street. There was something about those two words, *Today's Special,* that made people take notice, and Shane was a master at choosing decadent treats to feature. Today's special was the Chocolate Coconut Macaroon, and she knew they'd be sold out by day's end.

They were in the slow hours, after lunch and before the hunger of the afternoon set in. They'd spent many mornings sitting at the same round table next to the window, chatting before getting to work. Shane knew about the growing tension between her and Brian. He'd talked Junie down from many ledges over the years, and more recently, he'd been on her side with regard to Sarah and not giving up until a diagnosis made sense. Shane's nephew had been diagnosed with ADHD a few years back, and Shane swore that the medication took away his entire personality. Shane called it the R2-D2 disease, *Where the meds change children into robots*.

Junie was glad for the familiarity of their ritual. The tension in her jaw and shoulders relaxed.

"So tell me." Shane put his hand atop hers. "How's Ruth? How did Sarah do?"

"Leaving Mom felt like I was abandoning her, and it was a relief, all at once. I have all this." She waved her hand in the air. "I have my normal chaotic life to fall back into, and Mom has...nothing. She'll go through her life in an empty, lonely house." Junie thought about her words and silently promised herself that once she went back home, she'd make the time to be more present for her mother, rather than blowing her off as an unnecessary interruption. "Sarah's with Mom. Brian went home, but we're staying for a bit longer."

He cocked his head. "Should we worry?"

"About me and Brian?" Junie nodded, then shook her head from side to side. "I don't know. I don't think so. I think it's just Sarah and now this." She took a deep breath and relayed the last few days to him, tiptoeing over the flashes of memory like pebbles under bare feet. "What do you think about the memories?"

"That's weird."

"Yeah, that's what I thought, too. Brian is not pleased."

"Maybe you were just replacing yourself with Ellen? Do you remember your dad tickling you on the floor? Surely you went in the shed with him."

"No." Junie shook her head adamantly. "My dad was not a tickler. He was a science teacher. He was loving, but not that kind of loving, you know? He showed his love by sharing his knowledge and applauding my successes, but not with physicality. And as far as his shed goes, no way." She finished her baklava. "Got anything else?"

"More?" Shane lifted his eyebrows at her empty plate.

"No. Ideas about the memories of Ellen?"

"Nope, fresh out. What does Brian think?"

Junie thought about the way Brian had looked like a wounded animal when she'd yelled at him, mistaking him for her father and Sarah for Ellen. She could understand why his hurt had so quickly morphed to anger. "Brian thinks I'm trying to sabotage his relationship with Sarah. I wonder if I'm just losing my mind."

Shane lowered his voice. "We're not talking about Ellen here, are we?"

Junie shook her head, thankful that Shane didn't make her spell it out.

"Well, are you?" he asked.

"Losing my mind? Probably."

"No, are you sabotaging his relationship with Sarah?"

Junie held his gaze, her teeth clenched. "No, of course not." She drew her eyebrows together. "At least I don't think so." She escaped into the kitchen.

Shane followed.

"You just lost your father, and you're stressed about Sarah. Ellen is…revisiting you. It makes sense that you might be looking to avert attention from all of that, and maybe pushing Brian away is your scapegoat, your way to gain some space?"

Could she be driving Brian away on purpose? Was she so sick of battling with him about Sarah that she'd begun pushing him away? Maybe Shane was right. Maybe she was setting up obstacles, making it harder for Brian than it needed to be. Junie pretended to look over the daily order sheet.

"I don't think I am, but maybe. I'm so confused." She tossed the clipboard onto the counter and covered her face in her hands. "This thing with Ellen and losing my dad, it's just too much. I mean, I feel like I'm dealing with losing my dad better than I'm dealing with the memories of Ellen. Or maybe I'm not dealing with losing him at all. I haven't felt it hit me like a brick in the face, like it *should* hit me." She turned her back to Shane and said quietly, "I can't help but wonder if he was somehow tied into Ellen's disappearance."

"Sheesh! That's a leap, don't you think?" Shane leaned against the counter next to Junie. "Look, you're exhausted. This is your dad we're talking about. Ralph. The man who raised you, who taught you that adding detergent to your water, baking soda, and vinegar gives you a better eruption for your volcano."

Junie laughed.

"That doesn't sound like the same man who could've done something to your friend."

Junie wanted to believe him, but there was a nagging at the back of her mind that she couldn't shake. "You're probably right." She had to get the thoughts of her father untangled from her thoughts of Ellen, and the only way to do that was to figure out why she was having them.

She hugged Shane. "I think I just needed to touch base. Thank you."

"For what?" Shane asked.

"For being here. I'm gonna go see what I can dig up."

"I hope you mean that figuratively."

Junie slowed her speed as she came off the highway and drove down the quiet streets toward the Gettysburg library. She pulled into the parking lot and parked beside a row of hedges. This was it. This was the last place Ellen had been seen. Junie breathed deeply, wishing she were there for some other reason: a school project for Sarah, volunteering, anything other than hunting down clues to Ellen's disappearance.

Ivy laced the sides of the concrete steps leading to the once white building, which had grayed with age, making it look even more regal than she'd remembered.

The magnolia tree out front had branched tall and wide, blocking the view of the front window. Junie stepped from her car, thinking of Ellen skipping up the walk. A shiver ran up her spine. She considered turning back, driving away, and letting go of her need to discover whatever lay beyond her memories. But she couldn't turn her back; the pull was too strong.

Junie opened the heavy oak doors and stood in the entrance, breathing in the smell of aged wood and old books. The odor wasn't unpleasant or musty; it was simply distinct. She walked through the wide center of the building, wondering if Ellen had known when she left the library on that fateful day that something horrible was about to happen, or had she skipped away from the prominent building with a smile and been scooped off the street by some dangerous ex-con? Why did the police assume she was abducted? Was there any proof? She could have been abducted, but something felt incomplete, like when she substituted applesauce for butter in baked goods to make them low fat. Sure, it might go undetected by most people, but she knew it wasn't the best. Ellen's abduction felt fraudulent somehow.

Junie sat in a cubicle, facing the library computer, feeling bad for leaving her mother with Sarah even though she didn't seem to mind. She hadn't really lied to her. *I just have to run to the bakery.* She did have to touch base with Shane, but she also wanted to get a handle on the thoughts she was having. She glanced at her watch. She'd been poring over articles for half an hour and hadn't found much on Ellen's disappearance. She'd have to head back soon. According to the articles, Ellen had been at the library before she disappeared, as Junie had remembered. Then there was a gap in time before she was reported missing, a full five hours between when someone saw her leaving the library and when her mother had reported her as missing.

Junie and Brian had spoken about Ellen's disappearance only a handful of times. Talking about it made Brian angry and depressed, so Junie put away her own selfish need to talk about the memories of her best friend. She'd learned to compartmentalize her feelings for Ellen and her life with Brian. The two did not intersect often, and when they did, it was very short-lived. What she remembered from their brief conversations was that the day of Ellen's disappearance, he went home after lacrosse practice, and then his mother sent him to look for Ellen at the library. He didn't find her there, so he went back to the school, thinking she might be there; then he went to the park, but didn't see her there either. He said he walked all the way back to the library, which was about a mile and a half from the park, but he decided it was getting late and she would probably be home by then, so he turned around and went home. When Ellen didn't show up at dinnertime, her mother began to worry. Mr. Olson went looking for her after he returned home from work, taking Brian with him. Two hours later, Ellen was reported missing. Things were different back then. Unlike the couch potato youth of today, fixed to computers or glued to cell phones, back then children played outside, walked to and from friends' houses, and played sports for fun. Kids would leave the house in the morning, pal up with their friends, and come back later in the day. It was difficult to keep track of them, but it wasn't a time of fear. Without the Internet, pedophilia and abductions were rarely spoken of. Besides, the neighbors were pretty close-knit. Had there been anything unusual, they trusted each other to keep their children safe.

Junie thought about her childhood and how one day Ellen was there and the next day she wasn't. Not for the first time, guilt pressed in on her for having lived for all those years, happily going through each day, while no one even knew where Ellen was, or what had happened to her. Her mother always said that life was not fair. She thought about her father and how he and her mother had been waiting to retire to do all the things they couldn't while her father had worked. She thought about Sarah and her regression and subsequent silence, which no one could understand or accept. *No,* she thought, *life is not fair.*

Junie read through a few more articles, unearthing nothing more than a mention about neighbors and persons of interest being interviewed. She checked her watch—she wanted to talk to Mrs. Walters, the librarian, and she needed to check in with Shane—not because of the business, but because she just needed someone to lean on.

Mrs. Walters had worn only purple for as long as Junie could remember. Today was no different. Donning a light purple polyester pantsuit that buttoned up to her neck, Mrs. Walters stood behind the counter, smiling at Junie. "I wish I remembered more, Junie, but it was so long ago."

Another dead end. "Did you see anything out of the ordinary? Hear anything when she left? A scream?"

Mrs. Walters shook her head. Her thin, sharp nose and gray, professionally set, short poufy curls made her look a bit like a poodle. "Her brother and father came looking for her. You know, she was a spunky little thing. At the time, I guess I thought she was probably just playing at a friend's house and would turn up sometime soon." She shook her head, her eyes cast downward. "It's a shame, a real shame. Thank goodness there weren't any other abductions. Poor girl."

Junie's stomach turned. Little girls didn't just disappear—did they? She thought of Sarah and how quickly her personality disappeared. She pushed aside the ache of missing that unique spark of her daughter and wondered where she should look next.

Chapter Fifteen

Junie pulled onto the highway, heading back toward her mother's house. She couldn't shake the feeling that the memories of Ellen meant something. She glanced at her cell phone, wondering why she hadn't heard from Brian. She picked it up and speed-dialed his number. It went straight to voice mail. She called his office.

"Hi, Stacy. It's Junie. Is Brian in?"

The young receptionist's voice sang out in a breathy falsetto pitch. "Not yet, Mrs. Olson. He called and said he left your parents' house late, so he'd be in later in the afternoon."

Junie hung up the phone, wondering why her husband had lied and where he had gone. Could he have been too upset to go to work? She checked for missed calls—none. She wondered if something had happened, a car accident, maybe, then realized that she'd have been notified. Too annoyed to go back to her mother's house, Junie decided to pay a visit to the Gettysburg police department. Maybe they could clarify who the *persons of interest* were in Ellen's case, and she could get the notion of her father being involved out of her head.

Clouds moved across the sky, shading the sun and casting an ominous gray to the previously sunny day. Junie wondered if it might rain. She shivered, thinking of her father in the coffin, rain pelting the ground above him. "Okay, Junie, enough of that," she told herself. An hour and twenty minutes later, thanks to her heavy foot, she pulled into the police station parking lot.

Deputy Lyle sat behind a giant wooden and metal desk, the same desk that Junie remembered from her youth, when he had been *Officer* Lyle. He'd gone gray around the temples, and his once slim waist had expanded with age, but his welcoming grin and friendly eyes remained.

"Juniebug, how are you?"

"Well, I'm thirty-one, for one thing, so not really a bug anymore," she joked.

"Heck, you'll always be that smiling little girl who came into the station with her father, reporting a car that didn't stop for a passing turtle."

Junie sat in a metal chair across the desk from Deputy Lyle, feeling twelve years old again. She looked around the familiar police station, remembering the day her father had brought her in to report the turtle incident. He'd held her hand in his. He hadn't wanted to bring her in. He'd told her it wasn't an offense to not stop for a turtle, but she'd insisted. Her father had spent the next two weeks making TURTLE CROSSING signs with Junie and posting them up on trees around their neighborhood.

"I'm sorry about your dad. He was a good man."

Junie looked down at her lap. Her heart swelled with pride. Guilt tamped at that swelling. *Of course he was. I'm such an idiot.* "Thank you."

"How's your mom holding up?"

"Oh, you know, as well as to be expected. Dad's death was so sudden, it's still really fresh. She's not really used to it—none of us are."

"I don't think we ever get used to it." He leaned forward on the desk. "So, to what do I owe this pleasure? I haven't seen you since you brought that beautiful baby girl around."

Junie fiddled with her keys. Her face flushed. "Sarah. She's four now." Junie didn't want to talk about Sarah. When people asked how Sarah was, Junie had to decide if she was going to say all positive things, which is what most people wanted to hear—she's happy, loves school, has tons of friends—or if she was going to say the truth—I think she's happy, she only speaks to me, she isn't really accepted easily by other children, she wets her bed and sucks her thumb. Oh, and her dad wants to label her as emotionally disturbed. "I've been thinking about Ellen Olson."

"I wondered when you'd come around about that. You two were thick as thieves." He cleared his throat. "Your mom, the Getty Girls, they all worried over you day and night. Do you remember that?" He didn't wait for an answer. "We all wondered what would happen, if you would be okay."

Junie shook her head. She had no memory of anyone doting on her. She felt Deputy Lyle's eyes on her, as if he were gauging her reaction. "I have moments of memories. You know, Selma telling me not to worry, that sort of thing. I just can't remember anything around the actual event. I don't really remember what happened. The investigation, I mean. Brian hates to talk about it, so all I really know is that she was there one day and gone the next."

Deputy Lyle stood and opened the drawer of a filing cabinet. "That's pretty much what did happen, Juniebu—Junie." He removed a thick green file and leafed through it. He let out a long sigh and sat back down in his chair, eying the framed photograph of his daughter, just a few years younger than Junie, which sat on the corner of his desk. "You sure you want to dredge all of this up again?"

"That's the thing. There's nothing to dredge up. I have zero memories of what happened when she disappeared or afterward. It's like I blocked it out—and all the weeks around it, or something—and I feel like I've disrespected our friendship by not remembering." Junie hadn't realized that she'd been carrying that guilt until the very moment the words left her lips. As much as it hurt, she was almost relieved, saying the words aloud, as if she'd been carrying them around like a burden, and a great weight was lifted. She brushed her hair from her face and said, "I think I need to understand what happened. I mean, I know they didn't find her, but did you guys have any idea what happened? Who took her?"

Deputy Lyle set the open file down on the desk.

Ellen's seven-year-old face smiled up from the last school photo ever taken of her. Junie's heart jumped. She hadn't seen Ellen in so many years. The ache of missing her came rushing back. Junie's hand shook as she reached for the photograph. "May I?"

Deputy Lyle nodded. A gentle smile plumped his cheeks. "Junie, the way these things work, it's not like in the movies, where clues are left on sidewalks and wrapped up in a half-hour episode. We traced Ellen's whereabouts and came up with nothing. No witnesses, except the librarian who had seen her leave the library. She'd said goodbye to her, and Ellen had told her she was going home for dinner."

Junie stared into Ellen's eyes, barely registering his words. There she was, the Ellen she had spent every moment of her childhood days with. The Ellen she'd taken for granted as always being there—a friend at the ready, whether it was Saturday morning at seven a.m. or an afternoon after school. Ellen, whom she ached to talk to, to laugh with, to see.

Deputy Lyle cleared his throat, calling her attention back to him. "After that, she vanished."

Junie handed him back the photograph. "Vanished? People don't just vanish." Junie's heart raced. She thought of Sarah playing in the yard by herself and made a mental note not to allow her to do that anymore. *Vanished*.

"Right, we know that. We talked to...those we thought might have seen her." His eyes drifted to his lap.

"Like who?"

Deputy Lyle shifted in his chair. "People along the route home. People from the school, the library."

"The school?"

"Yes, in case she had gone back to the school. Brian had thought she might have gone there. Sometimes she stopped by to play in the playground, heck, all the kids did. We checked the creek, in case..."

"And did you find anything?" *Just ask him!* She fidgeted with her hands.

"It rained that evening, making it hard to find anything. Even the search dogs couldn't nail down a scent. There seemed to be a trail to the school and to the creek, but you girls used to go there all the time, and there was no indication of a struggle, or even that she'd been there."

"It just makes no sense." *I can't ask him. I have to.* Junie wanted to know about her father—had he been questioned? Even though Shane had put her father's integrity into perspective for her, Junie still needed to hear the truth from Deputy Lyle. She was afraid to ask. Junie loved her father, and part of her didn't want to disappoint him, even though he was no longer living. She didn't want Deputy Lyle to think poorly of her, either. Junie bit her lip and stifled the urge to ask the question.

"No, it doesn't make sense, but not all things do.

We're not far off the interstate. The thought is that someone might have scooped her off the sidewalk, and—'"

She had to do it. She couldn't keep herself from asking. Her heartbeat sped up, as if it might burst from her chest at any moment. "Did you question my father?" *There, I said it. Shit.*

Deputy Lyle squinted. "Your father?"

Junie knew he was waiting for her to say something, some rationalization as to why she'd asked. *I saw a vision of him. I have a funny feeling. I'm an idiot.* She sat in silence, feeling foolish for pursuing the question.

"Yes." He nodded. "We questioned your father. We questioned all of the teachers, neighbors, her family." He crossed his arms. "What's this really about, Junie?"

"I don't know. I just want to get a handle on it. Were there any primary suspects?"

"Is there something about your father that is troubling you?"

His eyes narrowed. He looked at her more intently, as if he could see into her thoughts. Was it her imagination, or had he straightened his back, sat taller, more in control of the conversation? Yes. She was sure of it. He'd changed into cop mode right before her eyes.

Junie sighed. "No. I just thought that understanding what had happened would help, but I'm left with the same questions that I had when I came in here." *I just want to know for sure that Dad wasn't a suspect.*

Deputy Lyle came around the desk and sat on the edge of it. He folded his arms across his chest and softened his voice. "There is little in life worse than when a child disappears, Junie. It's hard when we don't understand what happened, or why, but we have to accept it and move on. I know it's hard, without closure, and with losing your father, but let it rest, Junie. Don't make yourself crazy over the past. Your father was a good man."

What about when the past becomes your present? Junie stood to leave, feeling as though she now had more questions than she did when she'd arrived.

Chapter Sixteen

"We thought you'd be back ages ago," Ruth said sharply.

"I'm sorry, Mom. I got a little tied up at the bakery." Junie leaned over and kissed the top of Sarah's head, inhaling the soft scent of Johnson's Baby Shampoo. Sarah didn't look up from the game on Ruth's laptop. Sadness swept through Junie like rushing heat. She wished her daughter would wrap her arms around her neck and croon about how much she'd missed her.

"I wish you would have called. I was worried."

The tone in Ruth's voice made Junie realize how self-absorbed she'd been. She'd left her mother to care for Sarah, expecting it to be acceptable, and it was *acceptable,* but that didn't make it right. Ruth was strong, but Junie was expecting too much from her. She'd slipped into spoiled teenager mode too easily, leaving Mommy to deal with whatever she couldn't at the moment. She stood before Ruth and took both of her hands in her own. "I'm sorry, Mom. You're right. I should have called."

Ruth looked away, then back at Junie, and Junie watched her furrowed brow soften. "It's okay. I'm just—"

"No, Mom, it's not okay. I'm really sorry." She wasn't going to allow Ruth to let her off the hook that easily. She *was* being selfish. She needed to pay more attention to her mother's feelings. Was Junie mollycoddling Sarah in the same way? She had to wonder.

"It's fine, Junie. Really. I'm just tired."

"As well you should be. I'll try to be more thoughtful." Junie sat down at the table. "Have you heard from Brian? He was gonna call when he got back to Virginia, but I haven't heard from him." She tossed her cell phone on the table. "I was hoping it was a cell issue."

"No," Ruth said. "He's busy and probably upset. He'll call when he's ready."

Golden boy Brian. Why was she upset over the way her mother made excuses for Brian? Ruth saw the kindness in him, that he was a loving father and a generous husband, and he was all those things, but there was another side to Brian—a side that only a wife could see. Junie would be lying if she called him mean or even unloving, but there was definitely something that flashed cold at times when she needed warmth. *Ready may never come.* "I was thinking about taking Sarah to the park. Do you want to come?"

"No, I think I'm going to lie down for a while. What

about dinner?" Ruth opened the fridge and stared into it.

Junie stood and put her arms around Ruth, hugging her close. "We have more food from the neighbors than we could ever eat. Go, rest. We'll grab something ourselves, 'kay?"

Ruth nodded, and Junie wondered how she might ever get past her father's death. She'd heard about spouses losing their will to live when their partner died. The thought sent a shiver up her back and a wave of nausea through her gut.

"Want us to stay?" Junie asked.

"No, please, go. Sarah needs some activity." Ruth laid her hand softly on Sarah's head. Sarah didn't even flinch. "I'll be fine. I'm just going to rest a bit. If I need anything, I can always call Selma or Mary Margaret."

And just like that, Junie realized exactly how very apparent her inability to nurture was. She longed to be relied upon in that same confident way that Selma and Mary Margaret were. If her own mother wasn't feeling taken care of by Junie, was her own family?

Junie buttoned Sarah's yellow sweater as Sarah stood motionless, nonplussed. They stood before the swings, which hung still above a circle of mulch. The seesaw perched on its angled mount, lonely and bare, the blue paint chipped, names etched deep into the wood. Junie walked over until she stood next to its center. She reached out and ran her finger along the initials, long ago scratched into the seesaw with a sharp, gray rock. The etching, "E + J," was now filled with paint. Only the faintest outline of the letters remained. Fogginess bloomed in the back of Junie's mind, moving forward like dark storm clouds. Junie leaned against the seesaw, grasping the edge within her fingers. She could see Ellen's face, smiling, laughing at the edge of the woods. She heard her own, younger voice. "No, Ellie! We're not allowed!" Ellen turned and disappeared into the woods. The darkness in Junie's mind masked the evening with a blur filled with flashes of Ellen's screaming face, her arms reaching far above her head, palms out. *Shit. Not now.* Junie dropped to her knees, her face in her hands. The rhythm of the chains that held Sarah's swing grated at the edge of her mind. *Sarah.* Junie lifted her eyes, looking through her fog at Sarah's outline on the swing. She blinked again and again until her vision cleared and her heartbeat began to slow.

Sarah swung, oblivious to her mother's plight. She kicked her legs forward and back, swinging slowly.

What the hell is happening to me? Junie stood on shaky legs. Her eyes scanned the edge of the woods. She had to clear her head, figure things out. Deputy Lyle hadn't clarified anything relating to Ellen's disappearance, and Junie felt like she was at a dead end. Ellen had to be showing herself for a reason. She must be missing something.

"Sarah, let's go for a walk." She heard the tension in her own voice and mentally ticked it down a notch.

Sarah continued swinging, her gaze straight ahead.

"Come on, honey. Let's go to the creek." She slowed Sarah's swing and helped her down to the ground.

Sarah took her hand. Her eyes remained flat, but her lips curled into a smile.

The brush thinned as they walked hand in hand deep into the woods, toward the sound of trickling water. Junie's heartbeat slammed against her chest as Ellen's giggles played in her mind. *No, Ellie! We're not allowed!* Junie had spent her youth yielding to her father's warnings about the danger of being near the creek. *Only derelicts hang out back there. The creek is deceptively deep. Anything can happen.* She'd spent her teen years ignoring those same warnings, secretly spiriting away into the woods around the creek.

Trees were etched with hearts and initials from young sweethearts. They followed a well-traveled path, the dirt below them packed hard and bare. They passed Lovers' Rock—an enormous boulder that couples could climb atop to be out of sight when they were feeling amorous. Junie had visited the secret love nest only twice that she could remember. Both times were with Tommy Dee, a middle school crush. She'd tried to entice Brian into going there with her, a playful little jaunt to experience what it might have been like with him, lacrosse star extraordinaire, had they been together in high school, but Brian would have nothing to do with the *childish games*.

The familiar scent of damp earth became stronger as they neared the creek, inciting a trembling in Junie's limbs that she didn't understand. It dawned on Junie that she could remember before Ellen had disappeared, and she could remember starting school in the fall, but she was not certain how much time she had lost. Was it days? Weeks? How far back, how many details, did most people remember from when they were seven years old? As they walked toward the creek, she tried to retrieve particular memories to define just how much time she had forgotten—or blocked out.

Sarah pulled to the side and stopped walking. Junie continued forward, stopping when Sarah's arm became immovable. She turned around. "Sarah?"

The edge of Sarah's yellow sweater was caught on a bramble.

"Oh goodness," Junie said, and began pulling the poky spines from her daughter's sweater. "How'd this happen, sweetie?"

Junie followed Sarah's silent gaze beyond the bramble to the edge of the creek, where it arced toward a thick tree. Beneath the tree, a mass of large rocks spilled into the creek. Atop the rocks lay two red roses.

Junie's hand covered her gasp. Sarah struggled toward them. Junie squeezed Sarah's hand in her own, urging her back toward the park. Sarah whimpered, pulling toward the thorny brush.

Great. When Sarah got her mind set on something, it was hard to break her focus. "Sarah, let's go back. It's getting late." *And Mommy's getting anxious.*

Sarah would have no part of a retreat. She tugged with all her might, flailing her blond hair from side to side and clawing at her mother's fingers. Sarah loved roses as much as Junie loathed them. Sarah broke free from Junie's grasp, running on her tiny legs toward the flowers. Junie hurried after her, ignoring the spiky thorns as they snagged her jeans. A chill ran through her when Sarah picked up the carefully cut green stems and smelled the beautiful blooms.

Junie reached for the stems. "Honey, they're prick—"

At that very second, Sarah screamed, dropping the roses to the ground. She held her bloodied finger straight out in front of her, her eyes clenched shut, her pain-filled wail echoing in the woods.

Junie reached for her. Sarah fought and screamed, batting at her mother's hands.

"Let me help you," Junie pleaded. The setting sun streamed through a mass of trees, illuminating Sarah's tortured face. Junie froze. It was her daughter's voice that cried out, but it was Ellen's fearful eyes, Ellen's shaking hands before her. Junie tried to hear past the rush of adrenaline that coursed through her. *Ellen*. She knew it wasn't Ellen, and yet she couldn't see through Ellen's fright. Junie shook her head, trying to clear her mind. *Sarah. Sarah*.

"Sarah!" Finally her voice boomed from her throat. *Sarah, not Ellen. Sarah*, she silently repeated. She reached for her frightened daughter, who was caught up in a full-blown tizzy. They'd been through this before, and the familiarity didn't make it any easier.

Junie knew what she was in for—an hour of crying and screaming over three drops of blood. She looked toward the sky, silently pleading for guidance. All she wanted was to help her daughter, console her, take the fear away from her, and run from Ellen's image. She dropped her eyes to the roses. Her mouth formed a hard line. She stared at the roses as if they were the devil incarnate, wishing they'd ignite into flames and be gone. What the hell were they doing there, anyway?

Chapter Seventeen

Junie let out a loud sigh and fell backward onto the bed, thankful to have a moment's peace. Her arms splayed above her head; her hair surrounded her like a golden halo. The evening had been flat-out exhausting, between settling Sarah down and wrestling with memories—were they memories, and if so, could she trust them? Whatever they were, the images were wearing her out. She found it hard to concentrate on her daughter and her poor mother. Her mom was the one who really needed support, and Junie had basically left her to fend for herself while she tried to figure out the mess in her mind. *I'm a lousy mother and a lousy daughter.*

The cell phone rang on the bedside table. Junie sat up and looked at the name, then at the clock. *Really?*

"I thought you were going to call when you got there. I've waited all day." Why was she being such a bitch?

"Sorry. There was a lot to do. I was running all day long."

Junie pursed her lips. "Mm-hmm."

"How's Sarah?"

Exhausting. "Good. I called your office."

Silence.

"They said you left the area late. Where'd you go?" Junie was fueled by the aggravation of the images of Ellen, Sarah's fit, and the loss of her father...*God, Daddy*. She could barely see straight. She felt abandoned and hurt, and now angry. Brian was the lucky recipient of Junie's wrath. She knew she sounded like the quintessential jealous wife, someone she'd never been before, and at the moment, she didn't care.

"They were wrong. I was there all day."

"Stacy was wrong? Miss overly efficient Stacy? Really, Brian? What's going on?" Junie paced the bedroom, waiting for his answer and knowing that no matter what his excuse, she was in the mood for a fight and Brian would be the lucky recipient of her wrath.

"I guess. Anyway, I know we argued, and I wanted to apologize."

"Brian, Stacy doesn't get things wrong." Maybe the distance between them had already become bigger than she imagined. The thought of another woman prickled at the back of her neck. It was a crazy thought—she knew it was. Brian was trustworthy. He loved her. He loved Sarah. But lately, he'd been pulling away. She might be reaching for straws, but better to reach than to ignore them until they poked you in the ass. "Brian"—she hesitated—"is there someone else? I mean—"

"What? No."

Silence thickened between them.

"I stopped by Dad's office to say goodbye."

"You did?" Her anger softened. It pained her to see the space between him and his father, and she hoped that maybe this was Brian's way of reaching out to Peter. Maybe Brian was making an effort to patch thing up between them. Now she felt horrible. *I'm such a bitch*.

"Junie, we might have fought but God, I wouldn't ever cheat. Ever. I stopped for coffee, then swung by afterward. I just didn't want to go to the house. The memories are too painful. I must've just been out of the office when you called. I might have been a little late, but not much."

Junie ran her hand through her hair, snagging on a tangle. She looked at herself as she walked by the mirror. She had bags under her eyes, her hair was frizzy. She was a mess. She exhaled long and loud. "I'm sorry. It's just...losing Daddy, and now seeing Ellen—"

"You saw Ellen again?" he asked.

Junie nodded.

"June?"

"Yes, yes, I saw her again. The same thing. She was screaming. I took Sarah to the creek, and—"

"Why would you take Sarah to the creek? I thought I told you that I didn't want her going there," he fumed.

"What? You never told me that," Junie said. "You said you didn't want to go there with me. What's the big deal? We went for a walk." She sat on the edge of the bed, listening to Brian huffing angrily into the receiver. "I thought it might help me remember something about Ellen."

"Would you please stop with Ellen? Focus on the things that matter. Focus on filling out the papers for Sarah's doctor and helping your mother get through your father's death. She lost her husband, Junie. She needs you. Sarah needs you. Ellen is gone. Gone. You can't help Ellen, but you can help them."

Junie's head fell forward. Tears streamed down her cheeks.

"Junie?" he said tenderly.

"Yeah?" she whispered. "I just thought…what if it's a sign. What if, after all these years, she's trying to tell me something?"

"You've got to let it go. The past is the past. You can't bring her back."

"Maybe, but I can't just ignore it. It's driving me crazy. You just don't understand."

She was met with silence.

"Brian?"

When the silence stretched to the point of discomfort, Junie said, "I'll be here for Mom, but I have to follow my gut on this. I owe that to Ellen."

"Even if it tears your family apart?"

His words hit her like a kick to the gut. They were slipping apart, like a balloon rising to the sky, slipping through a child's fingers. Her throat was tight. Did she really have to make a choice? Could she make a choice?

On one side, she had Brian and Sarah, and on the other, Ellen's memories. It wasn't an easy choice. She wanted Brian and Sarah. She loved them, but she also loved Ellen, and she began to wonder why Brian was threatened by her memory. He had never been the type of husband to follow her every move or to complain about her decisions. Why now?

Chapter Eighteen

Junie settled Sarah in front of the television and sat with Ruth in the kitchen, drinking tea and reading the morning paper. Maybe there was some truth to what Brian had said—maybe Ellen *was* taking over her life. She needed to be there for her mother, mentally and physically. God knew that her mother had always been there for her.

"Mom, I thought we'd spend the day together. You know, maybe do a little shopping or something."

"I was thinking about sitting here all day and eating that entire cake that you made. You know, if you keep baking like that, we're all going to weigh six hundred pounds." A conspiratorial smile spread across her lips.

Junie laughed. "You're lucky. I wanted to bake last night, but I fought the urge."

"Did you hear from Brian?"

Junie closed her eyes against a wave of annoyance.

Brian. It's always about Brian. "Yeah, late last night."

"Everything okay?" Ruth asked tentatively.

Her mother was the only person Junie knew who could ask one hundred questions with just two words. She mulled over her answer. *I don't know. I wonder if we've grown too far apart to fix. Maybe he* is *seeing someone else. Maybe I'm just a bitch.* "Yup, it's all good."

"Still arguing about the questionnaire?" Ruth smirked.

"Wha…How?"

"Before he left." She ran her finger around the rim of her cup. "Brian asked me to convince you to fill it out."

"Great. Now he's got you in on this?"

Ruth leaned across the table. "She's my granddaughter." She looked toward the den. "Why not fill it out, Junie? So they find an emotional issue? Who cares? I didn't raise you to be one of those parents who thinks her kid is above…anything."

Junie stared into her mug.

"June, listen to me."

Junie lifted her eyes to meet her mother's serious gaze.

"There's no shame in that little girl, and don't you dare make it seem like there should be."

"I'm not." *Am I?*

"Yeah, well, the longer you wait to do this, the more she hears you and Brian fighting about it, the more she'll think something *is* wrong with her, and there's nothing wrong with that perfect little girl."

Junie looked away from her mother's direct stare. "See, even you don't think there's anything *wrong* with her."

"Wrong? No. Different? Troubled? Off? Yes. She's crawled so far into herself that she's a shell of who she used to be. Her personality has disappeared. Our little girl doesn't talk, Junie, she doesn't smile, laugh, or play."

Junie stood and went to the window. She spoke in a rushed whisper. "Don't you think I know that? Come on, Mom. I get it." She set her mug in the sink and crossed her arms. "What's the questionnaire going to change?" Junie sat across from her mother, leaning forward so their faces nearly touched. "She has no emotional issues."

"That hour-long fit last night wasn't an *issue*?"

Okay, maybe. "Pfft. She was upset, freaked out by the blood."

"The fact that she shies away from people, from her own father, isn't an issue?" Ruth pushed.

"She doesn't shy away." *Does she?*

"When's the last time she went on a play date?" When Junie didn't answer, Ruth asked, "Did you have to change the sheets this morning?"

I can't go down this path, not today. "Okay, listen, so she has some stuff to deal with. I get it, okay? But that questionnaire—they're looking to label her as something, and I don't think kids regress without some kind of physical issue. They've ruled out abuse, so it has to be something medical."

"Why, June Marie? Why does it have to be something medical? When did you get your medical degree?"

Junie stared her down, feeling betrayed and ridiculous all at once. The truth was, the more she thought about Sarah, the more she believed her issues might be purely emotional, but she just didn't want to accept that path. After all, wouldn't that indicate her faults as a mother?

"Can we please just enjoy our day together? I really need some downtime, and I'm sure you can use a distraction, too." Junie reached for her mother's hand.

Ruth put both hands around her mug.

Junie bristled. She felt as if she were running down an unfamiliar path toward a darkened cave, Brian, Ruth, and Sarah standing before the entrance to the cave, and Ellen just inside. As she neared the entrance, Sarah lifted lonely eyes, Ruth shook her head, making a *tsk* sound, and Brian whispered, "Make your choice."

Chapter Nineteen

They drove through the cemetery gates. Junie had convinced Ruth that they all needed a day of activity, and Ruth wanted to visit Ralph's grave before heading out. She pulled into the parking lot and immediately recognized Peter's Mercedes.

Junie helped Sarah from her car seat, watching her mother hesitate as she stepped from the car. Ruth peered in the direction of Ralph's grave. Her fingers gripped the edge of the door.

"You okay, Mom?" Junie stood beside her.

"Yes, yes, fine. I still can't believe he's gone," she said.

They moved slowly toward the grave, and Junie could feel her mother gathering strength. Peter stood, facing Ralph's grave, his shoulders rounded forward, his head bowed. Junie and Ruth approached from behind, linked together by Sarah's small hands.

"Peter, how are you?" Junie stood behind him.

He turned doleful eyes toward them, a bouquet of roses in his right hand.

Junie's breath caught in her throat. She took a step backward, casting her eyes away from the roses.

"He was a good man." He set the flowers on the freshly turned earth and embraced Ruth. "I'm so sorry."

Sarah slipped behind Junie's legs, tugging her mother's arm toward the parking lot.

Ruth wiped a tear from the corner of her eye, nodding. "Yes, he was a good man."

Junie turned toward Sarah, giving her a stern *Not now* look. The tips of Sarah's white sneaker touched the edge of Junie's dark shoes. Images hit her fast and hard—a white sneaker illuminated by the streetlight on the Olsons' driveway. Peter appearing from the dark backyard, stopping dead in his tracks when he sees the sneaker, jogging over and swooping it up. Disappearing again into the cover of the night.

"What do you think, Junie?"

Junie hadn't heard the conversation. She stared at Sarah's sneaker, her heart pounding against her ribs.

"Junie?" Ruth repeated.

Junie looked up, her mind reeling. *When was that? Did it mean something*? "Sorry, Mom. Um, what?"

"I was asking Peter about having dinner with us next week. Are you up for it?" she asked.

"Yes, yeah, sure." *Stop it! You're making yourself crazy, overthinking everything*. Junie wondered where the sneaker fit into her crazy memories. Why was it significant? Maybe it wasn't even Ellen's. She was definitely losing her mind. Surely she'd seen Peter picking up after Ellen a million times—hadn't she? She pulled at memories that must be there somewhere, but the only ones that appeared were of Peter huddled over his work, the lamp illuminating his desk like a beacon in the darkened den. She couldn't remember Peter ever picking up shoes or toys after Ellen, day or night. In fact, she could barely remember him being around. She had only vague memories of him arriving home in one of his dark suits, briefcase in hand, but he had never been a hands-on father with Ellen.

Peter turned thoughtfully toward the grave. "I just wanted to say goodbye. Ralph had been so kind to Ellen and Brian." Peter looked into Junie's eyes. "Do you remember the summer Ellen disappeared? He was preaching to you both about summer learning."

"No," she said. *How much of my life is missing?* Junie ran through her memories of the summer when Ellen disappeared. There weren't many, and she couldn't be sure of the timing. Near as she could tell, the last memory of Ellen that she had was them skipping to school the morning that she'd disappeared. She wondered about when she'd seen her at the edge of the woods, which she thought had to have been close to when she'd disappeared at the end of June—the trees were full, flowers in full bloom. She remembered the police and their questions, and her next memory was of her and Ruth buying school supplies, which brought her to the end of August. She was pretty sure that she'd lost the memories of almost the entire summer when Ellen had disappeared.

"Ralph had a way with kids. He was always teaching them something science related." Ruth's eyes softened. She looked down at Sarah. "Poor Sarah will barely remember him, if she does at all."

Sarah clung to her mother's legs, her face buried in the backs of her thighs.

"Life moves fast, Ruth," Peter said, "but somewhere in her mind, the memory of her grandfather will live on, if only as shadows. I'm sure she won't lose him altogether."

Like you lost Ellen? Junie instinctively grasped Sarah's hand.

"How's Susan?" Ruth asked Peter.

Junie watched their exchange. She knew that Susan had kept in touch with Brian in a very peripheral, duty-bound way. She called every year on Christmas, and each time she called, Brian endured the same strained and limited conversation: "Sarah's fine. Junie's well. Work's good." She had always assumed that it was the same between Peter and Susan.

"She sends her love. She wished she could have come for the service, but she just..." His voice trailed off.

"It's okay. I know." She nodded. "Too many harsh memories. Please, give her my love, too."

Junie realized that Peter and Susan must have been in closer touch than Brian and his mother, and she softened toward Brian, who now somehow appeared like the outsider in the family.

"I will." Peter turned to Junie. "Brian left?"

Junie's head snapped up. "Didn't he come see you?"

Peter let out a slight breath of a laugh. "No, he did not." He looked off into the distance. "I'm afraid too much has transpired in our lives. I think I remind him of all we've lost."

A pang shot through Junie's chest. "He...he didn't come to see you at the office on his way out of town?" *He lied?*

Peter shook his head. "Don't I wish." Peter turned to leave. He crouched down, smiling as he looked at Sarah. "Hey there, pumpkin. Grandpa has cookies for you at his house. Will you come visit me?"

"Of course she will." Junie's voice carried a note of worry. *What the hell is Brian up to?*

Sarah's eyes grew wide. She clenched her mother's hand so tightly that Junie gasped.

"Sarah!"

Sarah burst into tears, tugging her toward the parking lot, shaking her head vehemently from side to side.

Junie tried Brian's tactic. "Sarah Jane Olson, you stop that right now." Sarah continued to pull away, mews of discomfort coming from behind her clenched lips. Junie's chiding had no effect on Sarah, which left Junie feeling like a heel.

Peter forced a smile. "She's been through a lot. It's okay." He put a hand on Junie's arm for a brief second, sending Sarah into a full-blown tizzy of screams and kicking fits. "Tell Brian...well, just tell him I love him and I'm proud of him."

Oh, trust me, I will.

"That was flat-out embarrassing," Ruth said quietly. "Really, Junie, something has to be done."

It was embarrassing, but she'd tried the harsh approach that Brian thought Sarah needed, and it had done no good. Maybe what she needed wasn't tough love, but a more direct, meaningful approach. She looked down at her daughter, who had calmed down after Peter left, and she wondered why she'd had such a visceral reaction. What better way to find out than to ask?

"Sarah, honey," she said, kneeling in front of her. "Why were you pulling me away?"

Sarah's thumb was jammed in her mouth, her eyes cast downward.

"Sarah?"

Silence.

Junie stewed. Brian's words came back to her, and this time, she acted on them with a harsher tone. She reached up and yanked Sarah's thumb from her mouth. "Tell Mommy what you need. Say the words. You know the words. You were an early talker. You know the words. Remember the day you wanted to stay at the toy store and I wanted to leave? You were exasperated? You said, 'Mommy, I'm exasperated!' You can tell me what you need. I know you can."

Sarah didn't flinch. She didn't blink. She just stared at her mother in silence.

Junie put her hand to her mouth, her hope

shattering against her daughter's silence. *You're not making this better. She will talk when she's ready to talk.* Junie took a deep breath, then asked in a frustrated, stern voice, "Sarah Jane, what on earth is going on with you?"

"Junie!" Ruth touched her arm.

"No." Junie's body shook as she turned to face her mother. "Brian's right. This is foolish. She's got to be doing this for attention." She turned back to Sarah. "What is it? Are you afraid of Grandpa?"

Silence.

"I didn't think so." She put her hands on her hips. Sarah withdrew to the safety of Ruth's side. "Is it me? Are you angry with me and just trying to embarrass me?"

"That's ridiculous," Ruth spat, then lowered her voice. "We're in a graveyard, Junie. Don't you think she might be frightened by that alone?"

Junie was too annoyed to think rationally about where they stood. She zeroed in on her own inadequacies. "Is it ridiculous, Mom? Maybe it's not. Maybe she's sick of having a mother who isn't as strong or as forgiving as you."

Hurt traveled to Ruth's eyes. "Junie?"

Junie covered her face in her hands. "If Daddy were here, he'd tell me what to do. He'd take apart what I was seeing with Ellen until it fit some science"—she waved her hands in the air—"something understandable. He'd look in his books and figure out what was wrong with Sarah in about a minute!"

"Don't glorify your father, June. He knew about the

changes in Sarah—you told him yourself—and he didn't know what was going on with her any more than the rest of us." She put her hand protectively on Sarah's back, drawing her closer to her side. "You need to get ahold of yourself. This"—she waved toward Ralph's grave—"is hard for all of us. All of us, June, and you can guarantee it's equally as hard for your daughter and your husband as it is for you. Stop this nonsense and pull yourself together."

With that, Ruth took Sarah's hand and led her back to the car, leaving Junie alone, wallowing in self-pity.

Junie took a few deep breaths, tucked her shame away, and followed them to the car.

"I'm sorry," she said, clicking her seat belt in place.

"Ice cream."

Her mother always knew what to do.

They sat on the stone wall licking their ice cream cones in silence. Sarah's ice cream dripped down her hand. She licked it efficiently, then went back to work on the scoop.

"We were here when Ellen went missing, right?" Junie asked.

Ruth sighed. "Junie, do you think we need to talk about that right now?"

"Yes, I do. I want to understand what's going on, and I can't do that unless I understand what part of my memory is missing."

Ruth drew her eyebrows together.

“I can’t remember any of it. I remember being here with you, because Daddy didn’t come home that day, and the next day I remember you telling me she was missing, but I don’t remember the days, weeks, or moments around it all.”

“There isn’t much to tell. You waited for Daddy to take you for ice cream, and when he didn’t come home, I took you.”

“That’s the only time I remember him not coming home.” Junie tossed her cone into a nearby trash can.

“There were other times. You were little. You just don’t remember.”

“Okay, well, I remember you being mad.”

Ruth ate her ice cream without answering.

“Is there something more? Something I’m missing?”

Ruth looked at Sarah, then back at Junie, speaking quietly. “There is a lot that goes on in a marriage, Junie, as you know, and yes, you’re missing things, but not things I care to discuss.”

Okay, fine. “Anything about Ellen?”

“And your father? No.” Ruth pursed her lips, then softened. “Ellen went to the library. Brian went looking for her, then Peter did, then the police. No one found her. End of story.”

“But how can that be the end? People don’t just vanish.”

“People vanish every day,” Ruth said. “They never found a trace. They questioned Daddy, but that was ridiculous. They questioned all of the neighbors. Poor Susan, she just couldn’t take it anymore. Peter was rooted in his partnership, so he couldn’t move out of state, and he didn't want to disrupt Brian's good standing in school." She shook her head.

"What?"

"The golden boy. I love Brian—you know that—but I often wondered if Ellen ran away from home."

"That's ridiculous. She loved Brian." Junie watched Sarah nibble the last of her cone; then she wiped her hands and face with a napkin.

"Yes, she did, but she was always in his shadow." Ruth stood and took a few steps away from Junie, drawing one arm around her middle, the other to the bridge of her nose. When she turned back to Junie, her eyes pleaded for relief.

Junie lowered her voice, though there was no need. "Is that why Daddy didn't want me to marry Brian? Because he blamed him for Ellen's disappearance?" She'd never let Brian know about her father's one-time, quiet question. *Junes, are you sure* he's *the one for you, the right family for you?* But she'd never forgotten the meaning behind it.

"I don't know, Junie. Ellen was always second fiddle to Brian. Peter paid her no attention, even Susan—and I can't believe I'm saying this out loud—even Susan, though she treated her like she was a cute little girl, bought her dolls, dressed her up when Ellen allowed it, drew comparisons of Brian's brilliance to Ellen's childish ways."

"She was seven!" Junie fumed.

"Yes, she was, and we all saw that. But even at seven, Brian showed remarkable intelligence, and they couldn't help but compare."

"So it's Brian's fault? How could you not have told me all this before?" Her face flushed.

"It's not Brian's fault. He was also just a child, a smart child. It just was what it was. That's the thing about life, Junie. It's not all neat and tidy. What you see and remember as a child isn't necessarily what you see and recall as an adult. Who knows? Maybe Ellen never felt any of what we saw. Lord knows I could be wrong in this. I mean, a seven-year-old wouldn't make it far, would she? Especially in this small town."

Chapter Twenty

The next morning, Junie packed the car, determined to set things right with Brian and to make more of a directed effort with Theresa—maybe even complete the damned questionnaire and finally figure out what was going on with Sarah. What her mother had said to her made an impact. *What you see and remember as a child isn't necessarily what you see and recall as an adult.* She felt useless as a mother and a wife and felt even worse about leaving Ruth so soon, but Junie worried that if she didn't work on her marriage, she might not have one to go home to—and that was something that she wasn't ready for.

"I love you," Junie said as she hugged Ruth. "Will you be okay?"

"Of course. I'm a big girl, and you have to take care

of our little girl." She smiled at Sarah, who was buckled into her car seat. "Besides, I'm never really alone. Mary Margaret and Selma are ten steps away."

"I'll call you, and if you need me to come back, just ask. You know I'll come."

"Go. I'll be fine. I love you."

The house was quiet, with nothing out of place. Brian had obviously not cooked himself dinner the evening before or eaten breakfast that morning. Junie imagined him stopping for a protein bar and a cup of coffee on his race in to work, and her mind wandered to when they were newly married and they'd cherished every moment together. She'd wake early to fix him breakfast, and they'd talk about...what? She couldn't even remember. It made no difference what they talked about. They were happy. She distinctly remembered the ease in which they lived, as if every moment together was stolen and breathed new and exciting air into their relationship. Sure, Brian had long days when he was on difficult cases, and she had mornings when she'd have to race out the door early to the bakery, but they did so grudgingly, and they'd savored their goodbyes until the last possible second, when they'd reluctantly pull away from each other's grasp.

Junie sighed, hoping they could find a way to put the stress of life behind them and make their way back to happier times—even if they were a different type of happy. Navigating the changes in their daughter, and their lives, and forging a united front would be a good start. She called Theresa and scheduled an appointment for later that morning, then called Shane, who assured her that he was fine with handling Bliss for a few more days. He thought she was doing the right thing, focusing on Sarah and Brian, and wished her luck.

Dr. Theresa Don's office was filled with colorful photographs of faraway places and littered with toys and stuffed animals. The first time Junie had entered the roomy office, she'd noticed the "did he touch you here" dolls that the other therapist had shown Sarah. Thankfully, Sarah did not have to repeat that line of questioning, as the other therapists had reported that there had been no indication of any physical abuse.

"Junie, Sarah, how are you?" Theresa's eyes opened wide, her lips curved in a welcoming smile.

She is good at this, Junie thought. Sarah was immediately drawn to her.

Sarah jumped onto the couch, blanket in her fist, thumb in her mouth.

"I see you've brought your blanket today, Sarah. Were you feeling a little uneasy coming to see me?"

Sarah's thumb hung from her mouth, the tip of her nail clenched in her teeth. She didn't answer.

Theresa's eyes never left Sarah's face. "I heard that your grandpa died. Do you want to talk about it?"

Junie held her breath. Theresa was so direct. Had Junie missed the impact her father's death had on her daughter?

Sarah's eyes welled with tears.

Shit.

"It makes you sad, doesn't it?" Theresa asked.

A tear slipped down Sarah's cheek, pulling at Junie's heart.

"When someone dies, it's okay to be sad. It means that you loved that person very much, and I'm sure your grandfather loved you, too." She reached down to the table and picked up a drawing pad and pen.

"I heard, Sarah, that you wanted to come home with your daddy a few days ago."

Sarah sat stoically. Her eyes shifted from Theresa to her mother and back.

"Was that because it was too sad for you to be there? Or maybe you worried that Daddy might not come back?" She eyed Junie, as if to indicate that sometimes children make the correlation of losing someone to losing others they loved.

Theresa drew a sad face on the pad, then drew a face with an *O* for a mouth and big, open eyes; then she drew a happy face. She showed the pad to Sarah, pointing to each face. "This is sad, this is scared, and this one is happy. Can you circle the face that looks the way you felt? Or maybe you'd like to draw your own face?"

Sarah didn't move.

Theresa put the pen and pad down and turned toward Junie. "Sometimes these things take time. Why don't we let Sarah play awhile while we talk?"

Sarah slipped off of the couch and sat among the

toys. She kept her thumb in her mouth, blanket in her fist, and made no other movement.

Theresa and Junie left the room, leaving the door open. Theresa leaned forward, speaking in a quiet tone. "You mentioned that she reacted strongly toward Brian's father? This is a very difficult question, but do you think there could have been any emotional abuse by him? I realize that there is no indication of physical abuse, but the scars of emotional abuse are not as easily noticed."

"What? No, definitely not." Junie crossed her arms, then remembered therapists saw that as a defensive posture and dropped her arms to her sides, feeling foolish.

Theresa nodded. "And this wanting to leave with Brian, did Sarah say anything during the time he was gone that indicated she wanted to see him, or missed him?"

Junie shook her head. "She didn't say a word. Period."

"And how were you, when Brian was leaving? Might Sarah have picked up on any behavior between the two of you that would make her want to be with her father? Sometimes children can become protective if they feel one parent is...berating the other one unnecessarily."

"What are you implying? That I'm a mean wife and my daughter had to protect her father?"

Theresa touched her arm gently. "No, Junie, that's not what I'm saying at all. Parents argue, and with the death of your father, emotions are heightened. She could have heard you two and mistakenly thought you were upset with Brian."

Junie thought about when Brian left. They were arguing about the questionnaire. *Great. It's my fault...again.* She looked at Sarah, who hadn't moved, then sighed. "Yes. We were arguing about the questionnaire that you asked me to fill out." She bit her lower lip, then said, "I'm sure she heard us. God, I just suck at parenting."

"No, you don't." Theresa then asked, "Did you fill out the questionnaire?"

Junie shook her head, feeling like a heel.

"Do you want to do it now?" Theresa asked.

Junie laughed, imagining a comical scene. *Hey, ever had needles in your eyes? No? Well, how about you try it now, with me!* "No, thank you."

"Okay, I have another idea. Let's sit down and talk, just you and me." Theresa led her to an alcove by the window. She could see Sarah through the open doorway, but Sarah couldn't hear them.

"Junie, Sarah feeds off of you and Brian. You are her world. She will thrive when you thrive and she'll falter when you falter."

"So it is my fault." *Great.*

"No, but you and Brian do feed into her feelings at times, as all parents do. So when you and Brian argue—especially about Sarah's regression—you need to do it out of earshot."

Junie nodded.

"Easier said than done, I know." Theresa twisted her wedding ring.

Junie's stomach ached. She was exhausted and at her wits' end with regard to Ellen and Sarah. If she didn't get her worries out, she just might explode. "Theresa, can I ask you something? It's not about Sarah, so if you need to charge me for this time, that's okay."

"Sure, but I'm not an adult psychiatrist. You know that, right? My specialty is children."

"Yes, I know. But right now, you're all I've got." Junie told her about the images she'd seen and the inner turmoil the images caused her to feel. "I think she's trying to tell me something, but I don't know what."

"This is pretty far out of my norm, but my gut reactions go a few different ways. Ellen's disappearance is like the secret never told. You've carried the worry of it, suppressed the urge to figure it out, because Brian can't allow himself to talk about it. Of course it would bubble to the surface with your dad's passing. I assume this is the only person you've lost since her disappearance?"

"Yes. My mom's parents were in a car accident when I was young. I never really knew my dad's parents."

Theresa seemed to chew on that for a minute. "With Sarah's recent regression and your father's surprise passing, your stable base is threatened—cracked, even, which can lead to lack of sleep and almost a constant state of free-floating anxiety."

"Yes, that's exactly how I feel, but it's tearing me and Brian apart. He's acting angry toward Sarah, fed up with me. I don't blame him, but he's such a calm person in general. That's one of the main things that drew me to him. He could always see things analytically, separating feelings from issues and moving forward in the best possible way. That's what makes him such a good lawyer. But now it's like we're always on edge, and the last time I saw him like this—" Junie's jaw dropped open. Her hand moved to her mouth. "Oh my God."

"What is it?" Theresa asked.

Junie's eyes were wide. She glanced quickly at Sarah. "After Ellen disappeared, I tried to go over to her house a few times. My mom had told me not to, but I needed to. I *needed* to see that she wasn't there, see it for myself." She lifted her eyes to meet Theresa's. "Brian acted this way then. When Ellen was there, he'd hang out and talk to me. He was nice when I came over. But once Ellen disappeared, he'd chase me off. He was mean, yelling at me to go away and not come back. How could I have forgotten that? It hurt so badly at the time."

"You didn't forget it. You repressed it. It must have been too painful for you, so your mind buried it."

"Wouldn't it have come back before we got married? I mean, Ellen was my best friend. Her disappearance was a major event from my youth, my formative years. How could I have forgotten how radically Brian had changed? His personality completely changed. He became mean. I'd say *that* was pretty significant."

"Was it, or was it just a sad and angry brother missing his sibling? Perhaps you were a reminder of what he'd lost?"

"Then why would he date me? Marry me?" She

pressed her hands into her temples. Why hadn't she thought of that years ago? Had she purposely not gone down that line of thinking? Was she afraid of losing Brian? Had they been living in some warped, make-believe world where they pretended that Ellen hadn't existed? The thought sickened her. The reality of what seeing her must remind Brian of pained her. When she spoke, her voice was strained. It sounded distant in her own ears. "It must be painful for him to see me every day, don't you think?" Junie mouthed, *Oh my God,* and closed her eyes.

Theresa reached out and touched her arm, causing Junie's attention to be drawn to what she had to say. "Junie, you can't climb into Brian's head. You don't know what he feels, or what he felt, or even what he's repressed. To him, that initial anger and the reminder that you carried as a child, might have changed to a happier reminder, or it could have disappeared altogether. There's no way to know without talking to Brian directly, and even then, he might not understand what it all means, or what he feels." Theresa looked at Sarah. "In fact, he might be angry at Sarah for changing because in his mind, the reality that he can't protect those he loves might be coming back to haunt him."

Chapter Twenty-One

Junie wasn't sure if talking with Theresa helped her see things more clearly or if they confused her even more. On one hand, the idea of Brian seeing Sarah's changes as just another person he couldn't protect made total sense, but when she tore it apart, shredded his actions to get to the innards of the issues, something still didn't feel right. She had no idea what to believe. What if he'd married Junie for some warped reason, like to remind him of Ellen, to keep him close to her? Junie was so confused that her thoughts felt like Jell-O in water, slowly tearing apart, becoming transparent, until they were indiscernible.

Junie stepped from the shower and wrapped a towel around her body. There was only one way to find out. She dressed in a nightshirt, checked on Sarah, fast asleep on dry sheets, and went downstairs to wait for Brian to return from the office. She wondered if she'd ever get used to his working until nine or ten at night, and she hoped that was all he was doing.

The click of the dead bolt woke Junie from where she dozed on the couch. She glanced at the clock, eleven thirty. She listened to Brian's footsteps as he neared the kitchen, passing right by the living room. She sat up, listening not out of mistrust, but out of curiosity. He used to head straight upstairs, having missed Junie while they were apart. She heard him leaf through the newspaper, fill a glass of water, and eventually, walk back toward the stairs. As the moments passed, she grew agitated. When did he stop going directly upstairs to see her? Why did he? How could they have let their relationship slip away?

"Brian?" she called softly, fiddling with the blanket that lay across her lap.

"Junie?" He came into the living room and flicked on the light. "What are you doing down here in the dark?"

His accusatory tone bothered her. She had a right to wait up for her husband, didn't she? "Waiting for you." It came out sounding snippy, which hadn't been her intention.

"Is everything okay?"

Junie was wide awake now and suddenly feeling very combative. "Yeah, I just wanted to talk to you."

Brian sighed, grating on Junie's already irritated nerves.

"You're home so late?"

"Big case, you know that." He sat in an armchair and removed his tie. "I'm beat. What's up?"

"I talked with Theresa today."

"And?"

Junie resented his hurrying her. She was his wife, and she'd seen him for only a few minutes each day for the past month, not to mention having lost her father. Her blood simmered. "And she got me thinking about everything, about us." *How the hell can I phrase this without him walking away?*

"I told you that I'm not having an affair," he snapped.

"I don't think you are." *Do I?*

"What then?" Brian sat back, crossed his arms.

"Do I remind you of Ellen?" She held her breath.

"What the hell are you talking about?" He stood, as if to dismiss her.

"Brian, sit down, please. I just want to talk to you."

"About my dead sister. Why is it always about my dead sister lately?"

Junie was on her feet, fueled by anger. "How can you say that? You don't know she's dead. It's like you've given up on her."

"I have." His nostrils flared.

They stared each other down like angry dogs. Until finally Junie said, "Yeah, well, I haven't. But that's not even what I want to talk to you about."

"Then what the hell is it? I'm tired, and I have to be back at work in six hours. I don't have time for this nonsense."

His words shot through her heart like an arrow. "Nonsense? Your wife needs to talk to you and you call it nonsense? Well, I'm sorry I'm not one of your damned clients, Brian, but there are a few things I need to know." She crossed her arms to stop them from trembling. "When you look at me, do I remind you of Ellen—good or bad—in any way?"

Brian's jaw clenched. "You're crazy. Why are you even asking me this?"

"I'm not crazy. I just need to know."

"No, you don't remind me of my freakin' sister, okay? Not at all—until you bring her up; then, yes, you are like a beacon with her face on it."

Junie nodded, holding back tears. "When you see Sarah, do you see Ellen?"

"Junie." He turned his back.

"Do you?" she said through her breaking heart. *Please say no.*

He spun back around, fire in his eyes. "You have no idea what it's like. My family is falling apart and it's my fault."

Junie felt as if she'd been kicked in the gut. "It's not your fault. Sarah's regression has nothing to do with you."

"Junie," he said, his eyes damp. "I think you should take Sarah and stay with your mother for a while."

Junie's voice was caught beneath a giant lump in her throat. "What? Why?"

Brian shook his head.

"Why?" she yelled. "The last time you treated me this way was when Ellen disappeared."

Brian looked up at her.

"That's right. I remembered. You chased me away,

just like you are now."

Brian picked up his tie and headed for the stairs.

"Brian, don't walk away from me."

"Junie, just go. Please. I can't deal with this right now."

"Deal with this? *This* is your life, Brian."

"No, *this* is you trying to dredge up our past, not live our current lives."

Junie's lower lip trembled. How could they ever move beyond this moment if Brian was neither ready nor willing to deal with the past or help Junie to understand it?

Chapter Twenty-Two

Junie had slept on the couch and woken up when Brian left for work. She checked on Sarah, fast asleep on wet sheets, and decided it wasn't worth waking her. She'd bathe her after she called the babysitter.

Her eyes stung from crying herself to sleep, and she could feel the puffiness that remained. She had to make a decision by the time Brian came home; that much was clear. That gave her several hours to figure out if she should go back to her mother's or beg for forgiveness. She was leaning toward her mother's.

Shane carried a cup of coffee to the table where Junie sat, red faced and exhausted. He'd brushed back his hair, though it was so thick it still bubbled up in places. Shane wasn't what one would call lanky, but he was tall and his limbs were long. He was soft without being pudgy. Shane was comfortable. That's the word that seemed to fit his build, and Junie warmed at that comfort as he approached.

"Thanks." She feigned a smile.

"Tell me what I can do." Shane, her foothold to reality, offered strength when her husband could not. Junie felt guilty, leaning on him for support when she should be leaning on her husband, but she had nowhere else to go.

She shook her head. "There's nothing. I just needed to be here, I guess, to figure things out."

"So, you said the therapist thought Brian was somehow linking you to his memories of Ellen, like he married you to feel less bad about her being gone?"

"I don't know. It's all so convoluted, but at the same time, it makes perfect sense. He's just acting so weird. I mean, is he ending our marriage? Is this a separation?" She broke down in tears.

Shane came to her side of the table and embraced her. "Honey, it's okay. I'm sure he doesn't mean that." Shane held her until she stopped crying. He sat beside her. "Remember when we first met? You told me that Brian was the one who urged you to open Bliss. He supported your every move. And remember when Sarah started preschool? He had you take pictures at the house, at the entrance to the school, after school? That's not the sign of a man who doesn't care about his family. Before Bliss picked up steam and you wanted to quit, he was the one who pushed you and convinced you to make it work."

"Yeah," Junie whispered.

"This is just a bump in the road."

"He's never home."

"You knew that he would have times when he was never home when you married him. When we first met, you told me that you were proud of him for having the work ethic that his father had."

Junie thought about what Shane had said. She had been proud about Brian's work ethic, though she wasn't sure why. Peter was always working, never with his family. Why would she have thought that was a commendable trait in her husband? "Yeah, well, it sucks, and he lies to me."

"Lies to you? He's a lawyer. That's what they do." He smirked.

Junie lifted her eyebrows.

"Sorry. That was stupid. He shouldn't lie to you."

"He said he went to see his father, and he didn't. I have no idea where he went."

"Do you think—"

"No. I don't know what to think anymore."

Shane sat up straight and said, "Then there's only one thing to do. Go see him at his office, where he has to talk to you like an adult, without ultimatums. You can sit down in his office and hash this all out."

"You think?" Junie wiped her eyes with a napkin. Shane was ushering her out the door with a pat on the back.

He held his pinky and thumb spread out next to his ear. "Call me."

Chapter Twenty-Three

Junie sat in her car in the parking lot outside Brian's office. She folded and unfolded her hands, nervous about confronting him. Shane was right. She had to clear the air. She had to find out why he had lied to her. If he was out with clients, he'd have told her. He must have something to hide. Junie's stomach lurched. If he wasn't with another woman, where was he? She watched a car pull into the parking lot.

Peter stepped from his black Mercedes and headed toward the building, cell phone pressed to his ear.

Junie reached for the door handle, then stopped. Brian was coming out of the building, walking hurriedly toward his father. Junie dropped her hand and slid down in the driver's seat. Luckily, she was parked in a packed lot, where her van looked just like every other minivan.

She watched them, her heart pounding fast and

hard. They didn't shake hands. Brian stood with his arms crossed, legs spread slightly apart. Peter's hands were in his pockets. He looked from left to right, then nodded toward the side of the building.

They disappeared behind the building. Junie could no longer see them. She was dying to follow them, to hear what they were talking about. Were they making up? Why wouldn't Brian have told her about meeting Peter today?

Peter appeared from the side of the building and headed for his car. Brian looked around, then headed back inside.

Junie dug in her purse for her cell phone. She dialed Brian's cell.

"Hey," he answered.

"Where are you?"

"Work."

"What are you doing?" she asked.

"What do you think I'm doing? I'm working."

"I was going to come see you. Can you talk?"

"Can't. I have a client in my office."

Liar. "Who?"

"Junie, what's going on? Why so many questions?"

"I just—" *I want to know why you were with your father*. "Sorry. Anything good going on today?" *Tell me; please tell me*.

"No. Look, I gotta run. Are you on your way to your mom's?"

Junie's heart sank. He had meant it. "Soon."

"Drive careful."

"Wait—before you hang up."

"Junie, come on."

"I saw you with your dad just now."

Brian didn't answer.

"Brian, I saw you. What's going on? Why didn't you tell me about seeing Peter?"

"We're working on a case."

"A case?"

"Yes, a case." His voice was edged with irritation. "Look, I gotta go."

"Why didn't you tell me that you were working on a case with him? He said you never went to see him when you left Mom's."

"What are you talking about?" he snapped.

"The other day, when you said you went to see him and that's why you were late arriving back at work."

"I never said that."

He lied. Oh my God, there must be someone else. If he's cheating, it's over. "Brian, don't play attorney with me. I know what you said." How much more was he hiding from her?

"Look, you're confused. You're tired, and you're heartbroken. You misunderstood. I gotta go," he said in a curt, attorney-client tone.

The line went dead.

Chapter Twenty-Four

Junie peeled out of her mother's driveway, having planted Sarah safely inside. She was in no mood to be caring, nice, or in any way reasonable. She drove by the schoolyard, then the library, and finally, the park. She pulled the van over to the side of the road, her stomach tied in knots. Why was Brian lying to her? She picked up her cell phone, scrolling through her texts. There were no new messages. Junie had always thought they could weather any storm. Maybe she was wrong. She crossed her arms over the steering wheel and rested her head on them. Tears streamed down her cheeks.

If Brian has found someone else—oh God. She couldn't even think about it. He wouldn't do that. Would he? He had been working late for weeks, and she never questioned him. She'd never had a reason to. Had she denied Sarah's issues one too many times? Was Brian done trying? Done putting up with Junie's belief that

Sarah had medical issues? Did she have medical issues, or was she a master manipulator? And what about Peter? What the hell was going on between Peter and Brian? Was she making something out of nothing? No, she was sure she wasn't. She knew what Brian had used as his excuse for being late to work, regardless of his backpedaling—he did say he'd gone to see his father, and yet she knew he had not. But now he was lying about *having* seen him. Nothing made any sense.

Junie leaned back against the driver's seat, let out a loud groan, and wiped her eyes. She couldn't even be a good daughter. She'd run out on her mother yet again, leaving her as soon as Sarah was occupied. She just couldn't sit in the house thinking about Brian lying to her, or her father being buried, or the flashes of Ellen that attacked her at odd moments. She couldn't even take listening to Sarah's silence, and she didn't dare bring Sarah with her to the park. She couldn't deal with another one of her episodes.

I have to be the most unlikable mother in the world.

She looked at the glove compartment with disdain, then clicked it open and withdrew the questionnaire. Junie took a deep breath and began answering the questions. *I can do this.* When she got to the question about abuse, Junie dropped the questionnaire into her lap and cried. It was all too much for her to think about. She folded the questionnaire and stuffed it back into the glove compartment. Junie pulled her shoulders back and wiped her tears. She had to get a grip on herself. She was going to figure this out once and for all.

Junie headed into the woods, wrapping her arms around herself to ward off the mounting chill. The sun streamed through the trees, and Junie realized that the air wasn't cold at all. The chill was coming from inside of her.

The trickling creek she used to find soothing now felt threatening, like a witch holding a poisonous, yet tempting, apple.

She inhaled deeply, watching the water trickle down the modest slope, thinking of how the images of Ellen had suddenly consumed her thoughts. What was she chasing? Why was she chasing it? Junie knew there must be a reason she'd blacked out the painful memories. She wanted to forget them, but they begged to be remembered.

Only derelicts hang out back there.

"Not now, Daddy," she said to the quiet woods. *Daddy.* What on earth did he have to do with all of this? Why was he leaning over Ellen? She had to remember to ask her mother about that.

She pictured Ellen urging her into the woods. "Come on, Junes. It'll be fun." She'd said *no* more times than she could count, heeding her father's harsh command. She'd watched Ellen disappear into the woods. She remembered moving slowly across the park lawn and into the edge of the forest, but Ellen had disappeared. She stood at the edge of the woods, her heart beating as if it might explode inside her chest. She'd heeded her father's warnings, hadn't she? She hadn't gone into the woods. Had she? She couldn't remember. *Damn it! Let me see. Take me there!* she silently pleaded.

Junie pushed through the brush until she stood before the roses lying forgotten on the ground. The edges of the stems were cut clean across, just as she'd remembered. One of the stems had been trampled on. The petals were wilted, not brittle. Junie bent down and touched the edge of the petal. Her arms began to tremble. A tingle ran up her arms as clouds drifted overhead, shadowing the sun. The woods grew gray. Junie closed her eyes, willing herself to remain strong and not retreat from the hated flower or the rush of memories that now stirred in her mind. *Darkness, rose petals floating by in the wind. She was a little girl again, standing near the Olsons' garden, hidden beneath the flowering dogwood tree at the edge of the property. Peter stood amid the roses, his face buried in his hands.*

Junie felt dizzy. She turned at the sound of giggling.

A young couple was making the climb to the top of Lovers' Rock. The boy, dressed in cargo shorts and a long-sleeved polo shirt, couldn't be older than fifteen. He scaled the rock, then turned back to the girl waiting at the bottom, her short skirt hiked midthigh as she stood with one leg on the boulder, one on the ground. Her sweater fell open to one side, exposing a cocoa-brown shoulder, smooth as butter. She leaned toward the ledge in the rock, then clearly feigned her inability to climb, mocked a slip back down to the ground—giggle, giggle. *Shit.* Junie ducked behind a tree, her heart pounding behind her ears, waiting for them to climb out of sight.

Ten long minutes later, with the couple safely atop the boulder and out of sight, Junie hurried through the brush and out of the woods. What the hell was she doing, anyway? They were flowers, nothing more than flowers, probably placed there by some young couple in love.

Junie drove to her mother's house with tunnel vision, her mind focused on Ellen. She wasn't a believer in ghosts or spirits, but by the time she got to her mother's house, she was convinced that Ellen was guiding her toward something. The way her body tingled and her mind went foggy when she saw Ellen's image was just not normal. What it was that Ellen was guiding her toward, she had no idea.

She came through the front door to find Sarah curled up on the couch next to Ruth, who was flipping through pages of an old photo album, telling Sarah where each photo was taken. Sarah looked nonplussed.

"Feel better?" Ruth asked.

"I don't know." Junie threw herself on the couch next to Sarah and kissed the top of her head. "What are you guys up to?"

"A trip down memory lane." Ruth turned the page. Ellen's face beamed up from behind oversized sunglasses. Her cheek was mashed against Junie's, each girl missing a front tooth. "That is your mommy," Ruth said to Sarah.

Sarah looked up at Junie, then back at the picture, and up again.

"How old were we?" Junie asked.

"Seven." Ruth looked up, her eyes sad and thoughtful. "This was two weeks before she disappeared."

"Mom, tell me about that day." She watched her mother steel herself against the conversation. "Please."

Ruth let out a long sigh. "It was a day, Junie, just like any other day. You girls went to school. You went to visit Katie Lane after school; Ellen had gone to the library. You came home and waited for Daddy. It was Tuesday, after all. And well, as you know, he didn't make it, so you and I went for ice cream. Ellen never came home." Ruth shrugged. "There isn't much to tell. After that, everything changed. Suddenly our safe little neighborhood came under scrutiny, and the days of kids playing freely outside came to an end." Ruth looked away. "It was a shame. Nowadays, kids don't even play outside at all. Selma can't get her granddaughter away from the darn computer—and she's eight."

Junie didn't care what kids did nowadays. She was focused on the day Ellen disappeared. "I went to Katie's house? I don't remember that."

Ruth nodded as she turned the page. Her father stood with his arm around Junie, a test tube held up to the light. Junie was looking up at him with a wide grin.

"Mm-hmm. You had gone home with her after school. Daddy was going to pick you up there after work, but you decided to come home early, so you walked."

"Why?"

"How do I know why? That was a hundred years ago." She turned the page. Ralph stood before his shed with a bucket of tools.

"Why can't I remember that?" Junie ran her finger over the image of her father.

"I don't remember everything from when I was seven. I don't remember everything from five years ago. Junie, we age; we forget. Let it go."

Sarah glanced from her grandmother to her mother.

"Does Katie still live around here? I haven't seen her in ages." Maybe Katie had some answers. Suddenly her heart sank. "It could have been me that day. If I walked home alone, why didn't they take me? Why Ellen?"

"Why is the sky blue? I don't have the answers, but I'm certainly glad it wasn't you," Ruth said.

"Geez, Mom. I just got lucky, that's all." Junie got up and went to the computer.

"Now what?" Ruth asked.

"I'm looking up Katie's address."

"She's Katie Frank now, and she lives on Laurel."

Chapter Twenty-Five

Katie Frank looked nothing like the freckle-faced, red-haired, lanky girl that Junie remembered. Her hair was a mousy brown, obviously dyed, and she had gained enough weight that she had a muffin top hanging over her too-low hip-hugging jeans.

Katie squealed when she opened the door. "Junie Marie!" She wrapped her arms around Junie as if they'd been the best of friends. Junie couldn't remember ever being very close to Katie, but she went along with the charade.

"Katie! You look amazing!" She followed her inside the small rambler. "You have a beautiful home."

"Nah, but it suits me. It's just me, you know. Bobby and I separated two years ago."

"I'm sorry," Junie said, though for the life of her she could not remember what Bobby Frank had even looked like. She had a vague memory of a bulky, aggressive football player. Junie mulled over the word *separated.* She wondered if she'd be using that word soon; *Brian and I are separated. I'm separated. Oh God.*

Katie waved her hand through the air. "Aww, you're so sweet. It's a good thing. Bobby and me, we were just like oil and water."

They settled onto a worn flowered couch.

"So what brings you here? I hear you've got a daughter now, and you're a baker! Gosh, I wish I could cook. I could burn water." She laughed. "Probably one of the reasons Bobby left me." Her tone was light, but Junie detected a sad undercurrent. Katie perked up a moment later and said, "Why, I haven't seen you since you got married." A smirk formed on her lips. "How is that hottie hubby of yours?"

He hates me. "Great, working, you know."

"I couldn't believe you married him after everything that happened." She lowered her voice to a whisper. "With his sister, I mean."

Junie was too anxious to stomach being fake for much longer, so she cut to the chase. "I've been thinking about Ellen."

"Oh, that poor girl. Remember the rumors?" She winked.

Junie's stomach turned.

"Rumors spread that she was abducted and sold as a sex slave."

Sex slave? How could the people in this town go that far? How could they think of her in that way? Junie felt even more like her world, her past, was crumbling around her. Junie crinkled her nose. "Really? No, that can't be true."

"Well, of course not." She smirked. "That's what they said about fifteen years ago." Katie grabbed a piece of chocolate from a dish on the table.

"Do you remember the day she disappeared?" Junie leaned forward, eyeing the chocolate.

"Of course, like it was yesterday. It keeps me up at night, all that happened."

"Do you know something? Was there more than one person who took her?" Junie reached for the chocolate.

Katie popped another candy into her mouth and laughed. "Oh, we're still doing that? Okay, I'll play along." She spoke as if the two of them were part of a conspiracy. She lowered her voice, and her eyes darted around the room. "Nah, I just assumed, you know? I mean, one person would have to drive the getaway car."

Play along? Freak. You've got it all figured out. "What did we do that day? My mom said I was with you."

"You were with me for only about twenty minutes before you took off after Ellen. Don't you remember?" She looked at Junie expectantly.

Junie shook her head. "I don't remember a darn thing." *What the hell? Where did I go?*

Katie rolled her eyes, again acting as if Junie were privy to some secret between them. "We were playing out front when Ellen walked by and waved you over. You came back and asked if Ellen could play with us, and I said my mom would only let me have one friend over at a time. You watched her walk around the corner; then you took off. Oh, I was so angry at you for dumping me like that."

Took off? Junie had no memory of following Ellen. "I'm...I'm sorry I hurt you."

"No worries. I got over it."

"So, then what happened?" Junie asked.

"Really?" She flapped her hands in front of her face. "Okay. How should I know? You took off, and the next day the police were all over the neighborhood asking questions." Katie leaned forward. "Junie, don't you remember any of this? Sheesh, I can see it like it was yesterday."

Junie shook her head. "Not a second of it. It's like it never happened. Like you're telling me a story." Junie rubbed the knot in her neck that had tightened as she listened to Katie speak. She couldn't remember being at Katie's house, much less leaving and returning. She didn't know if she'd forgotten being at Katie's house or if she'd blocked it out, but either way, she hated that there could be anything in her life that she failed to remember and Katie did remember.

"I wish I were."

Junie wanted to push her for answers, but she held back. The fear of what she might hear was suddenly too much for her to deal with in front of Katie, and in some strange way, Junie wasn't sure that whatever Katie had to say would be the truth.

Chapter Twenty-Six

Junie lay awake in the guest room at her mother's house, wondering where she'd gone when she left Katie's house. The image of Ellen standing at the edge of the woods of the park kept coming back to her. Her father's voice—*Only derelicts hang out back there*—played over and over in her mind. She threw her blankets off and went downstairs, fully prepared to bake her emotions away. Instead, Junie found herself in the kitchen, staring at her father's keys, which hung on a hook on the wall.

Junie slipped the key ring from the hook, opened the back door, and headed out into the night. Crickets chirped in the bushes. The moon shone bright, casting an eerie glow on the backyard.

The shed was dotted with tiny rust spots, like freckles on a pale body. Junie touched the lock, feeling guilty for wanting to enter her father's sacred shed. *This is silly*, she thought, and turned back toward the house. She looked up at her childhood window, which overlooked the backyard. The room was dark, the curtains drawn. She looked at the next window over, her parents' bedroom. How many nights had her parents gazed out that window when she and Ellen slept in a pup tent? Times were so different back then. She couldn't imagine letting Sarah spend the night anywhere outside of the four walls of a locked house. She couldn't even imagine Sarah wanting to.

She turned back and contemplated the shed. Taking a deep breath, Junie fished for the small key among the larger ones. She pushed it into the lock and waited for the *click* of the gears. The lock sprang open, heavy in her hand. Junie nearly jumped out of her skin. Goose bumps crawled up her arms.

She pushed the lock through the clasp. The door remained closed. Junie grabbed the clasp and pulled. The door swung open slowly, easily, until there was nothing between her and the inside of her father's sacred toolshed.

She should have brought a flashlight, a candle, something. She reached inside, knowing there was no light switch, but grasping anyway. She took one step into the shed, feeling the presence of her father, as if he were looking down on her, ashamed of her. Junie bit her lower lip, then stepped back out of the shed. Something skittered along the ground in the woods behind the shed. Junie jumped.

She looked behind her, but found no one there. She

glanced into the woods and caught a glimpse of a raccoon disappearing into the darkness. She stepped back into the shed and felt around the wooden tool bench.

"Ouch!" A sliver poked her finger. She put her finger to her lips, pressing it there. Junie crouched, opening the wooden doors under the tool bench. She felt around until her fingers landed on a big flashlight. *Yes!*

In the beam from the flashlight, Junie saw the neat and organized tools that her father had cherished. She looked in the cabinets and found shelves filled with different sized screws, nuts, bolts, and nails, impeccably sorted into little plastic bins. She turned around and looked at the shelves her father had constructed. No clues to Ellen. Nothing. Junie wasn't sure if she was relieved or discouraged. She aimed the flashlight up to the roof and across the ceiling. The beam cast a shadow on the shelf above the door, a lumpy shadow. She was here, and she wasn't leaving until every inch of the shed had been searched.

Junie spun around, snagging the stepladder. She climbed up, hoping it wouldn't topple over, and felt along the shelf with her fingers, flicking dust and dirt into her eyes. She closed them, then brushed off the filth, thinking about how lucky her dad had been to be tall enough to reach that height without a ladder. She aimed the flashlight beam so it illuminated the shelf. Adrenaline rushed through her.

She reached for a mound of darkness, moving her fingertips along the shelf. Her hands trembled with anticipation. What she expected to find, she hadn't a clue. Torn between guilt and anticipation, she wavered. *What if I find something bad? Clues to an infidelity? Something worse*? She felt fabric beneath her fingers. Junie took a deep breath and pulled the bundle down from the shelf. She climbed down from the ladder and set the flashlight on the tool bench. Junie shook out the small sweater she held in her hands. She gasped. The image of her father leading Ellen into the shed flashed before her—Ellen had been wearing the tattered blue sweater Junie held in her hands.

The sweater slipped from her fingers, landing on the tip of her shoe. Junie stepped backward, covering her eyes, as if by doing so, she might hide from the memory that had now come true.

Chapter Twenty-Seven

Junie sat on the back porch waiting for her mother and Sarah to come back from the early-morning jaunt to the store they'd taken. *We both need cheering up,* Ruth had said.

She gnawed her fingernails down to the quick, staring at the shed as if it held the answers when it really only confused her even further. Why would Ellen's sweater be in her father's shed? She had to ask her mother.

Tires rolled onto the driveway. Junie listened as one door, then the other, opened and shut.

"Come on. Let's show Mommy what you got," Ruth said.

Sarah didn't respond.

Junie looked up at the sky and wondered just how much God wanted to test her and why. She thought she'd dealt with Ellen's disappearance long ago, and she now knew that she had just blacked it out, like a bad dream. She had no idea how to help Sarah, and today's round of changing sheets had just about put her over the edge. Had she become so complacent about Sarah's regression that she was actually enabling her?

Junie jammed her throbbing finger back into her mouth, cursing the splinter that had pricked it in the shed.

The door behind her opened. "There you are," Ruth said, and sat behind her. "What's going on out here?"

"Just thinking." Junie feigned a smile.

"Well, I didn't see any more baked goods, so I guess that's good." She laughed.

Junie turned to face her mother. "Thanks for taking Sarah out. I know I suck right now as a mother."

"I wouldn't say *suck*."

Junie laughed under her breath. "Stink, sorry."

"No, suck is a good word. I just don't think it describes you. I think you're sidetracked, overwhelmed, unable to set aside the hurt that Daddy's death has unearthed, that's all." Ruth put her arm around Junie's shoulder and sighed. "You know, June Marie, I think there's a lot in this life that can make us crazy. Don't let Daddy's death be one of those things."

"I have no idea how you do it, Mom. You lost your husband a few days ago. Where does your strength come from? How can you just turn off the hurt?"

"I don't turn it off. It's there every second of the day. I just don't let it own me. Daddy didn't love me because I fell apart easily, you know. He loved my strength, and I am just honoring that trait."

"Doesn't it hurt? Don't you want to cry and curl up in a ball and beg him to come back?"

Ruth withdrew her hand, fiddling with her wedding ring. "Yes. I have my moments, when I think I hear him coming down the stairs, or I wake up in the middle of the night and he's not there. But mostly, I'm thankful for all of the years we had together. Many couples aren't quite as happy as we were, so mostly I feel like I miss my best friend, but I was lucky to have had him in the first place."

Junie nodded, wondering if she'd ever feel that way about Brian again.

"Mom, I did something that I'm not proud of." Her face flushed.

"We all do," her mother said seriously.

"I'm not sure you'd be so forgiving of me if you knew what I did."

"You'd be surprised."

Junie lifted her eyebrows and cocked her head to the side.

"Junie, life isn't about always doing the right thing. It's about forgiving those who do the wrong things."

There you go again, being all that I cannot be. "Do you think Daddy ever did the wrong thing?" She watched her mother's eyes grow sad.

"Sure."

"Wrong, or bad?"

"Depends on your definition, I guess." Ruth sat up straighter and faced Junie. "Spit it out. What's on your mind?"

Junie shook her head. "Nothing." She couldn't bring herself to lay another layer of discomfort on her mother.

"It's okay, Junie. There isn't much you can say that would rock the boat now."

Junie hemmed and hawed, unsure if she should reveal her worries. Ruth was strong, but Junie didn't want to test her strength and possibly be the reason it failed her. She ran her finger along the step, then jammed it back into her mouth and began chewing previously gnawed skin.

"June Marie, say it already, before you bite that finger off."

"Okay, well, I keep seeing these images of Ellen...and Daddy."

"Normal. He spent a lot of time with and around you girls."

Junie bit her lower lip. "But did he spend too much time with Ellen?"

"What are you getting at?" Her mother stood, her voice terse.

"I don't know. I get the feeling there was more to this whole thing with Ellen's disappearance than just a stranger abducting her."

Ruth turned her back to Junie, then spun around. "If you're implying that your father had anything to do with her disappearance, then...then...I'm ashamed of you."

Junie had never seen her mother get truly angry—upset, yes, put off, sure, but red-faced anger, never—or so she thought. Memories came rushing back to her now of the day they'd gone for ice cream, when they'd returned home. It was hours later when Ralph came home. Ruth was as angry as she was now—red faced, disgusted. Junie remembered sitting on the top of the stairs, out of view from where they argued.

"Where were you?" Ruth had demanded.

"Work," Ralph answered, but even seven-year-old Junie knew he was lying. Her loving, scientist father, preacher of all things good, was blatantly lying to her mother.

"I called, and the school closes at four thirty. You were with her, weren't you?" Her mother's voice cracked.

"It's over. I told you that. Leave it alone!"

Junie's voice stuck in her throat like thick peanut butter. Her mother stood angrily before her, arms crossed, eyes piercing.

"I'm…I'm sorry," Junie whispered.

"You should be." Ruth turned to go inside.

Junie couldn't hold it back; she had to know. "Mom!"

Ruth spun around.

Junie stood.

"Who was she?" Every muscle in Junie's body stiffened. Time slowed as her mother's face turned from anger to hurt. The tension in her jaw slacked.

Ruth stared at Junie without saying a word.

Junie stared, wondering if her mother would answer. She had to know what was going on. The timing was too coincidental. Her father disappeared and Ellen went missing both on the same day?

"I remember—the fight the day Ellen disappeared. Was it him? Did he do something to Ellen?" Junie turned her back, crossing her arms over her stomach. "Oh God," she cried, unable to stop the tears. "Daddy was some kind of pervert, wasn't he?"

"June Marie!"

Junie turned to face Ruth. "I saw it, him leading Ellen into the shed, him leaning over here, doing God knows what. What did he do? What did Daddy do?"

Ruth shook; her arms, legs, everything trembled. Junie followed her gaze to the open back door, where Sarah stood, thumb in her mouth.

"I think you'd better leave," Ruth said, and disappeared around the corner of the house.

Chapter Twenty-Eight

Junie sat in Theresa's waiting room, feeling as though her life were over. She'd alienated both her husband and her mother. Sarah sat beside her, thumb in her mouth, blanket piled on her lap. Junie lowered her face into her hands. She'd screwed up her own daughter, probably beyond help, and now she had nowhere to go. Theresa wasn't even an adult therapist. She'd probably throw Junie out, too.

The office door opened and a mother and son walked out. The mother avoided Junie's eyes. *No need to be embarrassed. I'm far worse off than you could ever be,* Junie thought.

"Junie, come on in," Theresa said. If she were annoyed at Junie's requesting an additional meeting, she gave no indication.

Sarah followed them silently into the room.

"Sarah," Theresa said. "I have this great new

drawing center I've set up. Would you like to see it?"

Sarah's eyebrows lifted.

Theresa led her into an adjoining room, where an easel, colored chalk, and oversized erasers were neatly laid out. "Your mother and I will be right in here talking. If you need us, come into the room, okay?"

Sarah didn't respond.

Junie's body was going to explode; she just knew it. Anxious energy would cause her heart to pound right through her chest, and her memories would tumble out of her head, exposing horrible things about her father and her husband. Her daughter would be ruined forever. She could just picture Theresa standing above her, shaking her head and telling her mother, "It was bound to happen. She was too messed up to ever be right."

Theresa sat before her without saying a word. Junie knew she was waiting for an explanation to her frantic phone call. She'd said it was urgent, but purposely left out the fact that it had nothing to do with Sarah—although, if she really thought about it, it had everything to do with Sarah. All of her actions had an impact on her daughter, and lately, every impact was a negative one.

"Thanks for seeing us...me."

"You sounded desperate."

Junie flushed. "I have to admit, this really has more to do with me, but I didn't know who else to turn to."

Theresa leaned forward. "I don't mind helping you, but if you are going to be my client, we really need to get some paperwork out of the way. Your daughter is my client, and I have to be careful not to overstep boundaries on that end."

Junie was taken aback. Paperwork? Now she was a client? She flinched at what it implied about her—she was broken, maybe as broken as her daughter. "Of course. Whatever you need."

Theresa handed her the same paperwork she had filled out for Sarah, and Junie rushed through completing the forms, very aware at the cost of each minute. They could afford it; they were lucky. Finances hadn't been an issue for years. Brian's practice made more money than they could probably spend each year, and Junie's income from the bakery was what she referred to as fluff money. She was free to do with it what she wished, but the fact that she needed help dealing with emotional issues scared her. Could Brian use her becoming a *client* against her? She imagined future arguments including phrases such as *unfit mother* and *crazy*.

"Is this confidential? Whatever we talk about?"

"Yes, of course." Theresa took the completed paperwork and set it aside. "I know you are going through a difficult time, so I can't say I'm surprised to find you here on my couch." She smiled.

"I am." Junie bristled. "I mean, I never expected to feel so out of control. I've been thrown out by my husband and my mother." Tears pushed at Junie's eyes. *Not now, please*. She opened her mouth to speak and choked on sobs.

Theresa handed her a box of tissues. "It's okay. Take your time."

"I'm sorry," Junie said, wiping her eyes and feeling foolish. "What is wrong with me? I don't even know where to start."

"Does this have something to do with the memories that you've been experiencing?"

"I found something, and I'm not sure what to do about it, and Brian's lying to me." She looked out the window, then turned back. "About his father, of all things. None of it makes any sense, and I feel—overwhelmed."

"What did you find?"

"It was in my father's shed. I found a sweater. Ellen's sweater."

"And that's significant because?" Theresa picked up her pen, wrote something on a pad of paper.

"Because we weren't allowed in his shed, and I remember—or at least I think I remember—seeing Ellen walk in there one night."

"And Brian's lie?"

"That makes no sense at all. He lied about meeting with his father at his office. I saw them. I was right there in the parking lot, and after his father left, I called him, and he lied about the meeting." Junie bit her lower lip, then added, "And he lied about going to see him when he left after the funeral. It's like one lie after another."

"Why would he lie about that? What is their relationship?"

"They're distant. But why lie?" Junie sat back, crossed her arms protectively. A shield against the truth?

"Okay, so let's take this apart a bit. What would it mean if Ellen had been in your father's shed?"

Junie thought about the question. "That's just it. I don't know. That he was a pervert that liked little girls?"

"Do you have any reason to believe your father might have been a pedophile?" Theresa asked.

Junie flushed, waved her hands in front of her face. "No, that doesn't feel right," she said emphatically. "In fact, just the opposite. He was not overtly emotional. He was clinical. I think that's what's bothering me so much. I can't put the two pieces together. He was hiding something, obviously, but what?"

"I don't have that answer. So, what other plausible explanations can you come up with?"

Junie held her hands up in the air. "It was the middle of the night, I think, so he wouldn't be tickling her or playing a game. I just can't figure out exactly what else he could have been doing."

"Okay, let's talk about Brian for a minute. Why would he lie to you about his father?"

"Who knows?"

"Well, obviously he does. Did you ever talk to him about how he treated you after Ellen died?"

"I tried, but I didn't get very far."

Theresa nodded, then rubbed her chin. "Junie," she said thoughtfully. "How do you feel about hypnosis?"

Junie crinkled her nose.

"Yeah, I know, it sounds hokey, but for some repressed memories, it works to uncover the reasons why you have repressed them. It may help you to understand what surrounds the memories of your father and Ellen, and who knows? It could help you to understand what you've forgotten about Brian and his father, too."

Sarah walked into the room, dragging her blanket.

Saved. "Are you done drawing, honey?"

Sarah nodded.

"Let's go take a look." Theresa and Junie walked into the other room. Sarah stayed behind.

"This is beautiful," Theresa said. "Is this a garden?"

Junie stared at the picture. It looked remarkably like Peter's garden, but it could have just as easily been any garden. "Papa Peter's garden?" Junie asked.

Sarah was silent.

"Her grandfather has a garden in his backyard. Sarah likes to play back there, but this trip, it was a mess, covered with weeds." Junie wanted to run away, hide from the idea of hypnosis. If Theresa was bringing up hypnosis, that meant she thought Junie was crazy—she *needed* hypnosis. She turned to Sarah and used her for an out. "Maybe we'd better go home." *Oh God, where can we go?* She caught Theresa's eye and whispered, "I didn't get to tell you about what happened with Brian and my mother. Brian told me to stay with my mom, but she's pretty mad at me and basically told me to go home." She turned her back to Sarah. "I don't know where to go."

"Do you feel safe around Brian?"

"Of course," Junie said.

"He's not so upset that it might put you and Sarah in danger in any way?"

"You've met him. Of course not."

"I have to ask." Theresa flashed her most professional therapist gaze. "I would go home, then. A home belongs to the family, not just one family member, and Sarah needs stability."

Junie nodded. She could do this. "So, should I try to talk to Brian about his dad?"

"What do you think?" Theresa asked.

Theresa's question annoyed Junie. *Why would I be here if I had all the answers?* She thought about the question. Should she talk to him? What would she gain by doing so? It turned out she did have all the answers after all; she just didn't realize it. With a sigh, she said, "No. It would only cause conflict."

"Think about what I suggested. Let me know. I think it could help."

Chapter Twenty-Nine

Junie heard the front door open at six p.m., much earlier than usual for Brian to come home. She moved about the kitchen, focusing on stirring the spaghetti rather than the mounting fear that Brian might not want her there. Her chest tightened as his footsteps neared.

"Hey!" His voice carried a happy cadence, and Junie released the breath she'd been holding. He wrapped his arms around Junie's waste and kissed her cheek. "I'm glad you're here."

He kissed Sarah's head. "You, too, sweetie. I missed my girls."

"You're not mad?" Junie asked.

"Mad? No. But I don't want to talk about any of that. Can we just have a nice evening as a family?"

A nice family evening. Every inch of Junie ached for just that. She'd take it! She had begun doubting her own perception. It was certainly plausible that Brian and

Peter were working on a case together, and it was true that he hadn't been in the habit of telling Junie who he worked with.

Dinner was uneventful, and Junie enjoyed the peacefulness, the normalcy that had been lost over recent weeks. Brian was in good spirits and seemed sincerely glad that Junie and Sarah were home. When Sarah wet her pants after dinner, he didn't get upset and snap at Junie for herding her upstairs and into the bathtub, cooing, "Accidents happen."

Brian read to Sarah at bedtime and sat beside her while she drifted off to sleep.

"Is she down?" Junie asked when he came downstairs.

"Yeah, sound asleep."

The news came on, and Junie turned down the volume. She sat next to Brian, feeling his warmth, comforted by his arm around her shoulder. She'd missed that closeness, and yet she was afraid to mention it. She felt a bit like she was walking on eggshells—not because of anything Brian did or said, but because of her nagging desire to talk about the possibility of hypnosis. She knew Brian would be against it. The last therapist had suggested it for Sarah, and they both had nixed the idea without giving it much thought at all. So why was she considering it for herself?

The next morning, Brian left early for work, passing by Sarah's bedroom as Junie silently changed her soiled sheets. He didn't smirk or make a nasty comment, but the fact that he didn't even say goodbye bothered Junie. After the nice night they'd shared—they'd made love after Sarah had gone to bed, and sure, it had been rushed and maybe even a little rougher than usual, but she'd hoped it might be the spark of a softening between them. It had been weeks since they'd been intimate, and she was beginning to wonder if they'd ever find a path back to their sensuality. She'd hoped he might wake up in the same loving mood. Instead, he'd been unreadable, and in some ways, that was more difficult than him being angry.

Junie took Sarah to preschool, where Sarah stood silently to the side as kids played in small groups. Her teacher assured her she would try to get her involved in the day's activities, and Junie left, heading toward Bliss.

"She's back!" Shane announced when she walked in the front door.

Junie said hello to Mrs. Matz and her daughter, Caroline, Bliss Friday-morning regulars.

"For a few hours, anyway," she said to Shane. Junie went into the kitchen and looked over their order sheet. Shane had, as always, kept everything perfectly organized. She owed more than the bakery's success to her friend; she owed a slice of her sanity as well.

Once the customers cleared out, she sidled up to Shane and asked, "What do you think about hypnosis?"

"The kind that makes you squawk like a chicken?"

"No, the kind that helps you remember things you might have repressed." She slid a tray of cookies out of the oven.

"Ah, is that where we're headed?"

"I don't know. What do you think? I mean, I think it makes sense. Now that I'm having these flashes of memory, I can't really ignore them."

"No, I guess you can't." He slapped her fingers as she reached for a cookie. "Uh-uh. Those are getting frosting."

"Mm, even better." She waited for Shane to say more, and when he didn't, she asked, "Will you go with me?"

He lifted his eyebrows.

"For moral support. Please? I can't do this on my own."

He set the cookies on the cooling rack. "Isn't that what girlfriends are for?"

They'd gone through this before. Shane knew she had no girlfriends to speak of or to lean on. It was a running joke—a joke that recently turned to something that pained Junie more than she'd care to admit. "Sure, if I had any." Just another item for Junie's Things I Suck At list: maintaining female friendships.

"Your mom?"

Junie saw the hope in his eyes, and knew he would rather she took her mother. She also knew that she could count on him to go with her. "She's kind of pissed at me."

He shrugged. "Sure, if I can get a day off out of it."

Junie threw her arms around his neck. They'd call in the kitchen helpers for a day, even if they weren't great with the customers. She needed Shane, and even if they had to close the bakery for a day, they'd make it work. "I knew I could count on you!" She slipped an apron over her head and said, "Can we keep this between us? I don't know what Brian would think about it."

Chapter Thirty

Preparing for hypnosis was nothing like the dramatic scene that Junie had imagined. Theresa didn't turn down the lights; there was no soft music playing or any other dramatic flair. She and Shane sat in Theresa's office, side by side, and Theresa explained how the hypnosis would work, which was very clinical, as far as Junie could tell.

"Sometimes people can't be hypnotized," Theresa explained.

That'll be me, Junie thought.

"For some, it simply doesn't work. You'll need to be accepting of the process and completely relaxed, which I know is easier said than done."

"Is there any chance I will stay hypnotized?" Anxiety pushed her words out quick and sharp.

"Not a chance. I'll bring you out of it if I see you are feeling overly anxious. Some therapists believe you have to experience the pain of the past in order to learn from it. I'm not one of them. I think you simply need to remember the events surrounding the incident, or sometimes, the incident itself, but from the perspective of a bystander, not a participant."

"Fascinating," Shane said. "Can this have any sort of aftereffects?"

"I'm not sure what you mean."

Junie liked the way that Theresa included Shane. She was concerned that he'd be made uncomfortable since he wasn't her husband, and Junie didn't want any misunderstanding about their relationship. Surprisingly, they'd never been questioned about their relationship by anyone—not Brian, not Ruth, not the kitchen help. Junie considered them lucky in that regard. Gossip was not something she was comfortable with. That would be all she needed, another thing to worry about. She felt a little funny now, sitting in Theresa's office, doing something so intimate with Shane watching and keeping it a secret from Brian. It was the "secret" part that was bothering her. She wished that she could trust her husband to understand and support this new, confusing part of her life as it unfolded, but she feared he'd be angry with her for pursuing the memories of Ellen, and she couldn't worry about that right now. She had to focus, to let herself relax enough to allow herself to be taken under hypnosis.

"Might she have more flashbacks? Can you stir up memories that aren't really there, but fabricated by insinuation?"

Junie hadn't thought of that. She clenched her hands together. "Can that happen?"

"I won't lie to you. There's a lot of debate about hypnosis. Some believe that repressed memories are not real; others swear by them. I take them on a case-by-case basis. I'm very careful when a client is regressing not to put any ideas into their heads. I let them lead me down the trail they follow. I simply take them back to a certain time."

Junie looked at Shane, then reached for his hand. "What do you think?"

"You can't ask me that. This is your life."

"But I trust you," she pleaded. Part of Junie wanted him to tell her not to do it, but a bigger part wanted to see what the past revealed.

"I say go for it. I'll be right here. If I see you struggling, I can indicate that to Theresa and she can bring you out of it." He turned to Theresa. "That's right, isn't it? You'll respect my opinion?"

"Yes, of course. I'm not here to push Junie into anything, and I certainly don't want to cause her any distress."

"Can I just ask one thing?" Shane asked.

Theresa nodded.

"I thought you were a child psychiatrist? Where does this come in?" he asked.

"Good question. I am a child psychiatrist—one who happens to also do regressive therapy. I don't offer it up as a recommended treatment for children unless I firmly believe their issues are rooted in some type of event or abuse that if uncovered could help them heal. For Junie, with all that she has riding on these memories, I think it might help."

Shane raised an eyebrow toward Junie, and she nodded, as if to say she trusted Theresa and was going through with the hypnosis.

Junie lay on the couch, her eyes closed, hands clasped tightly together. *I'll never get hypnotized. No way.* She listened to Theresa telling her to relax. Her fingers loosened their grasp. She was aware of her shoulders relaxing into the cushions. Her mind was tingly, foggy.

It was the middle of the night. Junie woke up and looked at Ellen's sleeping bag. It was empty. She listened, expecting Ellen to flush the toilet and come back into the room. She didn't.

Theresa's voice floated by her. "What do you hear?"

Junie clenched her fists. "I don't know. Mewing, sort of."

"Where are you?" Theresa asked.

"I'm in my bed, but I get up and follow the noise."

"Do you see anyone?"

"No." Junie hesitated, her face tensing and relaxing in unison to her fists clenching and unclenching. "I'm going downstairs. It's dark. I'm scared."

"You're okay," Theresa assures her. "You're watching yourself; you're safe."

"The noise is getting louder. I'm following it, near the den. It's dark, except for the light from the moon." She licked her lips. "It's pretty, like in a romantic movie, but the noises are getting louder. I see something."

Junie grew silent; a groan escaped her lips.

"Junie, you're okay. You're not there. You're watching this happen. What do you see?"

A tear slipped down Junie's cheek. "What's going on?" she demanded. "What's happening?"

"Who do you see?" Theresa urged.

"Daddy. Daddy! What are you doing?" she yelled.

"It's okay. Calm down. He can't hear you, Junie. You're watching, remember? Tell me what Daddy is doing."

"Is she okay?" Shane whispered to Theresa.

"I don't know what he's doing. She's not okay," Junie said, answering Theresa's question. "Ellen? Ellen what are you doing?" Junie sat bolt upright. "Ellen? Daddy?" Junie screamed.

"Junie, what do you see?" Theresa asked.

"Get her out, please," Shane urged.

"I can't get her. Daddy? What are you doing to her? Daddy! No!"

"When I count to three, Junie, you will wake up, and you will remember what you saw. One, two, three."

Junie lay still.

"Is she okay?" Shane's words were slathered in panic. He went to Junie's side.

Theresa touched Shane's shoulder, held up her index finger.

"Junie, can you hear me?" Theresa asked.

Junie opened her eyes. Her hand flew to cover her heart. She breathed in fast, hurt pants.

"You okay?" Shane asked, his arm around her.

"Yeah," Junie said, laying her head on his shoulder. "Wow."

"Just relax. Sit for a bit, and don't try to talk."

Junie's body felt oddly light, and her senses felt as if they were on steroids. She smelled creek water, as if Shane had bathed in it. She sniffed his shirt.

"You okay?" Shane asked, leaning away from her.

"I smell the creek."

"I showered at home today, thank you." He pulled his shirt up to his nose and smelled. "Downy fresh."

"It's not abnormal for your senses to carry over from the hypnosis. Do you remember what you saw?"

Junie's face flushed. "Yes, I think so." She wrapped her arms around her middle. "It was like I was watching a movie. Weird and not at all what I expected."

Theresa's eyes trailed Junie's face, her body language. Junie knew she didn't want to put thoughts into her mind, so she relayed what she'd seen. "It was just like the flash of memory that I'd had. Ellen had spent the night, and I woke up in the middle of the night and her sleeping bag was empty. I went looking for her, and"—Junie cleared her throat, trying to wrap her mind around the reality of the memory—"I saw my dad leaning over her. It just makes no sense."

"What do you think your father was doing?"

"I don't know, but I do know that I have to find out." She reached for Shane's hand. "I'm glad you're here. I feel better not going through this alone."

Shane squeezed her hand.

"I was scared. Ellen was making these noises and

jerking her feet, and when I yelled at my father, he—"

Junie looked down at her lap.

"What did he do, Junie?" Theresa asked.

"He told me to go away. He said it mean, like, *Get outta here. Now!*" She shivered. "My dad never spoke that way to me. I can't believe it."

"Do you think it wasn't real?" Now Theresa sounded like a therapist, and it annoyed Junie.

"You're the therapist. Was it real?" She put her face in her hands. "I'm sorry. I'm a little overwhelmed. He's my *father*."

"I understand, and we can do a follow-up session next week to try to determine what it was that he was doing, which will give you time to think about it, and hopefully, it will stir your memory before then."

"This didn't give me anything more than what I had recalled before going under. Nothing new came of this."

"Sometimes the new memories come later. Think of regression as a vortex, a portal that you've now opened, to allow the memories to flow through."

Junie turned to Shane. "What do you think?"

Shane blushed. "I think it's all quite extraordinary. I was frightened, actually, watching you in this other state." He turned to Theresa and said, "Theresa watches you closely, Junie. I think you're in good hands. She didn't let you get frenzied, which is what I was afraid of. The real question is, can you wait a week? You're not the most patient person."

"She has to wait a week. I won't regress her any sooner than that. I want to see what she can recall naturally. Many patients recall information quite easily after their first session."

First session. Another week. What on earth will I recall naturally this time? The idea that she might face more memories, and face them alone, scared the hell out of Junie.

Chapter Thirty-One

Junie folded the laundry to keep her hands busy. She set the clothes in neat stacks on the bed, trying to figure out how to tell Brian what she'd done. She knew Brian would be angry with her about her trip to Theresa's office, but she wasn't sure if he'd be angrier about her being hypnotized and regressed or keeping it from him. She didn't want to tell him now, but the guilt had eaten away at her all day, leaving her with a dull headache. She wasn't used to keeping secrets from her husband.

Brian came into the bedroom and emptied his pockets, placing his wallet and a few stray dollar bills on the dresser. "How was your day?" he asked.

"I went to see Theresa today." *Shit.* So much for not blurting it out.

"What did she say about the bed-wetting? Does she have any new ideas?"

Junie fingered the seam of a T-shirt. "I went to see

her about me, actually." She bit her lower lip.

"You?"

Junie nodded. "I did regression therapy to try and see why I'm having these memories of Ellen." She took a deep breath, hoping that the nicer side of Brian that she was seeing might last. "Shane went with me."

Brian's hands stopped in midair as he lifted his shirt over his head, his back facing Junie. She watched his shoulder muscles tense and ripple down his lats. He drew his shirt back down over his head and turned slowly toward her.

"You did what?" His eyes pierced through her veil of confidence.

Shit. "I knew I shouldn't have told you."

Brian stomped around the bedroom, his face red and tight. "Shouldn't have told me? I'm your husband. Of course you should have told me." He stood before her, legs planted firmly, muscles tense, arms crossed.

"You don't feel the need to tell me everything. Why should I tell you?" *Damn it. What am I doing?*

"Is that where you want to go with this? This is your way of getting me back for not telling you about my father?"

"No, that's not it." *Is it?* "I told you because I wanted to. I didn't even plan to, but you were being nice to me again, and accepting Sarah, and I thought—"

"So you thought, *Let's piss off Brian and bring up Ellen again*. When you came back, I thought that was it. I thought you'd left all that stuff behind." He stormed into the bathroom and slammed the door.

Junie stared at the closed door. *Shit.* She sat on the bed and thought about how she could fix this mess. Was she sabotaging her entire life? She kicked off her shoes and waited for him to come out.

He yelled through the door, "And you made a fool out of me in front of Shane!"

"I did not. Why are you bringing him into this?"

Brian opened the door, his face freshly washed, the edges of his hair wet. "I didn't. You did. Who brings their business partner to a therapist with them anyway?"

"Like you would have gone?"

"No. I would have talked some sense into you. What's done is done. Your father's dead. Leave it alone."

"I can't. Why can't you understand that? I didn't ask for these memories. I don't want them."

"Then don't pursue them."

"I have to. Can't you see that? I need to put them to rest, no matter what they upend."

"You're willing to throw away your life, your family, for whatever your memories hold?"

"I guess I am, and you should support me."

"Your father didn't do a damn thing to my sister." Brian left the bedroom and headed downstairs.

"How do you know?" She was on his heels. "How do you know what my father did?"

"I was fourteen. I'd have seen it."

"Adults don't see abuse. How could you?"

"Now your father's a child abuser? I don't even know you." Brian picked up his car keys and opened the front door.

"Where are you going? It's eleven at night." Junie's heart sank. She'd done it this time. She'd never be able to untangle this mess.

Brian stared at her, teeth clenched so tight his lips pursed. His eyes narrowed and he shook his head.

"Don't go out. I'm sorry. I didn't mean to upset you."

"I'm going to the office."

Junie bristled with the slam of the door. Her heart shattered. She wondered if, on some subconscious level, she was pushing him away on purpose. Why couldn't she keep her big mouth shut? Who was she kidding? She'd known the outcome of the conversation would not be good, and she'd told him anyway. She was just no good at lying. Ironically, she had her father to thank for that.

Chapter Thirty-Two

Junie slept fitfully. She awoke in a cold sweat, a memory taunting her. She'd remembered the morning after Ellen had spent the night. She'd woken up in the morning to Ellen's empty sleeping bag. She remembered asking her mother where Ellen was, and she said she got sick in the middle of the night. It made sense to her. Ellen had been sick, a reasonable explanation.

She rolled over and looked at Sarah's curls on Brian's pillow. He hadn't come home during the night. Sarah lay on his side of the bed, a giant urine spot beneath her. Junie wiped the sleep from her eyes. *Not now.*

She carried Sarah into the bathroom and cleaned her up, then changed her linens and the linens in Sarah's bed as well. *Two accidents. That's not good.* Her actions were robotic; her mind weeded through her memories. Ellen being sick might explain what she'd seen, but what about Ellen's sweater in her father's shed? Why would he have tucked it above the door like that?

She brought the linens downstairs to the laundry room, passing Sarah on the way. She sat on the floor in the living room, a pad of paper in front of her, crayons spread across the floor.

"Be careful of the hardwood, Sarah."

Sarah didn't answer.

They had an appointment for Sarah later that afternoon with Theresa. Junie felt guilty for taking up so much of Theresa's time, but she reasoned that it was necessary. If nothing else, she was protecting her own sanity. Maybe what she really needed was marriage counseling, she mused.

She threw the laundry in the washer and went to sit with Sarah.

"What are you drawing?"

Sarah didn't move. She held a green crayon in her hand. The picture she'd drawn looked like the one she'd drawn in Theresa's office.

"Papa Pete's garden?"

Sarah popped her thumb into her mouth and looked up at Junie.

"You love that garden, don't you?"

Junie thought of her mother, how hurt she had been with her accusations about her father. She'd have to call her and apologize. She couldn't have her entire life falling apart, although it seemed to be heading that way fast.

"I feel like we're monopolizing your time." Junie blushed, feeling naked, as if she'd been overexposed during their last session. She wished she'd taken the time to do her hair instead of throwing it up in a rubber band.

Theresa wore wide-bottomed slacks and a T-shirt. Her dark hair hung in a thick mass to her shoulders. She was tall and slim and pulled the casual outfit off with panache. Jealousy tiptoed through Junie. With all that had been going on in her life, she would love to have a facade of ease for others to perceive. She saw herself as a pinched nerve lately, moving from one stressful moment to the next.

Theresa sidled up to Junie and whispered, "Life is beautiful even when it seems it's not. Hang in there."

Theresa's words soothed Junie, and for the first time in twenty-four hours, she was able to relax.

Theresa bent down to eye level with Sarah. "How are you today?"

Sarah clenched her blanket and the notebook she'd been drawing in.

"Did you draw more gardens?" Theresa held a hand out. "May I see?"

Sarah gave her the notebook, and Theresa studied the drawing. She narrowed her eyes, then said, "This is beautiful. I see that you really do love your grandpa's garden." She led them into her office, where Junie and Sarah sat side by side.

"Do you want to tell me about this picture? I still

have your other drawing up on my board. It was far too beautiful to erase."

Sarah watched Theresa.

Theresa waited, but Sarah offered nothing.

"Do you mind if I ask Mom about the garden?"

Junie liked how respectful Theresa was toward Sarah. She waited for Sarah to respond. Sarah sat silently beside her.

"Mom, what can you tell me about this garden of Papa Pete's?"

Junie adjusted herself in her seat, not sure what she should say—should she talk about how she and Ellen used to play around them, or did she just want to hear about Sarah's experiences? She chose the safe route and stuck close to Sarah.

"Papa Pete is very proud of his gardens, or at least he had been until recently. His backyard was like *The Secret Garden*. Do you know that book? His gardens weren't locked or anything like that, but they sure felt magical." She looked lovingly at Sarah. "Sarah has grown up playing in the gardens much like I did. Even though Brian and Peter aren't close, Peter has always reached out to Sarah." Junie thought about Peter and Sarah's relationship, and again wondered if Peter was somehow trying to make up for his coldness toward Ellen. It was a strange thought, but it somehow fit the situation. "The entire backyard is walled in by enormous trees and beautiful shrubbery." Junie used her hands to show the breadth of the bushes. "She'd play out there for hours." Junie smiled, remembering the happiness of her own younger days.

She looked at Theresa and asked, "Did you ever have a place when you were young where even your worst fears were put at bay, left at the entrance? The gardens are…were…that type of place."

Sarah nodded.

Both Junie and Theresa watched her with amazement as she bobbed her head. Junie's cheeks hurt from the smile that grew across them.

"Sarah, you loved them, didn't you?" she encouraged her, but Sarah withdrew. She stopped bobbing her head and looked down at the floor, sucking her thumb.

"Junie, you said *were*. What's changed?" Theresa asked.

"Peter. Peter's changed. I think it must all be too much for him now. He's all alone in that gigantic house. He's lost his wife, his daughter, and"—she leaned forward and whispered—"maybe his son." She thought of the pain the garden must have brought Peter even after all the years that had passed. "Something in him must have snapped. You'd think that after all these years, he would be used to it, but I think he finally just gave up on the garden. Maybe it's his way of finally letting go of Ellen. Maybe my dad's passing made him realize that after all these years, she was not coming back."

Theresa glanced down at the picture again, vibrant green and reds against the dark brown of the table.

"Sarah, I noticed something in this picture. You have one black mark drawn between the flowers. What is that?"

Junie picked up the picture and looked closely.

Sarah didn't answer.

Junie stood. "May I?" She nodded toward the other room.

"Sure."

Junie walked into the other room and studied the other picture that Sarah had drawn. The same black image was drawn, almost a tiny scribble, as if she'd begun drawing something and then stopped.

"A rock, maybe?" Junie drew her eyebrows together, trying to remember what she'd seen in the garden. Then she remembered Sarah hadn't visited the gardens during their last trip. The last time Sarah had seen them, they were meticulously manicured.

Theresa nodded. "A rock. Perhaps that's it." She switched gears and asked Sarah about her father. Why did she want to leave her grandmother's house with him? Sarah didn't answer. Was she glad to be home?

Sarah nodded.

That little movement sent a rush of adrenaline through Junie. She recognized the soaring emotion that followed—hope. She had hope. Sarah had responded. That was huge.

Upon completion of their time together, Theresa asked Sarah if she'd come back the following week, and Sarah grabbed her mother's hand, thumb jammed in her mouth, and stared down at the floor without responding. Her blond ringlets bobbed up and down, the slightest of movements. Had Junie not been looking for it, she could have missed it. Her heart soared.

"Yes, yes, we'll be back. Most definitely," she gushed.

On the way home from the appointment, Junie could barely conceal her delight. She rattled on and on to a silent Sarah about how proud of her she was and how she hoped Sarah felt safe enough to talk to Theresa someday.

Then her chest tightened. She realized that Sarah's face had once again become a blank slate. Had she said too much? Was she too pushy? Damn. Parenting was so hard. She needed a handbook.

She settled Sarah in at home and called Brian from the kitchen.

He answered with a snappy, "What?"

Junie paid no attention. She boasted about Sarah's progress. "You should have seen her. She responded! She actually nodded. Brian, this is huge."

She waited for him to respond, to be as thrilled as she was and maybe even forgive their argument.

He was silent.

Junie swallowed her excitement. She bit her lower lip, contemplating what to say next. "Brian? Aren't you even the littlest bit happy about this?"

She heard him sigh and could envision the disappointment in his eyes. Maybe he was waiting for an apology. Could she give it? Was she sorry for wanting to find out what was driving her memories? No, she wasn't.

"Okay, well, just wanted to let you know," she said.

The phone went dead.

Chapter Thirty-Three

Sarah sat on the swing in the backyard while Junie vented her frustration by pulling weeds. She would rather be baking, but after Sarah's breakthrough and Brian's attitude, she felt she might explode if kept indoors.

She wrapped her fingers around the thick weeds and yanked, feeling the release of her angst as each weed pulled free from its tethers. How could Brian be mad at her for trying to figure out what was going on? Could she be way off? Maybe Ellen was just taken by a stranger, driven away and sold as a sex slave, as Katie had indicated. But what if she wasn't? What if her father had had a double life?

She yanked another weed and tossed it aside.

She pulled at her memory, begging it to come forward. Why was Ellen's sweater in the shed? She really needed to ask her mother. She thought of the conversation that might take place.

Mom, I found Ellen's sweater in Dad's shed.

So what?

So, we were never allowed in the shed.

So he found it on the ground one day and thought it was yours, stuck it in there. Who knows?

No, I'm sure it was Ellen's.

Damn it, Junie. What do you want from me? Do you really think I'd have stayed married to a man who did something to that young girl?

I'm sorry, Mom.

She could never have that conversation.

Junie grabbed hold of a thick, thorny weed. She tugged and pulled, to no avail. "Damn it," she said, and crouched on her haunches. She pulled, leaning all of her weight back on her heels. "Come on, sucker." Tears sprang from her eyes. *Who are you? What are you?* She realized she was no longer thinking of the invasive weed, but of her father, and her husband, and maybe even her daughter.

She fell backward with the weed between both hands, a big clump of dirt attached to the root.

"Son of a bitch," she mumbled. The sun beat down on her from above. She lay on her back, watching the clouds go by. Her legs began to tingle. Her arms relaxed to her sides as the memory trickled in. Ellen walked with her father in the dark, toward his shed. She looked back over her shoulder and up at Junie's window. Junie could feel the cold glass pressing against her palm. The shed door shut behind them.

Chapter Thirty-Four

"I can't wait another week. I have to know. It's killing me." Junie was at the bakery with Shane, who was trying to talk her out of doing another hypnosis session before a week had passed. Brian had slept at his office again the night before, and Sarah had not only wet her bed in the morning, but she'd thrown a fit when Junie had left her at preschool.

Shane was helping a customer who couldn't make up his mind. *A middle-aged man pretending to care about his expanded waistline. What else is new?* He hemmed and hawed over the low-fat brownies or the regular brownies. Junie turned her back toward the customer and raised her eyebrows to Shane, as if to say, *Another one? Just get it over with and take the full-fat brownie and move on.* There were customers who truly cared about their figures but loved sweets; then there were customers who wished they could care enough about their figures to make changes to their diets but weren't quite adept at doing so. This man was one of *those* customers.

"You heard Theresa. She said she always lets a week go by, so you can see if any memories appear naturally," Shane said quietly.

Junie smiled at the man, who was now eyeing the chocolate éclairs. "They're appearing all right, and I don't like it."

Shane asked the man if he was ready to order, and he shook his head. Shane leaned against the counter, staring wide-eyed at Junie. "Do tell," he urged.

Junie shook her head. "It's crazy. It's all my dad and Ellen. He's walking into the shed with her. Why? Why would he take her in there?"

"I'm ready. I'll take two éclairs and a low-fat brownie."

Junie raised her eyebrows at Shane. *See?*

"My children will love these," the man added as he handed Shane the money.

"Thanks for stopping by. Enjoy the treats," Shane said. He flashed his most cordial smile, then quickly turned back to Junie. "What else did you see?"

"Nothing." She plopped down in the chair beside the counter. "That's just it. She looked back at me, like…like she was proud. Almost like she was teasing me. *See where I can go!"* Junie mocked in her best seven-year-old voice.

"Maybe she was."

"Pfft." Junie swatted the air. "My father would no

sooner take her into the shed—" Junie's jaw fell open.

"What?"

"We were in there. Me and Ellen. I remember. We snuck in one day. I stole the key one afternoon when my parents were upstairs and we snuck in." She bit her lower lip, remembering how cool it was to be in her father's shed. "We were crouched in the back of the shed, looking at his stuff."

"Stuff? What did he have?" Shane sat next to her, holding his doughy hands out in front of him to keep the mess from his clothing. "What did you find?"

Junie shook her head. "I have no idea. I don't remember..." In light of the unhappy images she'd been seeing, this memory made her happy. "I remember giggling. We were doing something we shouldn't have been." She covered her heart. "My heart raced like never before. I knew we were dead if my dad caught us."

"You naughty girl!" Shane laughed.

"Yeah. We...we looked through his tools, his shelves. I don't remember finding anything. Ellen had on that sweater, the one I found."

She looked at Shane, then let out a whooping, smack-yourself-on-the-forehead laugh.

"She took it off! I remember! She was hot, and we didn't want to leave the shed until we'd looked through everything, so she took off the sweater. I told her to shove it behind the tool bench. I remember. I remember! Do you know what this means?" She grabbed Shane's arm. "Daddy didn't do anything. He probably found the sweater and tucked it up there. It would be just like him not to want to embarrass us or something. Who knows."

"But what about him leaning over her in the den?"

Junie rolled her eyes. "I don't know, okay? I don't have it all figured out, but this is a piece. I just know it. I have no idea why he wouldn't have given the sweater back, but I do remember her taking it off. I remember." She sighed, then whispered, "I remember."

Junie had picked up Sarah from preschool and they'd gone to Chick'n Dip'n for lunch. She tried to coax Sarah into playing on the play set, but Sarah ate in silence. When her cell phone rang Junie was thankful for the distraction.

Mom.

"Hi," Ruth said in a soft voice. "Do you have a second?"

"Yes, of course." Guilt flushed Junie's cheeks.

"I've lost your father. I don't want to lose you, too."

The hurt in Ruth's voice sent chills down Junie's back. "Mom, you could never lose me. I'm so sorry about accusing Daddy."

"Your father—" Ruth inhaled deeply. "Your father was a good man, June. He wouldn't hurt Ellen. Hearing you say that just killed me."

"I know. I'm sorry. But I do have questions." Junie sucked in air through her teeth, instantly regretting her words.

"We need to talk," Ruth said.

Junie told Ruth that she was in a fast-food

restaurant and she'd call her when they got home. Then she gathered Sarah and her leftover french fries and headed home.

Skype was a valuable tool when you just needed to look into someone's eyes and see the truth that they held. Junie was thankful that she could see her mother for this conversation. She didn't think that words alone were enough, because she knew she had to ask the tough questions that were nagging at the back of her mind. The conversation was not going to be a pleasant one, but at least it could be an honest one.

"How's Sarah?"

"Fine, but let's talk about us, Mom. I'm hurting; you're hurting because of me. I'm so sorry." Junie touched the computer screen. She watched her mother drop her eyes, and when she lifted her gaze, there was something sorrowful, almost scared, behind it.

"Honey, I would rather have this talk in person, but, well, thank goodness for technology."

Junie watched Ruth gather her thoughts, suddenly feeling nervous. She fiddled with her fingers, and as she opened her mouth to speak, her mother's voice came through the computer.

"Daddy was a good man, Junie. You know that. He loved you, and he loved me. But he wasn't perfect."

Don't tell me. Please don't tell me. I'm sorry. If he hurt her, I don't really want to know.

"What you remembered about when Ellen

disappeared, that was right. He didn't come home until later, and I was mad. But that wasn't the only time he'd done that. Your father—" Ruth moved her hand to her mouth. Junie watched it tremble.

"Mom, you don't have to—"

Ruth held her hand up, shushing Junie. She nodded. "Yes, yes, I do. I've covered it up for too many years, and you have a right to know. Or maybe I just feel like I have a right to get it off my chest."

"Mom, whatever it is, you don't have to tell me."

"Yes, yes, I do." Ruth looked right into Junie's eyes.

Junie held her breath.

"Your father had an affair. It wasn't still going on when Ellen disappeared, but the hurt and mistrust took a long time to get over. I accused him of still carrying on, and he didn't come home because of that."

No way. Not Daddy. He loved me. He loved you. Junie listened in horror as her childhood fell apart before her.

"That day, he wasn't doing anything wrong. He'd gone to visit Peter at his office, to make amends."

"Peter?" *What the hell?*

Tears streamed down Ruth's cheeks. "You're going to think less of me, but I have to tell you. I can't let this tear us apart, but even more important, I can't let you think that your father did something to that little girl."

Ellen.

"We fought that afternoon. He'd been acting strange, but I found out later that it had to do with his work, not with...the affair. God, I can't believe I've said it out loud. The *affair*." She took a deep breath.

"Mom, you don't have to tell me."

"Yes, I do. Now, please, let me finish." Ruth spoke quickly, as if the words had been begging for release for far too long. "He went to see Peter to confess the affair."

"Peter? He had an affair with Brian's mother? Susan?" None of it made any sense. Junie listened as her mother told her that it had happened years ago, right after they had moved into the neighborhood. Peter was working every evening and Ruth had been caring for Junie, who was just a baby.

"I'd been neglecting him, I guess."

"Mom, this isn't your fault. All parents neglect each other when they have new babies. I can't believe Daddy was so selfish. The bastard."

"No, it was more than that. I had postpartum depression, but it had gone undiagnosed. I was mean, angry all the time."

"I don't remember that."

"Of course you don't. By the time we figured out what it was, Daddy had found comfort with Susan."

"But how could you not know? She was our neighbor!" Junie was thoroughly disgusted with her father. She wanted nothing more than to hit rewind on her life and not have to know about the affair.

"He helped her out when Peter was at work, little things here and there. She needed help with gutters, a few things fixed, and none of us had any money."

"Peter had money. He was a frickin' attorney." Junie fumed.

"Yes, he was, but he had an expensive house and an expensive car."

"All luxuries *they* chose. Geez, Mom, can't you see this?" What was wrong with her mother?

"Yes, they chose them, and for whatever reason, your father and Susan were drawn together."

"Why'd you stay there? Why didn't we move? I would never have stayed." *I'd have left him! Wouldn't I?* she wondered. Junie thought about Brian, his lies, the way the lies made her feel unworthy and even a little bit stupid, but she wasn't ready to leave Brian. Would she have the strength to leave him if she found out he really was cheating? She wasn't sure.

"Things were different then. You didn't just leave. We couldn't afford to leave. We were lucky to afford this house on your father's salary—teachers don't make much money, and if we moved, we'd have lost our investment and never been able to buy another house." Ruth wiped her eyes. "Besides, it's important that you know they never slept together."

"What? Mom? You just said they had an affair. You *believe* they didn't sleep together?" *What is wrong with you?* "Didn't Selma or Mary Margaret tell you that maybe you were wrong?"

Ruth blushed. "I didn't tell them. It was too embarrassing. June, I know what it looks like, but I also know your father. He swore to me that it never got that far. He was torn apart by the emotional affair, which he admitted went on far too long. They'd talk on the phone, or they'd meet for coffee. Believe me, it just about killed me. I hated your father, but I also loved him."

"I hate him." She felt like an angry teenager who

was being punished. She hadn't asked for this information, and she certainly didn't want it.

"No, you don't. You don't hate your father. Marriages are complicated, June. You know that. They don't always wrap up as neat and tidy as the Cleavers or the Brady bunch. Your father had every right to feel underappreciated and lonely, and God knows Susan did, too."

Junie felt heat spread across her chest and climb her neck. "How can you take their side? How can you not hate her, and him? They cheated, even if they didn't sleep together."

"Because I have to take responsibility for my part. I was awful to your father, truly awful."

"It was medical! Postpartum depression!" Junie stood and paced.

"June Marie, sit down. You need to hear this."

Junie sat, crossing and uncrossing her arms, uncomfortable hearing this side of her parents' marriage.

"Your father spent every day of his life after the affair was over making me happy. He went to great lengths, for years, right up until the day he died—"

Junie watched her bite back tears.

"Until the day he died, he made sure that I always knew where he was, what he was doing, and he communicated when he was unhappy. As a wife, you can't ask for more than that."

"Yes, you can." Junie felt the respect she had for her mother diminishing with each defensive word she spoke. "You can demand fidelity. It's your right as a wife." Junie couldn't believe her mother hadn't been strong enough to stand up for herself, for their marriage. "Mom, you are the one who taught me to stand up for myself and that I deserve respect. How come you don't believe the same about yourself? It's so...so weak." Junie felt guilty the second the word flew from her lips.

"Weak? Is that what you think of me? Let me tell you something, missy. It takes more strength to stay in a broken marriage, to accept responsibility, to fix yourself and fix the marriage than leaving ever could. Nowadays marriage means nothing. It's someone you spend time with, someone you can take or leave when they bother you too much or cause you too much pain." Her mother crossed her arms, then uncrossed them, her jaw clenched, then unclenched. "Marriage today is shameful. Nothing is more important than loving the person you choose to marry and meaning your vows when you say them." Ruth's voice escalated. "Had he slept with her, yes, I might have gone home to my mother, which would have been my only choice with a newborn in tow, but he didn't, and truth be known, I loved him, adored him."

"I'm sorry, Mom, but now it's my fault?" Junie asked.

"No. God, no. It's not your fault. It's not really even my fault. Things in life evolve around circumstance. Good times wax and wane. What happened between Susan and your father tore apart more than just our family while it was going on. When your father told

Peter, their relationship was hurt. Do you think Susan left town because of Ellen?"

"Yes. She couldn't take it anymore."

"No, she left town because her husband couldn't take the infidelity, and losing him again—the first time to work, the second to the affair—was too much. She came to see me before she left. She said she was sorry for what happened, that it was all emotional comfort; no physicality occurred. She said"—Ruth paused to wipe a tear from her cheek—"she said I was the luckiest woman around. That my husband loved me, and *you*, more than we could ever know."

The tightness in Junie's chest spread to her arms and legs. Her entire body was one constricted muscle. How could her father put her mother in this position? Junie was trapped in her discomfort. She needed to be there for her mother even if she couldn't help but feel she was hearing something that, as a daughter, she shouldn't be privy to. Her father's affair didn't answer the questions that remained about Ellen. *Ellen.*

Junie wished she could reach for her mother's hand. "Mom, you've carried this secret for so long. I'm sorry."

Ruth looked down at the crumpled tissue in her hands. "There's more."

Junie's heart sank. *Please don't tell me Ellen was his child. Please don't say Mom was wrong.* "More?"

"You know him, and you know that he would have felt a lot of guilt about what he'd done to their family, even though he believed that Peter was really the death of their family unit."

"He couldn't have felt too guilty. He did it, didn't

he?" Junie turned away from the screen.

"Look, you can't change what Daddy did any more than he could have, and believe me, he would have if he could have. But you can listen to what I have to say, and then you can make a decision about what type of person your father was."

Junie kept her eyes trained on the keyboard.

"Your father always believed that the reason Peter didn't pay any attention to Ellen was because of him."

"Was she his?" Junie asked.

"No, of course not. We moved in after you and she had already been born, but Peter treated her as if she were the reason Susan had fallen apart, and he and Daddy didn't see eye to eye after that, as is to be expected."

Junie let the silence settle between them; then, after a moment, she said, "Fallen apart?"

"Susan had a mini breakdown, I guess you'd call it." The edges of Ruth's lips lifted. "I guess we both did. Susan blew up at Peter just before her...tryst...started. Peter thought that having an infant and a young, energetic boy was too much for her. He always had an edge about him when he was near Ellen, and I think it was because he blamed her, as the infant, for Susan's breakdown."

Junie thought of Ellen, always vying for her father's attention, trying to be the perfect child. *Shh, my Dad's working. Don't disturb him. My daddy never sleeps. He's such an important man. He has to work all the time. Daddy, look for me! I'm hiding!* Yes, she could see the distance between them.

"He adored Brian, some say, a little too much."

That didn't get him far.

"Anyway, your father took it upon himself to be like a father to Ellen."

"Didn't that bother you? I mean, staying in the neighborhood alone must have killed you, but seeing Ellen—" Junie's hand flew to her mouth. "My God, me and Ellen. She was around every second of the day."

Ruth lifted her eyebrows. "Like I said, it wasn't easy, but it wasn't Ellen's fault. That sweet girl was a gift to you. You needed a sister, and I, well, I couldn't give you one."

Junie knew about her mother's fertility issues and wanted to tell her how sorry she was that she couldn't have more children, but she was afraid of making the already painful discussion even more painful. Instead she said, "She was like a sister."

"I was thankful for that. You needed a sibling." Ruth let out a long sigh. "What I have to tell you next will hurt. You're not going to want to hear it, and you might wish I never said it, but I've never taken the easy road, and you need to know why your father did what he did."

Junie couldn't imagine what could be worse than what she'd already heard. She braced herself against the chair.

"The summer that Ellen disappeared, your father was teaching her about photosynthesis."

Junie waited. There had to be more. *That* was the big, bad, terrible thing?

"O-kay." *And?*

"Well, he wasn't teaching you, his daughter," Ruth said softly.

"So?"

"So, you aren't upset that he was teaching Ellen and not you?" Ruth's face contorted with confusion. "You were his little girl. I always felt bad for you because I thought he should take you under his wing, not Ellen."

"I might have been Daddy's little girl, but he taught me stuff all the time. Why would I be mad about that?"

Ruth let out a relieved *whew*. "You sort of zoned out during his science lessons."

"I did not! I loved listening to him." Junie swore under her breath. "I did!"

"Junie, think about it. When Daddy was talking about bee pollination, you were thinking about brownies and baking. When he tried to focus your attention on plants and photosynthesis, you made up every excuse in the book to not listen."

Junie laughed. "I did?" She squinted. "I don't remember that."

"Apparently there's a lot you don't remember."

"So Ellen going into the shed—"

"A lesson in photosynthesis. He asked you to go, too, but you didn't want to. Whether you remember it or not, he did ask you, practically begged you, to take part in it."

"That explains the way Ellen looked at me." Relief swept through Junie. "She looked at me like she was special and I wasn't."

"Unfortunately, we all picked up on how Ellen

played you with regard to your father, but that's what girls did, I guess. Sisters compete for attention all the time, and you two were as close as sisters, so we didn't feel that we had to put a stop to it."

"She did not *play* me." Junie didn't remember feeling that at all.

"Oh, yes she did, and you were pretty pissed at her. We thought you'd eventually handle it in your own way. You know your father didn't believe in mollycoddling. He wouldn't have let me intervene if I had tried to. I think after Ellen disappeared, you sort of let all that jealousy go. You memorialized a glorified recollection of her, just as you've done with your father. It's not a bad thing. It just is what it is."

"Was there any bad in her?"

"Oh, she could be such a little snit."

Junie laughed. "Really? Tell me. I don't remember that."

"Oh, she crossed a few lines. Even at seven, she could rile up her brother, teasing him about girlfriends and then running and hiding behind her mother. She'd get into a conversation with your father and look at you—if looks could kill, you'd have sear marks through your heart. It used to infuriate me, but she was just a little girl. She didn't know any better, and she—" Ruth looked down. "I felt bad for her."

"Because of Peter?"

"Yes, at first, but then because she had a medical issue."

Junie didn't know anything about a medical issue. Could there be any *more* about her life that she had been blind to? "What are you talking about?"

"The weekend before Ellen disappeared, she was sleeping over. It was the first time it had ever happened. She got up to get a drink of water, and your father found her seizing on the floor."

"Seizing?"

"Yes, she dropped to the floor as he was coming out of the den. Once he realized what was going on, he rolled her onto her side and he had to hold her jaw open. He was afraid she'd swallow her tongue."

The memory.

"Susan had taken her to the doctor a few hours later. They thought she might have had Tourette's. The testing was scheduled for later that week, and then—"

"She disappeared."

Ruth nodded.

"Mom, I'm so sorry. No wonder you were so mad at me. I feel like an idiot." Junie looked into her mother's eyes, seeing years of pain that she'd only made worse in recent days. "You are right. You were strong, not weak. I'm so sorry for all that I said. I had no right to judge you."

"Oh, Junie, you've said much worse than that to me. Don't you remember your teen years?"

The tension eased, and they began to reminisce about little things she and Ellen had gotten into as children, and they pondered what life might have been like had Ellen not disappeared. Ruth thought Ellen might have turned into a conniving teen, and they'd have grown apart. Before talking to Ruth about Ellen, the real Ellen, not her apparently glorified memory of her, Junie wouldn't have been able to imagine such a turn of events. Now she wasn't so sure.

"There's just one thing that I have to ask you, and this time you might get mad at me. I went into Daddy's shed the other day."

"I know."

"You know?" *How?*

"Junie, you have never been good at snooping. You found the sweater, right?"

"How could you know?"

"Because when you put the key back, it was set differently. Your father always left the key ring on the inside, against the wall. It was his *thing*. I thought you'd get better at snooping, but it seems you're no better at it now then you were at seven."

"You knew?"

"About you and Ellen in Daddy's shed? Yes, we knew. We were watching you girls from the bedroom window."

"No way! We were sure we went undetected." Junie remembered how they'd snuck back into the house, feeling as though they'd broken into Fort Knox, and how they'd laughed uncontrollably afterward.

"Hardly. When you two girls giggled and whispered, we knew there was trouble brewing. Your father found that sweater tucked behind the workbench right after Ellen went missing. He didn't have the heart to bring it over to Susan. He told me about it, and he didn't want to bring it into the house, because he didn't want to upset you. So he must have just put it away and forgotten about it. I remembered after we fought the other day. Then I noticed the keys. I should have said something, but I just didn't have the strength to get into it."

Chapter Thirty-Five

Junie plucked the stems off of the black cherries at a slow, even pace, thinking about the Skype call with her mother. Her father had had an affair. Okay, no big deal, right? Junie wasn't so sure. If her mother could forgive him, why couldn't she? Why did she feel her father's betrayal of her mother as if it were her he'd betrayed?

She tried to retrieve memories of him not being present, working late, or simply letting them down, but no matter how hard she tried, the memories just weren't there. How could she not remember that? Her mother had said she was just a little girl, and children's perspectives were different from adults'. Boy, was she right about that, but surely she'd have some memory of an absent father. Or had she been too selfish to notice then, too? Selfishness seemed a running theme in her life these days.

She twisted and yanked the stems, her muscles

growing more taut with each passing thought. She thought of how her father's affair was hitting a little too close to home with the recent turn of events between her and Brian. Was she being weak? Was she being stupid? Could he be taking advantage of the freedom in their relationship? Junie tossed the plump cherries into an orange plastic bowl, flicking the stems directly into the trash. She needed about six cups of cherries for the crumble she was making, and she had all afternoon free to make it—her appointment with Theresa wasn't until four p.m. She still couldn't believe she'd talked Theresa into seeing her so soon. Words like *emergency* and *breakthrough* always got a therapist's attention.

She answered the phone with a terse, *Hello?*

"Well, well," Shane quipped. "Are we a bit testy today?"

"Please. Wouldn't you be?" Junie closed her eyes and took a deep breath, wiping her hands on a towel. "I'm sorry. I'm a bit overwhelmed at the moment."

"And you're baking what?"

Junie smiled. He read her like a book. "Cherry crunch bars, I think. If I don't mangle the cherries in the process."

"Breathe, Junie. Breathe. I was thinking, if you want me to come with you to see Theresa, anytime, I will. You know that, right?"

"Yeah, of course. No worries. I know you've got my back."

Shane let out a breath. "Are you okay, Junie? I mean, really okay? You have so much going on."

“Shane, I’m fine, really.” Junie bit back the tinge of sadness she felt when she wished Brian could be as intuitive as Shane was.

“Okay. I know you have a lot on your plate, so don’t worry about the shop. I’ve got it covered.”

“You always do, my dear. It’s the one thing in my life I can count on.” Junie realized how true that was. “Thank you, Shane.”

Junie carried no guilt that afternoon when she let Sarah watch television and play her computer games. She needed a little mommy time, and as wrong as she knew it was, she was again thankful for the quiet. *Maybe I’m looking at everything all wrong. Maybe God knew my life was about to upend, and he’d done this to Sarah knowing I couldn’t deal with a rambunctious four-year-old.* Junie closed her eyes. *God, I am selfish.*

With the stems removed, Junie sat down at the table to pit the cherries. She dug into the sweet pulp with a toothpick, feeling it nudge against the pit, then digging below and flicking the pit out the end where the stems had been. By the fifth cherry, she was mangling the damn things, jabbing the toothpick in so hard it came out the other end and mumbling under her breath, “Bastard. Cheater.”

She mixed the cherries, sugar, cornstarch, water, and almond extract and set it aside while she mixed the dry ingredients. Junie raised her eyebrows, choosing to hand beat the dry ingredients instead of using the mixer. She mashed her frustrations in with the flour, salt, and baking powder. Having creamed the butter and sugar, she dropped each of the three eggs in separately, enjoying the exertion it took to blend them in one at a time.

She prepared the sweet crumble topping, dipping her finger in the brown sugar and butter mixture and popping it into her mouth. If her father were there, he'd say, "What Mom doesn't know…" That saying now held a totally different meaning, stirring up Junie's pulse once again.

"Damn it, Daddy."

Junie spread the fruit in the bottom of the baking pan, buried them with batter, then added the crumbles to the top and slipped the pan into the oven.

When the phone rang, Junie jumped.

Brian? She wiped her hands on a towel and reached for her cell phone.

"Hi." Her voice trembled.

"Hey." Brian breathed hard into the phone. "Look, we need to talk. I shouldn't have left. I'm sorry."

"It's okay. I haven't exactly been the best person to be around either."

"I'm happy that Sarah is making a breakthrough. I was a prick, and I'm sorry. It's just that there's all this emotional crap that came up lately, and—"

"It's okay," Junie said, though she was still angry about his lies. She mentally kept her anger at bay. She wasn't about to ruin the chance they had at reconciliation. How bad could it be? He'd lied about his father, and with their relationship in such a state of unhappiness, if he needed to keep the rebuilding of that bridge to himself for a while, she could respect that.

"No, it's not, and I'm sorry. Can I come home tonight?"

"I'm not the one who made you leave. This is your house. Of course you can come home." Junie bit her lower lip, then said, "But can we talk from now on instead of storming out?"

"You bet."

Junie heard the smile in his voice when he told her he loved her. Even the silence of the line going dead seemed happier than it had before.

As she set her cell phone on the counter, guilt tightened around her chest. She purposely hadn't told Brian that she was going back to see Theresa, and she wondered what she might make of her omission.

Sarah hadn't reacted one way or the other when she mentioned that their neighbor Clara Konel would be babysitting for a few hours. In fact, Sarah hadn't given any indication that she'd even heard her mother. Clara, a sixty-seven-year-old widow, had a gentle way about her, and since Sarah had started regressing soon after their move to the neighborhood, the Sarah that Clara knew was the only Sarah she had ever known. Clara treated her as if she didn't have issues. She chatted to her while they sat together even if Sarah failed to respond, and if Sarah found herself tied in knots over something that didn't sit right, Clara spoke softly, consoling her and letting her know she was safe. Junie thought Clara had the patience of a saint, and as she left the house that afternoon, she wondered if maybe Sarah didn't have any medical issues at all but simply preferred being treated like the baby she once was. She'd have to remember to ask Theresa about that.

Junie sat on the edge of the couch, legs crossed, her foot bouncing up and down nervously. What had she been thinking, coming alone to see Theresa? She needed Shane's support, she realized, swiping at a bead of sweat that formed across her forehead. Maybe she should just leave, tell Theresa she'd made a mistake. *I have no idea what I'm doing here.*

"I can't say I'm surprised to see you back so soon."

Theresa's voice startled Junie. "Am I that transparent?" *That much of a loser?*

"No." Theresa laughed. "Hypnosis sometimes sneaks up on people, unearthing memories that come back too quickly, or need exploring sooner rather than later."

Junie shook her head. "You know, it's not really because of the hypnosis—or maybe it is. My mom and I talked today, and I just found out that my father had an affair."

Theresa shook her head, her smile fading to a serious line. "How does that make you feel?"

"Angry, like a fool. I don't really know." Junie sat back, relaxing into the cushions of the couch. "It's funny. I knew you'd ask me that exact question, and trust me, I've asked myself that at least one hundred times in the past two hours, but I still don't have an answer." She realized that her leg was still; she was no longer nervous. She needed to clear her mind.

Theresa leaned one elbow on the arm of her chair. "You know, Junie, I'm a therapist, but I'm a normal person, too. I'm sure I ask all of the typical therapeutic questions, but I don't judge you. In fact, if anything, I put myself in your place. I think about how I would feel if that happened to me, and then I try to figure out how I can help."

"So, how would it make you feel?" Junie smirked.

"Angry, I think, and like my past were not real, as if it had all been a farce maybe."

Junie nodded. "I do kinda feel like that. There's this piece of me that feels betrayed, but then again, I know I shouldn't. I wasn't his wife. There's another piece that feels like I want to protect my mom, and so I'm angry because he hurt her." Junie still hadn't told Theresa that the affair was with Brian's mother, and she wasn't sure she was ready to reveal that information. She wasn't ready to add it to the list of things that could possibly wedge a wider gap between her and Brian.

"That's all very natural."

"Natural, or normal?" Junie asked.

"Do you need a difference? Who's to say what normal is?"

Now she'd struck a nerve. Junie bristled. "I actually hate that word, *normal*. I don't know why I said it. So, I guess natural is a good choice."

"Do you want to talk about your father's affair?"

Junie thought about the question. She rubbed her

temples, weeding through the urge to lie. She pushed away the crap and decided to shoot from the hip. “Not really. I mean, yes, I want to talk about him and what I feel. I think that’s important, but what I really want to do, I think, is find out more about what I repressed.”

Theresa’s eyes grew wide. “You want to talk about something that you’ve remembered?”

“No.” Junie clasped her hands together to keep them from shaking. “What I remembered, my mom explained to me. I want to see what else I can remember. The initial image I saw of Ellen before the hypnosis, when I was in the yard with Sarah. Ellen’s arms were above her head. She was screaming—that’s what I want to explore.”

“Okay. Let’s talk about this a bit first. What do you think you might remember? What do you hope you might remember?” Theresa sat back, picked up a note pad, and scribbled something.

Junie tried to make out what she was writing but was unable. She shifted in her seat. “I have no idea. I mean, I never would have guessed that my father had an affair, or that Ellen had seizures. I feel like…as you said, what I remember from my childhood might not be real.” She thought about what she was saying. Was it true? Did she really feel like her memories were not accurate? She wasn’t sure what she thought. Maybe. “The more I think about Brian, and the way he behaved after Ellen disappeared and the way he treated me after my dad died, the more I feel like something is…off.”

“What do you mean?” Theresa asked.

"I don't even know what I mean." Junie threw her hands up and sighed. "I never lie to Brian—ever. That's just how I roll. I'm like Honest Abe, but today he called to apologize, and I didn't tell him I was coming here."

Theresa tilted her head. "Do you think you were afraid that he'd judge you, or be angry that you were coming?"

"Maybe. Yes," she admitted. "He would be angry. He would judge me."

"Was he upset that you brought Shane?"

"Yes, a little."

"Is that why you came alone?"

"Do you ever ask easy questions?" Junie fidgeted. "What's my favorite flavor of ice cream? Do I prefer jeans or skirts?"

"Jeans. I can tell."

They both laughed.

Junie leaned forward, her voice softening. "I'm not really sure why I came alone. Maybe I didn't want to piss Brian off even more. I don't know. I knew I wanted to come, so I made the appointment. I'm not sure I gave it much thought at all." Junie felt relieved by the words she spoke. She'd been brave enough to come to the appointment, she had yet to run out, and she was dead set on going through with the hypnosis. "I believe in this, if even to open a tiny little view into my childhood. I don't really like what I've found out so far, but it's put my mind at rest with regard to those awful thoughts about my father. Now I'd like to do the same with the rest of the memories."

"And what if you find something less savory?"

Junie felt the heat of Theresa's gaze. She knew she was looking beyond the words Junie spoke. She was looking for nonverbal clues to what Junie was thinking. Junie raised her arms to cross them, then remembered that the action would signal her discomfort. *Sheesh, she could tell that the minute I walked in.* She crossed her arms.

"More unsavory than my father having an affair? The way I see it, if I've repressed something more, something about Ellen that connects to her disappearance, then I can help put closure to it all for Brian, which would help our marriage, too. Besides, I think I knew something was wrong with Ellen. I think I repressed that memory of my father leaning over her because I didn't want to think about what it meant—that she had something wrong with her. Does that make sense?"

"Possibly." Theresa's voice carried a thread of doubt. "Before we get started, do you want to talk about Sarah and her recent acknowledgments?"

"I'm afraid to." Junie leaned forward. "Was that incredible, or what?"

"What do you think it means?"

Junie shook her head. "I don't know, but it does make me think that maybe there isn't something medically wrong with her."

"Have you completed that questionnaire yet?" Theresa asked.

"I started to, but I just couldn't deal with it. I will now. I'm not afraid to face it anymore." She remembered her earlier thoughts. "Do you think there's any chance that she just prefers to be treated like a toddler? That she's doing this volitionally?"

"Volitionally?" Theresa looked up, considering the question. "Selective mutism, that's a consideration."

"Selective mutism? I've heard of that, but doesn't that have to do with being able to talk in some situations and not in others, like panic attacks?"

"It can, but not always. Selective mutism is usually driven by some sort of trauma, and it can vary in degrees. Some people don't speak at all. They just stop altogether, while others might speak only around those she or he feels safe around."

"Like Sarah talking only to me." Junie uncrossed her arms and thought about Sarah's silence. "But she hasn't been through any trauma."

"It's not always driven by trauma. Some children—and adults—simply decide to remain silent, for whatever reason. Sarah is regressing, too, so that complicates the diagnosis. We'll keep working with her and keep this in mind, but regression does not usually accompany the mutism."

Junie's hope deflated. She looked down at her lap.

"Junie, whatever is going on with Sarah, we'll figure it out, but there's no magic bullet. A diagnosis, whatever it ends up being, does not always equate to a cure."

Junie nodded, wishing she could cover her ears and yell, *Nanananana. I can't hear you.*

Falling under hypnosis was easier this time than the last. A tingling sensation came over Junie's limbs, and the darkness behind her closed lids lit up with tiny sparkles until she felt numb. She wasn't scared. Her body felt as if it were floating, light, unencumbered.

"Where are you?" Theresa's voice sounded far away.

"I'm at Katie's house." Junie stood beside Katie in her front yard. The bright yellow shutters of Katie's house sparkled in the sun.

"What are you doing?"

"Katie is showing me her new bike, but she won't let me touch it." Junie watched her younger self look over the bicycle. "I want to touch it. I want to try it, to ride it. She says I might break it."

"What do you feel?" Theresa asked.

"Mad. I feel like she's being a snot." Junie's body lay still; her fingers began to twitch. "I hate when she does this. She acts better than me. I hate when she does that."

"Junie, do you know when it is? What day, or what time? Is it daytime?"

"Yes."

"Do you see anyone else?"

Junie's index finger shot out. She lifted her hand. "Ellen. She's across the street, crossing over toward us." Junie smiled. "She's whispering to me. She wants...she wants to play with us."

Junie's face pinched; her jaw clenched.

"Junie, what is it? What do you see?"

Junie shook her head. She fisted her right hand.

"Who is there?"

"Me. Ellen. Katie." Junie breathed harder. "Katie's being mean. She won't let Ellen play with us. She called her a name."

Theresa waited. When Junie didn't elaborate, she asked, "What did Katie say?"

A tear slipped down Junie's cheek. "She said…she called Ellen a snitch." Junie clenched her fist again. "She's saying mean things. Ellen is yelling at her. I…I can't hear what she's saying."

"Junie, you're watching. It's okay. Take a deep breath." She waited while Junie took a deep breath. "Good. Now, what happens next?"

"Ellen is running away. No! Don't go, Ellen." Junie made little panting noises. "Ellen, wait! I hate Katie. I hate her."

"Junie, stay with me a minute. You're watching Ellen. What else do you see? Do you see any cars on the road?" Theresa leaned forward, listening.

"Yes, a van. A gray van, down the street."

"And where's Ellen?"

"Walking toward the van, toward the park." Junie panted again. "Ellen, wait!" She licked her lips. "I can't catch her. Katie is calling me names. I turn around and I want to shut Katie up."

"Junie, forget Katie. Can you look back down the street? Do you see or hear Ellen?"

"I hate Katie. I stick my tongue out at her; then I turn back and look for Ellen. I can't see her. Ellen?" Junie broke out in a cold sweat. "Ellen!"

"Junie, concentrate. Where is the van?"

"Driving by me."

"Can you see who is driving?"

Junie shook her head. "The windows are dark. I

can't see." Junie clenched her fingers together. "I see her. I see Ellen. She's in the field behind the seesaw at the park."

Theresa let out a relieved sigh. "Good, okay. Junie, I want you to breathe in and out slowly, okay? Let's do this together. Breathe."

Junie took a deep inhalation and blew it out slowly.

"Good. Let's do it again."

She repeated the breath.

"Now, remember, you are here with me. You are watching Ellen. Where are you?"

"Walking past the park, on the sidewalk."

"Where's the van?"

"Gone. I don't see it." Junie gasped. "Ellen is calling me. She's at the edge of the woods." In a thin voice, Junie said, "She's calling me over."

Junie was trapped. She wanted to follow Ellen, but she knew she wasn't allowed. They'd done it once before, gone into the woods and spied on the kids at Lovers' Rock. They'd been lucky not to get caught.

Junie kept walking, ignoring Ellen's taunts.

Ellen slipped into the woods. Junie panicked. Her heart beat fast and hard. "I can't let Ellen go in there alone. She might get in trouble. She needs me." Junie became aware of Theresa's voice.

"Junie, where are you now? Are you still on the sidewalk?"

"I'm walking home. I didn't want to leave, but my father said bad things could happen in the woods."

"You're walking home. Do you see the van

anywhere?"

Junie shook her head. "There are no cars. My chest hurts. I feel horrible for leaving Ellen. I wanna go back. I need to go back. Daddy said bad things could happen. I don't want her to get hurt. I'm so scared."

"Junie, you're safe. You're here with Theresa, in my office. You're watching the scene with Ellen. You're safe."

Junie breathed fast. Her feet jerked. "I need to find her. Daddy would be disappointed if I let anything happen to her. He told me. He said she was rascally, and that I needed to keep her on the straight and narrow."

Theresa lifted her eyebrows. "Your father told you that? Okay, what are you doing? Did you go find her?"

Junie nodded. "I'm hurrying. I don't see her. A bush prickled me, but I pushed through anyway. I can't see her!" A tear slid down her cheek. "Where is she? Daddy will be so mad."

"I want you to take another deep breath and blow it out slowly, Junie. Okay?"

Junie did as she was instructed.

"You're in the woods. Take me there. What do you see?"

"Trees, bushes, Lovers' Rock."

"What do you hear?"

Junie squinted. She angled her head away from the couch, listening. She whispered, "A boy. I hear a boy. I'm scared. I want to go home."

"Do you recognize the voice?"

Junie's hands trembled. She shook her head.

"Do you see Ellen?"

"No. I see...woods. Trees." Junie was silent, her eyebrows furrowed. "Water. The creek. I can smell the creek." Junie clenched the sides of the cushion. "Someone is there. I hear him. I hear talking."

"Who is it? Do you recognize the voice?"

Junie hesitated, trying to figure it out. "I don't know. Where's Ellen? I can't find Ellen." Her lower lip quivered.

"Junie, I'm going to bring you back now."

"No." Tears streamed down her cheeks. Her chest heaved up and down with each breath.

"Junie, we can continue this another time. I think it's time I brought you back. I'm going to count to three, and when I say three, you will be back here with me, in this room. You'll remember what you saw."

Chapter Thirty-Six

The voice haunted her, but it was the words that cinched it for her. How many times had Junie heard him call Ellen "squirt"? That had to be the day that Ellen disappeared. She'd been at Katie's house, which was not a common occurrence. There was no other explanation.

Junie concentrated on what she'd remembered as she sliced through the cherry crumble bars, now draped in a thick, hardened layer of chocolate and pistachios. *Life sucks*, she thought to herself. *Life Sucks Bars*. Just like that, the cherry crumble bars had a new name. Junie's best names came when she was baking—usually baking out of frustration or elation. The Midnight Madness Bars, thick blueberry, cream cheese, and fudge brownies that were concocted and named the night she found out she was pregnant with Sarah, had been born much the same way.

Ca-chunk, ca-chunk. Junie sliced through the thick

bars.

Brian never told her he was with Ellen. He said he couldn't find her. Maybe it wasn't Brian. Maybe she was mistaken—she'd been wrong about her father, about the shed.

Ca-chunk, ca-chunk.

Junie didn't know what to think.

Sarah walked into the room, a paper in her hand.

Ca-chunk, ca-chunk. Squirt.

Sarah laid her drawing on the table and walked out of the kitchen.

Junie glanced at the paper, realized it was a drawing of some sort, but couldn't concentrate on foolishness. She went to work releasing her frustration in the cutting of the bars.

The front door opened. Junie's heartbeat throbbed in her ears. *Ca-chunk, ca-chunk. Squirt.*

She listened as Brian said hello to Sarah. Her hands began to shake.

Ca-chunk, ca-chunk. Squirt.

His footsteps neared, stopping at the threshold of the kitchen. Junie ground her teeth together, her eyes trained on the Life Sucks Bars.

Brian put his hand on the small of her back and kissed her cheek. She stiffened, closed her eyes.

"You okay?"

"Mm-hm." *Don't touch me.*

"Sorry I'm a little late. What'd you make? Smells delicious." He reached for a bar.

Junie's knuckles turned white, the pads of her

fingers clenched around the handle of the knife.

"These are amazing," Brian gushed. "You"—he kissed her cheek—"are amazing."

Ca-chunk, ca-chunk. Squirt. She felt confined. Brian stood too close. *Ca-chunk, ca-chunk.*

Relief swept through Junie when Brian took a bar and left the room.

Chapter Thirty-Seven

The next morning, Junie ripped the sheet from Sarah's mattress with such force that the edge of it caught and tore along the seam. Junie gathered the sheet in her arms and sat down on the edge of the bed. She looked around Sarah's room. She loved being a mother even if she wasn't a very good one. Tears welled in her eyes. Ellen never had a chance to experience being a mother. She never had a chance to fall in love for the first time, or make out at Lovers' Rock. She didn't get to go crazy at college, drinking until the room spun or sleeping with guys she didn't remember in the morning.

Junie brought the dry part of the sheet to her cheek, held it there, collecting her tears.

Squirt.

There must be a mistake. She hoped there was a mistake. Surely she was remembering wrong, had the days confused. Ellen's frightened face flashed before her. Peter picking up her sneaker in the middle of the night. Brian's voice echoing in the woods. It was all too much. Junie dropped the sheet on the floor and fell across Sarah's bed, sobbing into the pillow.

She felt Sarah's hand on her back, barely a weight, more of a presence. She turned red eyes toward her daughter's worried face.

"Oh God. I truly suck," she cried into the pillow. Junie wiped her eyes and sat up, sniffling through the tears that remained. "Come here, honey. I'm okay." She lifted Sarah up onto her lap and held her tight. *Please don't let it be Brian*.

Brian passed by the open doorway, then came back and stood in the doorway. His eyes trailed over the bundled sheets that lay at Junie's feet, then over his daughter, her arms around her mother's neck, cheek against her chest. Their eyes locked. He shook his head.

Junie buried her face in her daughter's soft neck as she listened to his footsteps fade down the hallway. She closed her eyes, hoping she was wrong and fearing she was right. She squeezed Sarah when the front door thumped shut.

Chapter Thirty-Eight

"When will the weekend get here?" Junie asked Shane.

"Something going on this weekend?" he asked.

Junie closed the oven door and sighed. "No. I think I want to go visit Mom, make sure she's okay."

"You guys made up?"

Junie knew that Shane secretly craved strong familial relationships, and she saw the hope for Junie and Ruth's reconciliation in his eyes. His own family was a bit cantankerous toward one another. "Yeah. Turns out my father was teaching Ellen about photosynthesis. Mom says I was not so interested."

"Gee, what a surprise."

Junie swatted him with a baking cloth. "What's that supposed to mean?"

"Come on, Junie." He grabbed the clipboard and pretended to read it, then rolled his eyes up toward the ceiling. "You think I don't know you by now? Anything fact oriented, organized, learning, you hate it. Think I don't see you fading out when you're reviewing the orders and deliveries? I know you scan. You don't even know how to reconcile."

Junie frowned. "Of course I do. I'm not an idiot."

"Nope, far from it. In fact, I think you might be brilliant, but you didn't get that way from studying, or even from listening intently. I think you're brilliant about what interests you, and all other things, well, let's just say you're right brained. If it isn't interesting to you, you don't clutter your mind with it."

Junie sank down into a chair. "Am I that shallow?" She thought about all of the areas of her life that were systematically coming apart at the seams. Had she caused them all? Had she been too self-centered, not involved enough with her daughter and her husband? Did she ignore the important things in life because she was disinterested? She thought about her recent conversations with Brian and realized that for the past few months, they'd spoken of nothing other than parenting and, more recently, Ellen. Was that her doing? Did she dismiss other more important things he might want to talk about? Was that why he seemed so distant? *Oh God. Does he think I don't care about his job? His happiness? Am I perpetuating the rift between us?* Brian's voice came back to her from the memory she'd recalled. *Squirt!* Her guilt instantly vanished.

The front door chimed, and Shane went to greet the customer.

"Junie, there's someone here to see you," he called

into the kitchen.

Katie stood with her back to the counter, a black purse thrown over the shoulder of her flowing tunic.

"Katie?"

When Katie turned around, Junie saw that she was upset. Her eyes had dark circles under them; she fretted with her hands. Junie took her arm and led her to a table in the corner.

"Are you okay?" Junie didn't know what to make of Katie's surprise visit. They weren't friends, and Junie hadn't even told her the name of her bakery. "Shane," Junie called. "Can you please bring some coffee?"

Katie sat with her purse in her lap, folding and unfolding her hands. She tucked a curl behind her ear and leaned forward, whispering, "I'm sorry. I just—it's been so many years. I need to talk to you."

"Okay, sure." The bakery suddenly felt very large, as if her words might echo.

Shane brought two mugs of coffee. "Would you like a muffin? Fresh from the oven." He furrowed his brow at Junie.

Junie shrugged.

"No. No, thank you," Katie said quickly, then looked back down at her lap, which was in sharp contrast to the overly enthusiastic woman Junie had spoken to the other day.

"Katie, what's wrong? Did I do something the other day? Did I somehow offend you?"

"Oh, no," she said. "It's nothing like that." She took a sip of the black coffee, wiped her mouth on a napkin, then said, "Is it okay to talk here?" She looked around the bakery.

Shane had disappeared into the kitchen.

"Yes, of course. I mean, I don't know what you want to talk about, so I assume it's fine." *What the hell?*

Katie scooted forward until her rib cage rested against the table, her purse tucked beneath it. She spoke in a hushed tone, causing Junie to lean forward and turn her head to the side so she could catch every word.

"I wasn't sure if I should tell you or not, but I took your visit as a sign. You know?"

No, I don't. Junie's stomach tightened. She didn't like the direction Katie's tone was taking. Hadn't she had enough drama in her life lately? She looked outside at the people walking by. She couldn't help but think they were lucky. Her life was falling apart in droves, and those people were walking around with smiles on their faces, oblivious to the trauma that was unfolding, the memories that were strangling her, the old friend who most certainly had news that Junie didn't want to hear.

"Well, when you came to see me, my first thought was, *Yay! Junie's here*. But then"—her smile faded—"it all came back to me. Years of self-imposed torment."

Oh my God. What did I do? "Katie, I'm sorry for anything that I did or said. Please understand. We were kids. I didn't mean any of it. I'm having all this trouble remembering much from certain parts of my childhood, and if I was ever cruel to you—"

"Junie, no, hon, you weren't cruel to me." She swatted the air. "Sheesh, girlfriend, how could you even think that? We were like this." She crossed her fingers.

We were? "I don't understand, then. What do you mean by torment?"

"Junes," she whispered, looking around the bakery. "Don't you remember?" She opened her eyes wide, nodding her head, as if Junie *should* remember.

Junie tried to recall something, anything that might explain what she meant by self-imposed torment. She came up empty. "Boys?"

"Oh, Junes, you really don't remember, do you?"

Junie shook her head. A shiver ran up her spine. She was afraid to hear what Katie had to say. She didn't know how much more bad news she could take. What had she done that was so terrible that she'd caused this poor woman pain and torment?

"I've kept this inside me for so long, I think I started to believe it myself. But when we talked and you were asking." She mouthed the word *Ellen*. "Well, I knew. I just knew it was meant to come out. I mean, I don't know about you, but I can't live with this anymore. It's been too long."

"Whoa, Katie. I have no idea what you're talking about. Slow down, please." Junie's head was spinning. Ellen? Meant to come out? What the hell was going on? She held on to the edge of the table as she listened to Katie describe the afternoon in a much different way than Junie had remembered.

"When you came back, you were shaking, in tears. Gosh, can't you remember us hiding in my backyard? In the playhouse? I think we were back there for at least an hour."

Junie just shook her head. *I went back to Katie's?*

This isn't happening. What have I done? She tried to speak, but no words came out. The bakery began to fade away, as if she were listening to Katie talk in slow motion, each word drawn out, magnified.

"I was so shocked to see you come back. I thought for sure you were gone for the afternoon, but you came back." She nodded. "You were so upset. I didn't know what had happened. Then you told me, and my goodness. Junie, please tell me you remember this."

She could see the pain in Katie's eyes. She'd done something horrid. No wonder she'd repressed the memory. *Oh God*. All Junie could do was shake her head. Her hands trembled. Everything sounded as if she were underwater. Rushing blood pumped past her ears, blocking out any discernible language. Junie felt a hand on her shoulder. As she tilted her head up, her world went black.

The ceiling needs to be painted. That was the first thought that came to Junie as she lay splayed across the floor of the bakery. Shane hovered over her, his face a mask of worry. His eyebrows were furrowed, and his mouth gaped in fright. His hands clenched her upper arms as if he wanted to shake her awake.

Junie blinked, trying to clear her mind. *What happened?*

"June, sweetie, you scared me to death," Shane said.

Panic rushed through Junie. She turned toward the voice. *Katie*. Their conversation floated back piece by piece. *Ellen*. It hadn't been a dream. *Damn it*. Junie let her eyes drift closed.

"Uh-uh, Junie. Open your eyes. Stay with me."

Let me be. Junie wanted nothing more than to disappear. Maybe she could keep her eyes closed. Go to sleep and never wake up. She didn't want to believe that she'd hurt Ellen, although that's not exactly what Katie had said. Someone hurt Ellen. There had been a rock, a giant rock. *Oh God, the rock*. She could see it flying through the air. She could smell the creek.

Junie's eyes sprang open. She reached for Shane's hand, hyperventilating. He sat her up, holding her against his side. "Get a bag, under the counter, quick."

Katie rushed behind the counter and returned with a paper bag held out in front of her. "Oh my goodness. Is she okay? I shouldn't have come," Katie fretted.

Shane snagged the bag and put it over Junie's mouth. "Breathe, Junie. Just breathe long, slow breaths."

Junie did as he instructed until her breathing returned to normal, and she pushed his hand away. She blinked up toward Katie, who looked as though she might faint.

"I'm fine. I'm okay." Junie flushed. She tried to push herself to her feet.

"Oh no, you don't. Just sit and relax," Shane said, gently holding her against him.

"I'm so sorry, Junie. I didn't mean to upset you." Katie crouched by Junie. "What can I do?"

Junie wanted to scream, *Go away and never speak of what you told me!* Instead, she said, "Nothing. I'm fine."

Chapter Thirty-Nine

Junie paced outside of Sarah's school. She had to pull herself together. What did she see? Did she throw the rock? If not, who did? What happened to Ellen? Damn it. There were so many gaps in her memory that she almost wished she'd left it alone in the first place. The saving grace was that Katie had never said Brian's name. Did that mean that Junie made up having heard him that day? Did Katie just omit that part, trying to save Junie any further anxiety? She felt as if she were losing her mind.

Kids streamed out the front door, little girls holding hands, waving goodbye to the teachers. Junie looked for Sarah's red dress. She didn't see her.

Great, now I've lost my daughter?

"Junie, can we see you inside for a moment?"

Junie looked down at Ms. Coler, one of Sarah's teachers. She wondered if she'd ever get used to her four-foot-ten stature. Her petite frame and the dainty way she carried herself made Junie feel like an awkward giant.

"Sure. Where's Sarah?" *What has she done now?*

Inside the classroom, Junie found Sarah leaning over a small round drawing table, so intent on coloring that she gave no indication of hearing Junie when she said hello to her. Sarah was wearing a pair of shorts and a familiar pink T-shirt. The T-shirt Junie had packed in her bag of extra clothes that she kept at the school. Junie's heart sank.

The table was littered with drawings of gardens. Green bushes and overly bubbled flowers drawn with such force that the crayon looked thick, like wax. More drawings were strewn across the floor.

Junie knelt beside her daughter and picked up one of the drawings. She looked up at Ms. Coler.

"She's been drawing all morning. We tried to entice her to join the group, play outside, read with us at circle time, but she'd have no part of it. We were going to call, but—"

"That's okay, really. She's been enthralled with gardens for a week or so. I'm actually glad you let her draw." Junie scrutinized the drawing she held, then picked up another and another. Each drawing featured a similar garden and the same dark mark she'd seen in the drawings at Theresa's office.

Ms. Coler turned her back to Sarah and lowered her voice. "You know, I think we need to talk a bit about Sarah, if you have a moment."

Great. "Sure. Now?"

"If you don't mind. We can go into the front office." She touched Sarah's shoulder. "Sarah, honey, we'll be right back."

Sarah didn't budge.

Junie had known the discussion was coming. She'd been waiting for it. She sat across the desk from Ms. Coler, whose feigned smile annoyed Junie. *Just say it*. She waited, her muscles tensing with each passing second. She wanted to take the drawings and head straight over to Theresa's, but she knew she'd be busy with other clients, and she'd already run up a pretty hefty bill. These were more than just drawings. She could feel it in her bones. *But can I trust my feelings?*

"Junie, we love Sarah, as you know. And we know she's going through a hard time right now. We've been willing to work with her through wetting her pants even though our policy states that children must be potty trained." She gave Junie a condescending look.

"Yes, and we really appreciate all that you've done. You've been wonderful." *Please don't kick her out.*

"We haven't complained when she requires more…attention than some of our other children."

Junie dropped her eyes. *Here it comes.*

"It's been several months now, and I know you are working on figuring out what's going on, but we're…concerned."

"Yes. So are we. I understand." Junie felt as though her heart were being ripped through her chest. *Please don't make Sarah get used to another school. That would be the worst thing for her*. "We're working with a new therapist, and we think we're onto something," she lied.

Ms. Coler's eyes lit up. She ran a hand over her cropped brown hair, patting it with her palm. "Good. That's wonderful news."

Junie hoped that would be enough to buy her a little more time. "We're hoping for a breakthrough very soon." *She's not some new drug, you idiot. She's your daughter. Stand up for her*. Junie looked at the drawings in her lap, then said, "Stability is very important for Sarah right now. Sarah loves it here. She's comfortable here. Please don't tell me she's too much for you." Suddenly she felt the heat of tears tumbling down from the corner of her eyes. "I'm sorry." She snagged a tissue from a box on the desk.

"Junie, goodness, no. That's not what I was suggesting."

Junie sniffled, looked up. "It's not? But—"

"No. I was just going to suggest that you ask her therapist about Asperger's syndrome." She flushed. "I don't profess to know much about these things, but we had a child two years ago with Asperger's, and the behaviors are quite similar."

"Asperger's." Junie let out a little laugh under her breath. "I thought…I thought you were kicking her out." Junie brought her hand to her heart. "Oh, Ms. Coler, thank you." *Asperger's?* Junie knew that most aspects of Sarah's regression didn't mimic Asperger's, but she'd say just about anything to keep Sarah in a safe environment where she felt comfortable. The last thing Sarah needed was a change of schools.

Ms. Coler stood and hugged Junie. "I'm sorry your family is going through this. I know that you know how special Sarah is, and I hope that you know we all just adore her."

"Thank you," Junie gushed, and she meant it. She was truly thankful that something was finally working out in their favor.

They returned to an empty classroom. Sarah's chair had been pulled out from the table, the remaining drawings gathered into a small pile.

"Sarah?" Junie called.

"I'll check the bathroom." Ms. Coler hurried down the hall, calling Sarah's name.

Junie looked in the connecting classroom and passed by the window. She saw Sarah outside, standing beside a large tree. Junie rushed outside. "Sarah. Sarah, are you okay?" Her heart raced. She didn't know what she would have done if Sarah had disappeared. She pulled her to her chest.

Sarah put her fisted hand behind her back.

"Sarah? Why are you out here? What have you got in your hand?"

Sarah didn't answer.

"Sarah Jane? Show me what you have, please."

Sarah stared down at the ground. She didn't budge.

Ms. Coler came out of the building. "There she is. You scared the daylights out of me." She looked at Junie, then at Sarah's rigid stance. "Is everything okay?"

"Mm-hm. I just want Sarah to share what she has behind her back."

Ms. Coler smiled. "I'll bet I know what it is. Sarah, do you have Kayla's earring?" she asked.

Sarah bit her lower lip.

"It's okay. You're allowed to look at it, but it does belong to Kayla, so you can't take it home." She turned to Junie and explained. "Kayla wasn't here today, but her mother called to tell us that she'd lost an earring yesterday. This is a big deal because she just got her ears pierced a month ago, and this was the first time she'd worn something other than the little studs they'd pierced her with." She turned to Sarah. "Sarah found it in the classroom, and she's been enamored with it ever since. Now, I'm not sure, but I think Sarah here wishes she could have pierced ears. Don't you, Sarah?"

Sarah shook her head from side to side.

Junie's heart leaped. She'd responded! She grabbed Ms. Coler's arm. "Did you see that? Sarah? You don't want your ears pierced?"

Again she shook her head.

Junie laughed. "Okay, then, no ear piercing."

"I should say not," Ms. Coler said. "Sarah, may I please have the earring?"

Sarah shook her head.

Junie crouched before Sarah, not wanting to alarm her, as she had in the car. She held on to the drawings she'd picked up in her right hand and held out her left. "Sarah, may I please see Kayla's earring?" She reached for Sarah's hand, flipped it over, and opened her little fingers. Within her palm lay a tiny silver hoop.

Junie felt as though she'd been kicked in the stomach. She fell backward, holding on to the ground for support. The wind rushed out of her.

"Junie, what is it?" Ms. Coler asked.

Junie shook her head. "I'm okay. It's nothing." *I'm just looking at the exact same type of earring that my missing friend was wearing when she disappeared more than twenty years ago.* "It's been a long day."

Chapter Forty

Junie didn't care if they had to put the house up for sale. She had to get another appointment with Theresa—fast. If that made her crazy, then so be it. She could no sooner navigate alone the memories that accosted her than she could figure out what was going on with her daughter. She was adrift in a sea of worries and intangibles. She'd drown without a lifeline.

She'd left an urgent message for Theresa hours ago and had yet to hear back. When her cell phone rang, she jumped for it without looking at the caller ID.

"Hello?"

"Let's go away for a few days."

Junie stiffened. She'd almost forgotten what she'd heard. *Squirt.* Why was he suddenly being so nice? What was he up to? "Um, I'm trying to reach Theresa, for Sarah," she added quickly. "Her teacher wants me to talk to Theresa about Asperger's." *And I can't talk to you right now.*

"Oh, well, our court date was postponed, so I am coming home around five. Why don't you make it a little later and I'll go with you?"

Junie's jaw dropped. "You will?"

"Yeah, I've been thinking. Whatever Sarah's going through, she can't do it alone, and you've just lost your dad, so—"

Was he actually trying? Junie felt like such a bitch. How could she have thought Brian had something to do with Ellen's disappearance?

"I thought we'd go to Deep Creek for the weekend, get away."

What?

"Hello? Junie?"

"Yeah, I'm here," she said quietly.

"My family's cabin. It's miles away from anywhere. Just the three of us."

Call waiting buzzed through. "Hold on a sec," she said, and answered the call.

"Junie, it's Shane. I gotta talk to you. I think I made a big mistake."

"Shoot, okay. Hold on a sec."

"Wait. I'm late. Let me tell you quickly. I called Brian. I was worried about you, about what happened, so I called to tell him to be sure to take care of you, but he was pissed."

"You *called* him?" Junie realized just how worried Shane must have been. The only other time he'd taken it upon himself to call Brian was when she'd come to the bakery sick every morning—before they'd realized it was morning sickness.

"I thought he'd be there for you, but he was furious that Katie had come to see you. I think I did something really wrong. I'm so sorry."

Why didn't Brian mention the call?

"No, you're fine. Okay, look, I gotta run. Brian's on the other line." She heard Shane apologize as she clicked back over to Brian.

"Sorry about that," she said.

"No problem. Was that Theresa?"

"No." *Oh God.* Junie closed her eyes and lied. "Sales call."

"So, why don't you pack and I'll pick you girls up in a bit, and if Theresa calls, we'll go there first."

"Um, I think we should stay around here, in case she calls later." *I don't want to be alone with you.*

"Don't be silly. She won't work on the weekend. Be ready," he said in a tone that Junie heard as, *We're leaving when I get home. No questions asked.*

Junie panicked. What if Brian had been involved? What if he thought Katie told her something that confirmed his guilt? What if she was involved—she still wasn't sure what had happened, and all Katie had done was cloud her memories. What if Brian knew it was her who did something to Ellen? Did she do something to Ellen? Junie thought her mind might explode, and Brian would come home and find her brains splattered all over the living room floor.

She tried Theresa again and reached her answering machine. She picked up the phone to call her mother, then realized how stupid she'd sound, *Mom, I think I hurt Ellen, or maybe Brian did. I'm afraid to be alone with him. I'm afraid to be with myself. Oh, and Sarah's teacher wants me to ask her therapist about Asperger's, but her therapist thinks Sarah might be selectively mute. Did I mention that she was holding the same exact earing as Ellen was wearing when she disappeared? Shoot me now.*

She threw herself down on the couch, buried her face in her hands, and decided she needed a plan. First she made a mental list of the things she had to figure out: *Why was Sarah so enamored with the earring? Was it just a coincidence that it looked like Ellen's? Why was she drawing Peter's garden? What did I see at the creek? Was it Brian? Did I hurt Ellen?*

Then she listed a few things that were bothering her: Brian's voice at the creek. Gray van? Ellen's shoe? Asperger's? Selectively mute?

She had to work through each item to reclaim her sanity and understand what was going on—or at least that was her plan.

Junie picked up the phone and called Katie. After listening to her gush about how sorry she was, she finally got a word in.

"What exactly did I tell you? What did you feel you had to hide all these years?"

Katie didn't answer.

"Katie, please. This is important. I *need* to know."

"Junie, you passed out today. I think I made a big mistake. I don't think I should have said anything. I'm so sorry for unearthing something so painful. Really, it's our secret. I promise not to bring it up again."

"Our secret?" *What the hell?* Junie wondered when they'd had the type of relationship that had secrets. "Katie, please!"

"All I can say is that if you don't remember, then maybe you shouldn't remember. You get my drift?" Katie's voice wavered.

"Katie, listen. I need to know if I hurt Ellen. Did I hurt Ellen? Did I do something? Why did she disappear? Please, if you know, I need to know."

"I can't do this anymore, Junie. I wish you never came back. I should have said something years ago."

"Said what?"

"Why don't you ask your husband?"

The phone went dead.

Chapter Forty-One

Brian came in as Junie was changing Sarah's clothes. She stuffed them in the bottom of the hamper, not wanting to deal with any of his snarky comments. Every nerve was on fire. Her chest tingled. She moved about the room like a firefly, unable to settle down.

Junie sent Sarah to the living room to watch television as she carried the hamper downstairs.

"I thought I'd throw a load in before we go," Junie said, slipping into the laundry room.

"Another accident?" he said.

What happened to your good mood? "No, I just don't want to come home to dirty laundry. How was your day?" *Tell me about Shane.*

"Uneventful."

Liar. "Sorry about court."

"No big deal. We'll get the guy off. They're just buying time. How about your day?" he asked.

"Uneventful." *Call me on it. Come on, please.*

"That's good, I guess."

The air between them was charged with negative electricity. Junie heard every word Brian said as a taunt, every omission of his conversation with Shane as an admission of guilt of some kind, a threat to her safety, only she didn't know why. She'd never been afraid of Brian before, and she hoped she was being foolish now, but she couldn't shake the feeling that something had changed. His personality was forced, his kindness feigned. Katie's words echoed in her head. *Ask your husband.*

Brian's cell phone rang. He answered it, moving swiftly into the other room. Junie strained to listen.

"Now? I can't. We're…busy."

She breathed in slow, quiet breaths.

"Right now? Damn it. Why do you do this? What's so important that I have to leave right this instant?"

Silence. Brian paced. "Shit. Fine. One hour."

Junie heard him coming back and she quickly picked up Sarah's drawings, as if she'd been leafing through them.

"I gotta go out." Brian looked up, his eyes stuck on the drawings.

"Okay." *Good. That gives me time to think.* "Where are you going?" She took a chance. "Maybe we should postpone the trip."

"Naw. I'll be back early enough to go. Just meeting a client at the office, exchanging files."

Junie followed his stare. "Sarah drew these at

school. Didn't she do a great job?" She held on to a thread of hope that even now Brian would show some enthusiasm toward Sarah's efforts. "I think she's really coming along."

Brian took the stack of drawings and looked through them. He began to breathe harder, his chest lifting and falling with each measured breath. He snapped his eyes toward Sarah, who sat silently on the couch, blanket in her lap, thumb in her mouth.

"Nothing special there," he said as he opened the door. "Be ready in two hours."

Chapter Forty-Two

Junie sprang into action. She called Clara, thankful that she could come right over. She sat down with Sarah and asked her why she liked Kayla's earring so much. Sarah didn't answer. Junie tried a few more lines of questioning, but finally gave up when Clara arrived.

"Thank you for coming over so quickly. I'll be back soon." Junie snagged her keys and headed out to her car before she could get wrangled into small talk. *Ask your husband*. She'd ask him, all right, but not in front of her daughter.

The wind whistled through the telephone lines. Junie put her head down and steeled herself against the rush of fear that ran through her. She had to be stronger than her childish insecurities. *It's only wind*, she told herself, and headed toward Brian's office.

The roads were empty as she neared his office parking lot. Brian's car was nowhere to be found. Junie was not surprised. She picked up her cell phone and called him.

"Yeah," he snapped.

Junie listened for background noise. "Hey, um…can you bring me one of those folders that Stacy has, you know, the accordion ones? I want to coordinate some of the articles I pulled up about the things Theresa has brought up."

Brian didn't answer. Junie smirked.

"She's not here."

"Well, I figured that. She keeps them in her right drawer. She showed me last time I was there."

"I'll see if I can find it. I gotta run." Brian ended the call.

Junie heard a train in the background. *A frickin' train?* Junie could think of only one place that Brian could be, but why would he drive halfway to her parents' house at this time of night? She pulled out her cell phone and called Clara, who agreed to stay with Sarah for an extra hour and a half; then she lead-footed it to the highway.

Junie pulled off the exit when she passed the train station, thinking of Sarah's high-pitched voice calling out *choo-choo!* each time they passed the station and how much the missing *choo-choo!* alert had saddened her when they'd driven by the other day. She had no idea what she was doing, or why she felt compelled to chase down her husband, but Katie's words echoed in her head. She pulled down the darkened street to the illuminated station, feeling like a derelict. What the hell did she expect to find? She had no clue. Some tawdry meeting with a thug? Another woman? Junie suddenly felt sick to her stomach.

She took one quick spin through the parking lot, then headed back toward home, admonishing herself for acting like the star of a reality show. *Who does this?*

She waited for the light before the ramp to change, wishing she had a cup of coffee. She spotted a Dunkin' Donuts up ahead and decided to whip into the drive-through. She waited behind a blue Jetta full of teenagers, listening to them hoot and holler at one another. She debated parking and ordering inside. She glanced through the front window, and her heart skipped a beat. Brian sat across from Peter, his face red, pinched. His jaw was set in a hard line.

Shit. Junie pulled out of the line and into a dark corner of the parking lot, watching them through the glass.

Peter leaned forward, his elbows on the table, his hands outstretched and flailing, as if he were describing something. He brought them together beneath his chin and closed his mouth, watching Brian.

Brian stared down at the table. He ran his hand through his hair, then turned away.

Junie slumped down in the car. What the hell was going on? How long had he been lying to Junie about his father? Was the whole thing a put-on? Were they pretending to be cold toward each other? At least he wasn't with another women, she reasoned.

Junie had had enough crap for one day. She dialed Brian's number and watched as he withdrew his cell phone, looked at the display, then pushed a button. She was instantly sent to voice mail.

There had to be a good reason for this. He'd said he was meeting a client, and the other day he'd said that he and his father were working on a case together, but she didn't see any files. Maybe she'd confront them while they both sat together. Now.

She couldn't move. She jumped when her phone rang. *Clara*.

"Hi, Junie. I'm sorry to bother you."

Junie could hear Sarah screaming, out of control, in the background.

"What happened? What's wrong?" *Oh God, please let her be okay*.

She listened as Clara described her daughter moving from one houseplant to the next, spoon in hand, digging in the pots. She'd asked Sarah what she was looking for, but Sarah hadn't answered, and she'd finally taken each plant and put it out of reach on top of the refrigerator. Sarah now stood before the refrigerator, screaming.

Junie started the car and took one last glance into the Dunkin' Donuts. They were gone. She scanned the empty parking lot. *Shit*.

Clara left only minutes before Brian came in the front door.

"Junie?" he called.

Junie lay listening to Brian look for her, her arm wrapped protectively around her sleeping daughter. Clara had let Sarah cry herself to sleep, something that Junie had never been good at, but at that moment she was supremely thankful for it. Sarah's curtains were closed, and by the time Brian found his way upstairs, Junie had decided to take the easy way out and avoid a confrontation. She pretended she was sleeping. No Deep Creek, no confrontations.

With her eyes closed, she listened to him breathing heavily in the doorway.

"Junie," he whispered.

She lay still.

"Damn it."

She listened to him walk away.

So much for her plan. Now what? She'd sleep with Sarah. That much was decided. She snuggled in to her daughter's side, feeling torn. What had Sarah been doing, digging in the plants? Why was she so upset over not being able to reach them? Why was she enthralled with Kayla's earring, and what the hell was Brian doing with Peter in the middle of the night? Junie thought her head would spin all night long, but when she rolled over on her back, it took only a few minutes for her to fall into a deep sleep.

Chapter Forty-Three

The house phone rang. Junie looked over at Sarah, sleeping peacefully beside her, and was thankful that they'd decided not to hook up a landline in the bedroom. She climbed over Sarah's sleeping body and made her way downstairs to the kitchen.

"Hello?" she said sleepily. The clock above the stove read 6:00 a.m.

"Junie, hi. It's Peter."

"Peter? Hi, how are you?"

"I'm good. Listen, I need to talk to you. Is there some time later today we can meet?"

The urgency in his voice woke Junie up. "Is everything okay?"

"Come on, Junie. It's time to go. We need to get on the road." Brian stood behind Junie, his arms crossed.

Junie looked at the telephone, then back up at Brian, deciding if she should tell him that Peter was on the phone. Or maybe he already knew?

"Junie?" Peter's voice pleaded. "Later today?"

"Um." Junie looked at Brian. "Maybe we should skip Deep Creek. Sarah had an awful night last night, and I'd still really like to get her in to see Theresa."

"It can wait a day or two." Brian crossed his arms.

"Junie, your bakery?" Peter asked.

Everything inside Junie screamed to get out of the house and leave father and son to battle out whatever was going on, but Junie was frozen. She couldn't answer Peter, and she couldn't look away from Brian's stare. Her stomach ached. What could possibly be going on between them?

"We'll go today and be back Sunday night," Brian said.

Junie answered Brian. "Okay."

"Good, I'm on my way," Peter said.

Shit.

Chapter Forty-Four

Sarah stood before the refrigerator, staring up at the plants.

"Sarah, honey, let's go outside for a bit." Brian had taken the car to get gas—or so he said—leaving Junie with a little thinking space. If she met Peter, she had about an hour before she'd have to leave. She'd just tell Brian she'd had to run into the bakery to tie up a few loose ends. First, though, she had to help her daughter pull out of whatever was spiraling her into regressing, or rather, she had to find out what was circling in her daughter's mind, and the only way to do that was to try and get Sarah to talk about it.

They walked across the grass toward the rock garden that lined the fence, stepping over roots from the giant oak tree Sarah had named Weird Harold the summer before.

"Careful of Harold," Junie said. "What do you want

to do here? Want to see if there are salamanders or ants under the rocks?" Finding bugs was just one of the activities that Sarah used to enjoy with her grandfather. Junie crouched beside Sarah, missing her father with an ache so big it felt like a rain cloud hovering above her.

She watched Sarah touch the rocks, then pick up a stick and dig in the mud.

"Sarah, honey, why are you digging so much?"

Sarah flicked dirt up into the air with the tip of her stick.

"Are you looking for something?"

Sarah didn't answer. Junie let it go and decided that maybe letting Sarah play out her frustrations would pay off in the long run. She picked up a stick and began digging. Sarah stopped digging and looked at her mother.

Junie pretended to use all her strength to dig, moving from side to side, pushing down on the stick she held within her fist.

Sarah mimicked her movements. She'd mimicked her movements before, so Junie didn't see her daughter's aping her movements as a golden ticket, but mimicking was a form a communication, and that was a start.

Junie tried to get Sarah to speak to her. She asked her what she was digging for, if she liked the flowers, which rock was her favorite, and several other open-ended questions.

Thirty silent minutes later, Junie stood, wiped off her hands, and surveyed the holes that ran down their yard. It looked like a bad scene from *Gophers Gone Wild.*

Junie's cell phone rang. *Katie.* Junie answered the phone, walking away from where Sarah was digging.

"Junes, I'm really sorry about snapping at you. I don't know what got into me. We're friends, right?"

The hope in Katie's voice got on Junie's last nerve. She pressed her hand to her temple, took a deep breath, and decided to confront her head on. "Katie, I have no idea what you were talking about. I can't remember a damn thing, and I can't get any straight answers. I feel like I'm losing my mind."

Katie remained silent.

"Ugh! I'm sorry, okay. I'm a bit frazzled right now." She looked at her torn up yard. "My daughter is going through a rough time, and this whole thing with Ellen has me distracted."

Katie cleared her throat. The tremble in her voice made Junie believe she was holding back tears. "I'm sorry about your daughter. I didn't know."

"I know. It's not your fault. It's not anyone's fault. It just is."

Sarah picked up a giant rock and held it above her head. "Sarah, put that down," Junie said instinctively. The rock magnified before her...*Squirt! Get outta here!* Brian's voice echoed in her head. She leaned against a tree. The rock flashed again and again over his head, a bad rerun. Ellen's shriek raced through her ears. Junie froze.

"Junie, are you okay?"

She dropped the phone and crumbled to her knees. Katie's voice seemed very far away.

Junie stretched her fingers, reaching for the phone as if in a haze. She lifted it to her ear as Katie rambled on.

"Junie? I'm sorry, okay? It's just that this pact is killing me. It's been years."

Junie's eyes drifted to the garden. Suddenly she saw herself as a little girl, her hair blowing in the wind, drizzle hitting her cheeks, thunder roaring above. She was freezing, lonely, sad about Ellen being gone. It was pitch dark outside. Her bare feet sank into the wet ground. She stood at the back of the Olsons' garden, shivering in a thin nightgown that hung to her ankles. Hidden behind a large tree, she stared up at Ellen's window. Ellen had to come back; she just had to.

Peter's sobs drew her attention. He knelt at the edge of the rose garden, his shoulders hunched, his knees sunk deep into the wet earth. "I'm so sorry," he cried.

Junie's chest constricted.

A gust of wind came across the hill, blowing rose petals across the yard. Several blew by her face, floating slowly down and landing near Junie's feet. One lone petal clung to her thin nightgown.

The phone slipped from her hands as the world turned black. Junie faded in and out of consciousness. Strong hands lifted her under the arms, guiding her toward the house. Her mind drifted back in time. The smell of the creek surrounded her. She needed to find Ellen.

Chapter Forty-Five

Junie awoke in a full-blown panic. Sweat poured feverishly down her forehead.

"Junie? Are you okay?"

She blinked, bringing Brian into focus. *Brian.* She used the heels of her feet for traction as she scooched toward the headboard—away from Brian, and then turned her face away from his reach.

"What's wrong with you?" Brian asked, backing away from the bed. "June, it's me, Brian."

"I…I know who you are." She caught sight of herself in the bedroom mirror—her hair stuck out in tangled knots, and her cheeks were marked with dirt. She looked at her hands, also covered in dirt, mud packed tight under her nails. "Where's Sarah?" She looked frantically around the room.

"With my father."

"Peter? He's here?" She pulled the blanket up to her

chest.

"He got here about an hour ago. He said you were supposed to meet him, and when you didn't, he got worried and came over."

Junie watched Brian swallow hard, then close his eyes.

"Junie, we need to talk."

"Not now," she said. She was not up for any more drama. "I need to get cleaned up."

"Can't that wait? I have something that I need to tell you."

Junie was so confused. She wasn't ready to hear what he had to say. She needed to know what she was dealing with first, make sure Sarah was safe. Make sure *she* was safe. Her life had turned inside out. "Can you call my mom?"

"Your mom? Are you sick? Do you need me to take you to the doctor?" Brian moved closer to her—she flinched, pulled away.

"I'm…not feeling well, and I just want her here. Is that too much to ask?" Her voice escalated and trembled.

"Junie, I just want to talk to you."

Junie sat up straight on the bed. "Brian, not now. I'm in no shape to talk about anything." *I don't know who you are.*

Brian reached for her cell phone, dialed Ruth's number, and handed the phone to Junie.

She watched him walk out the bedroom door and waited for the door to close before she spoke.

"Mom?" she said quietly. "I think I'm in trouble. I need to talk to you."

"June? What's wrong? What's happened?"

Junie laid all of her memories out for Ruth. She told her that she wasn't sure, but she thought Brian might have hurt Ellen.

Ruth was silent for a moment. Junie waited, twisting the blanket around her finger.

"Honey, I want you to know that I hear you. I understand what you are saying, and I can hear how serious you are. I'm taking what you are telling me very seriously."

"But?"

"But I know Brian. I've known him since he was a toddler. He couldn't have hurt Ellen. Besides, how could a fourteen-year-old make a little girl disappear? It just doesn't make any sense."

Junie bit her lip, thinking about what her mother said. "That's seems right, but what about my memories?"

"Oh, Junie, look at what you thought about your father, and you were way off base, right? You can't throw your marriage away. Brian adores you. If you want to know what I think, I think you are flat-out exhausted. You haven't slept in months. Your heart is ripped out day in and day out because you don't know what's going on with Sarah, and for some reason, your brain is twisting things around."

"Do you really think so? I mean, I am so tired I can barely see straight, and I feel so useless as a mother." She struggled to get words out around her tears. "I...I can't even help my daughter figure out why she's doing all these weird things." Junie wept. "Mom, do you think I'm a terrible mother? I mean, is Sarah trying to be a baby because it was easier for her then than it is now? Was I nicer then? Did I give her more attention when she was a baby?" She wiped tears from her cheeks, feeling like a complete failure and hoping her mother would say something, anything, to make her feel better.

"June Marie, take a deep breath. You are an excellent mother." Ruth spoke as if she were giving a directive, then asked, "Did I ever tell you about your fourth-grade graduation?"

"No," Junie said, already feeling a little better. She hadn't realized how much the rifts that had occurred, first with Brian, then with her mother, had drained her. Sarah's regression had also been slowly sucking the life out of her, and her suspicions about Brian had her tied in knots. Losing her father had kicked off a tornado of memories, and when the hurt and confusion of the mess that had become her life intersected, she was sucked into the eye of the storm. Her mother's voice, her mother's confidence in Junie's mothering skills, was the life vest she needed.

"Well, I missed it. I had a flat tire on the way to the grocery store, and back then, there were no cell phones, so I walked two miles to the gas station, then had to wait for the guy to drive me to my car. It was just a nightmare. Anyway, by the time I got home, I was in no mood to be around anyone, so your dad took you."

"I don't remember that."

"No, I don't suppose you would. You were busy with your friends and giddy over the trip to the ice cream store afterward. I tormented myself for weeks. Every time a friend would bring up graduation, I'd feel sick, guilty beyond belief. But you." Ruth laughed. "One day you told me that you were glad that I didn't come to your graduation."

"Oh, that's really nice. Sorry, Mom."

"No, you didn't say it meanly. You said that all the other mothers were so plain that I would have made them feel bad."

Junie smiled. "I said that?"

"Yes, my dear, you did, and please don't tell me that you didn't mean it. That one comment pulled me through your teen years." She laughed.

"You always make me feel better."

"I always tell you the truth. You make yourself feel better," Ruth answered.

"Maybe you're right about Brian, but there's one thing that doesn't make sense, and it's driving me insane. Remember Katie? She called me after I went to see her, and she told me that I left her house that afternoon, that I went after Ellen, and that when I came back, we made some sort of a pact not to tell something. She said I should ask Brian what she was talking about."

"Junie, Katie Frank is a little snark. Don't you remember how jealous she was of you and Ellen?"

"Mom, I feel like I must have floated through my younger years without a care in the world. I don't remember jack shi—" Junie cleared her throat. "I don't remember anything."

"Well, I wouldn't worry yourself any about Kate. She probably never got over the fact that Brian married you. She had a thing for him. *Whew!* If young girls only knew how foolish they looked when they were in that hormonal stage. She used to walk up and down our block in those hot pants of hers. I can't believe you don't remember. Up and back, up and back, just trying to get Brian's attention."

"Nope, nada. I don't think Brian and I even spoke much after Ellen disappeared until after college."

"Yes, you're right there. He sort of boxed himself off from everyone." Ruth made a *tsk* sound. "It must have been grueling for him, to lose a sister like that."

Junie closed her eyes against a wave of guilt. "I'm so glad I have you, Mom, and I'm so sorry that I've been too wrapped up in my own crap to help you when you need it most."

"You're fine, Junie. Since you were a little girl, you could get wrapped up in things and think you had them all figured out. You...you like chaos, I think. Or maybe you like mysteries. I don't know what it is, but give yourself a little break. You've let your imagination get the best of you. I love you, and you know what? I'm just fine. I hug your father's pillow at night, and I talk to him like he's still there, but I'm a tough old bird. I'll get through it."

After she hung up the phone, Junie lay on the bed, staring at the ceiling, wishing she could be more like her mother: always in control, the right answer perched on the tip of her tongue.

Brian knocked at the door, then opened it a crack. “Is it safe to come in?”

“Yeah.” Junie sat up and decided to trust her mother’s judgment above her own. Ruth seemed the more rational of the two. “I’ve been thinking, maybe we should take that trip.”

Brian’s eyes sparkled. “Really?” His smile sank into his most serious look. “Junie, my dad wants to talk to you. I have something—”

Junie swatted the air dismissively. “Whatever is between you and your dad is between you and your dad. Can you please tell him thank you for coming, but that I’m too tired to talk right now? I’ll catch up with him when we get back.”

“Are you sure?” Brian sat on the edge of the bed.

Junie nodded and Brian wrapped his arms around her, pulling her close to his chest. A rush of anxiety swirled through her. She closed her eyes against it. She was determined to have a few good days. They deserved that.

Chapter Forty-Six

For the first time in what seemed like forever, Junie was able to relax. She sat in a rocking chair on the front porch of the rustic cabin overlooking the lake. Sarah was busy digging holes near the water's edge, and Junie made a conscious decision not to worry about *why* Sarah was digging. Thankfully, Sarah had gone without an accident since the evening before.

The whir of Brian's cast broke through the peaceful silence. It was a comforting sound, coming from the edge of the dock where he stood. He wore a pair of jeans and an open flannel shirt over a dark T-shirt. Junie watched him with interest. Her eyes followed the line of his back to the curve of his rear. *Not bad,* she thought, and realized how much she missed him. How much she missed *them*. Life had become such a cacophony of issues that their time together, the closeness that they'd once shared—the secret smiles, stolen kisses, and late nights spent making love—had been replaced with angst and worry and a distance that had become almost too vast to bridge.

Junie sauntered down to the dock, kissing Sarah on the top of her head as she passed.

Brian's fishing rod arced as she approached, and Brian let out a shout of surprise. He arched his back, drawing the rod toward him.

"Wow, you got it. You got it!" Junie squealed. "Sarah, come see Daddy's fish!"

Sarah lifted her head in Junie's direction.

"Come on. Come on," Junie urged.

Sarah walked slowly toward them. When she reached the edge of the dock, she stopped.

"Come on!" Junie waved her up.

Sarah moved slowly toward them, her eyes locked on the fish.

Brian lifted the fish out of the water and lowered it onto the dock. "Whoa, it's a beauty! Look at that pike. Sarah, come here." Brian grabbed a pair of needle-nose pliers from the tackle box. He stepped on the tail of the fish with the toe of his left sneaker, latched the pliers on to the end of the hook, and wiggled and pulled until the hook tore free. Drops of blood splattered onto the deck. "Dinner!"

Sarah screamed, a guttural, terrified scream that echoed in the mountains. She grabbed the sides of her head, her face beet red.

Brian whipped his head up, his arms following. The hook caught in the webbing between his index finger and thumb.

Junie ran to Sarah's side. "It's okay. It's all right, Sarah." She tried to wrap her arms around her. Sarah pushed her away, stumbling backward on the wooden decking and falling into the deep water. "Sarah!" Junie watched in horror as her daughter's arms flailed in that second before she broke the water and shot beneath the surface. Junie reached for her arm and missed.

In that split second, when disbelief met with panic, Junie thought her heart might stop. Sarah disappeared into the murky water. The world spun around Junie; darkness pushed at the edges of her vision. The hook was lodged in Brian's hand, tethering him to the fishing pole. He tore at the fishing line, trying to break free. "Jump, Junie. Get her!" he commanded.

Junie was paralyzed with fear. Ellen fell backward. *Ellen*. *Ellen* echoed in her head.

"Go!" Brian commanded. "Now!"

Brian's voice called her back to the present. She jumped off the edge of the dock into the icy cold water. She dove under, looking for Sarah. The water was too deep, too murky to see. She popped back up to the top, gasping for air, dog-paddling to the best of her ability. The image of Ellen's lifeless body seared into her mind. She gasped, falling under the water, then popped back up again. Brian ripped the hook free and dove into the water.

Junie went under again, searching for Sarah. It was Ellen's face she saw beneath the water. She opened her mouth. *Ellen,* she said. Her lungs filled with water. *Ellen, Ellen.*

Brian came to the top of the water, holding Sarah under his arm. He lifted her to the dock, scrambling up next to her.

Junie thrashed wildly, her head bobbing in and out of the water. She coughed and choked.

Brian lay Sarah on her left side; water dribbled from her mouth. She coughed up water, sobbing between gasps. Brian dove back into the water, fishing around for Junie. Junie's body convulsed, then went limp. *Ellen.* She felt her body being pulled out of the water, felt her chest heave with a giant cough. She choked, pulling herself onto her hands and knees and throwing up what felt like gallons of water.

Brian rushed to Sarah's side.

Junie fell to her stomach, panting and coughing, reaching for her daughter's hand.

"She's breathing. She's okay," Brian said. Tears streamed down his cheeks. "Holy shit," he said, looking up toward the sky.

Chapter Forty-Seven

That evening, Ellen's body floated through Junie's dreams, her eyes staring blankly up toward the sky, her arms dangling from her sides. Flashes of Brian interrupted the gruesome scene; his arms above his head, giant rock in hand.

Morning found Junie sitting up in bed, the covers pulled up to her chin. She inched away from Brian, clutching the blanket to her chest. Her heart throbbed against her ribs, set off by her mounting fear. The hero shine from yesterday that had made Junie look at Brian with new, schoolgirl-crush eyes had been washed away with her dreams, exposing a dangerous stranger that lay beneath.

Junie thought of his behavior of late. Brian had been like Jekyll and Hyde. Her mind traveled down dark paths, back to the images she'd seen when Sarah fell into the water, her dreams from the night before. Was he playing her to get her and Sarah alone in the remote cabin? Had she been swayed too far by her mother's advice? Junie's heart raced. She had to get out of there. She slipped from the bed and rushed through her shower.

In the kitchen, Junie made coffee and tried to think up an excuse to go home. She couldn't say that Sarah had an appointment with Theresa. It was Saturday. Maybe she could use Bliss as an excuse. No, Brian knew it was rare that there was an emergency that Shane couldn't handle. Shane. She could call Shane and have him show up to protect them. She nixed that as just plain stupid. Shane was no match for Brian.

Sarah walked into the kitchen, blanket dragging on the floor behind her.

Sarah. Junie would be damned if she'd let anything happen to Sarah. She scanned her daughter's clothing, silently hoping that she hadn't had an accident. She was dry. *Dry*. Sarah was doing better—and her mother was falling apart.

Brian sauntered into the living room and kissed Sarah on the head.

The hair on the back of Junie's neck stood up. She couldn't look at Brian without seeing him as an angry teenager, a giant rock held high above his head—aiming at Ellen. She felt Brian looming behind her.

He put his arm around her lower back and whispered, "Can we talk?"

Junie stiffened, swallowed hard. The last thing Sarah needed was to see an argument between her parents. Junie closed her eyes against her thoughts. *You hurt Ellen!* "Sure."

He took her hand and led her onto the porch. Junie looked at the landscape that was so beautiful just twenty-four hours earlier. Now, as she gazed at the lake and the backdrop of the mountains, she saw places that a body could disappear. Was Ellen's body there somewhere, decaying in a shallow grave or eaten by fish in the same deep lake that Sarah fell into? A shiver ran up her spine.

No, he saved us yesterday. If he had intended to hurt her and Sarah, he'd have let them drown, she reasoned—unless he wanted to torture them. *Oh God*.

"I think we should go home." Junie's words came fast. "Sarah should see a doctor after yesterday, and I'm not feeling great, either."

"Really?" He wrinkled his forehead. "She seems fine to me. She didn't even have an accident. I think she's okay."

Damn it. Junie bit her lower lip, trying to figure out how to get home.

"Besides"—he reached for her hand—"there's some stuff we need to talk about."

Junie withdrew her hand.

"Let's go for a walk."

"No—" She stood up and opened the door. "We can't leave Sarah."

Brian jumped up from his chair. "Junie, I just meant down to the lake. We'll be gone for five minutes. If she comes outside, she can see us."

Junie walked into the cabin. The screen door

bumped against her butt. "I need to make breakfast." Junie wasn't taking any chances. She would pack their things and get home.

While Brian showered, Junie packed their belongings and threw the suitcase in the car. Brian was coming out from the bedroom when she came back into the cabin. He stood between her and the small kitchen, his face a mask of seriousness.

"Junie, we really need to talk before we go back."

She knew he was angry. His shoulders rode high, and the veins in his arms stood out. "We can talk in the car," she offered, then walked around him and grabbed the trash from the morning's breakfast.

"June." He glanced at Sarah and raised his eyebrows.

She ignored him and went outside to the dumpster at the end of the driveway. She lifted the lid, a sickening ache tearing through her stomach. *Ellen*. Had he gotten rid of her this easily? She closed her eyes and thought of her mother and father, the way Ruth would pull back her shoulders, gathering strength, and her father's simple and steady confidence in her. Junie's shoulders drew back. She could do this.

They rode home in silence. Junie watched the muscles in Brian's jaw clench. She didn't care how angry he was. She wasn't letting anything happen to Sarah. She'd be damned if she'd just disappear like Ellen did.

She glanced in the backseat, where Sarah watched a

movie. When they got home, she'd take Sarah and go straight to her mother's house. There, she could call Theresa and figure out what was going on. One more hypnosis regression and maybe she'd understand the whole picture.

New panic swelled within her chest. She pushed herself against the passenger side door. Was she living with a killer? Suddenly the late nights took on whole new possibility. Had other women gone missing over the years? The prospect of her husband's dark side solidified in her confused and terrified mind.

Brain looked over and smiled. "I'm sorry. I shouldn't have gotten so upset."

She couldn't speak.

"We can talk when we get home," he said.

She glanced over her shoulder at Sarah, mentally planning how they would escape. She didn't even need to pack anything. They had enough in the car. When he went inside, they'd remain in the car and just leave. Satisfied with her plan, she turned her back toward Brian and gazed out the window. He helped criminals. He was a criminal. How could she have been so blind?

Chapter Forty-Eight

Junie sat in the driver's seat, talking to Brian through the open window, Sarah securely strapped in her car seat in the back of the van.

"Mom sounded like she was falling apart. I just need to be there for her." Her lie carried a whisper of guilt. She pushed it aside, not wanting to give Brian a chance to dissuade her. "I'll call you when we're settled," she said as she pulled away from the curb.

Junie shot a glance in the rearview mirror, watching Brian standing curbside, his arms held out, palms skyward. She let out the breath she'd been holding.

"Junie, you're exhausted. You're letting your imagination steal your sanity." Ruth sat in her reading chair, leaning forward, fatigue hanging under her eyes like bags.

Junie shook her head. She whispered, "I don't think so. I saw Ellen floating. She wasn't breathing. I saw him with a rock. I know something happened."

"They didn't find her body, Junie. Really, do you think that A. Brian is capable of killing his sister, or B. that at fourteen he could dispose of a body so well that even the police couldn't find it?"

Junie shrugged. She knew it sounded far-fetched, but as much as she hated the thought, she trusted her instincts.

"You know," Ruth said gently, "everything you do will affect Sarah."

"So I should ignore that her father might be a killer?"

"Listen to yourself, June."

Junie turned away. "I've been thinking. Sarah's behavior changed after we visited at Easter, right?"

Ruth nodded. "Right after you moved."

"Yes, but what if her behavior changed because of something that happened here, not because of some medical issue and not because of the move."

"What could possibly happen here? She loves it here."

"I know she does, but look at the timing."

Sarah came into the living room with a drawing in her hand. She handed it to Junie, her eyes trained on her mother's face.

Junie forced a smile and put the picture aside.

Sarah picked it up and handed it to her mother again.

Junie sighed. "Not now, Sarah."

Urine streamed down Sarah's legs.

"Sarah Jane!" Junie swooped Sarah into her arms, holding her away from her body as urine dripped from her legs. "I'm sorry, Mom," she called.

She brought Sarah to the bathroom and ran water in the tub. "What were you thinking?" she snapped.

Sarah clung to her mother's sleeve, tears slipping down her cheeks.

Junie closed her eyes and sighed. "I'm sorry," she said, and pulled her daughter close.

Junie set Sarah in the tub and carefully washed her.

"June?" Ruth stood in the doorway, Sarah's drawing in hand. "Sarah's been drawing this for a while now, hasn't she?"

"What, Mom?" She snapped her head back to Sarah. She didn't have time for this nonsense. Couldn't her mother see that she was a little busy?

"The drawing. Sarah wanted you to see it. Maybe there's a reason."

"I think Brian's right. She's doing this for attention. I've been too wrapped up in everything to see her actions for what they are." Junie sat back on her heels and put her hand to her temples. Her hair formed a veil around her face. "I just can't do this anymore. It's all too much," she cried.

"Take a deep breath. You can do it, and you will. Sarah needs you to."

Junie did as her mother said. "How do you do it, Mom? You lost Daddy and I never see you fall apart. I wish I were half as strong as you."

Ruth reached for Sarah and lifted her from the tub. "We all need to be a bit stronger as this little pumpkin gets bigger." She wrapped Sarah in a towel and walked her into Junie's childhood bedroom.

Junie dragged herself behind her mother, exhausted, feeling as though she'd like to go to sleep and never wake up. This had to be a nightmare.

She watched Ruth dress Sarah in a pair of red leggings and a striped top. "What do you think, little missy? Is there something you want to show your mama?"

To Ruth's surprise, Sarah nodded.

Ruth grasped her thin arms. "There is? Well, okay, then." She glanced at Junie, who was leaning against the doorframe.

"Do you hear that? Sarah has something to show you." Ruth opened her eyes wider, indicating the urgency in her words.

Sarah brushed by her mother and went into the bathroom. She lifted the drawing and handed it to her mother.

"Yes, I saw this sweetie." She sighed. "It's beautiful."

Sarah grabbed her mother's arm and squeezed.

"Ouch!"

"I think your daughter is trying to tell you something," Ruth urged.

Junie crouched down and looked into Sarah's eyes. "Tell me."

Chapter Forty-Nine

Sarah's silence did nothing to answer Junie's questions. She ran her hand through her hair, staring at the drawing. She reached for Sarah's hand. "Come on. We're going outside."

Sarah's legs moved quickly to keep up with her mother. Ruth walked beside Junie.

"Where are we headed?" Ruth asked.

"Peter's garden."

Sarah stopped.

Junie spun around. "Let's go, Sarah."

They stood at the bottom of the hill that led up to Peter's house. The green grass lay before them like a red carpet, inviting and intimidating all at once.

Sarah shook her head.

Junie and Ruth shared a concerned glance. Junie knelt down, Sarah's small hand safely held within her own. "Sarah, you obviously want me to see something.

Let's go see. You can show me." Junie kept her tone upbeat.

Sarah wasn't buying it. She shook her head.

Ruth touched Junie's shoulder.

Junie stood.

Ruth crouched beside Sarah. "Do you want to show Grandma?"

Sarah looked down. Her curls swayed from side to side with the shaking of her head.

Junie let out a long, loud sigh. She looked up the hill toward Peter's house, feeling the pull of the garden. "How can I help you if you won't help me? Why did you want me to see the picture if you won't go see the garden?"

"I can probably answer that." A voice startled Junie.

"Peter?"

He nodded.

"Dad!" Brian ran across the lawn, his eyes trained on Peter. "Don't."

Sarah hid behind her mother's legs. Junie looked from Peter to Brian. "What is going on?"

"Maybe I should take Sarah inside," Ruth offered.

Sarah held Junie's shirt in her clenched fist. She pushed her body against her mother. She was not going anywhere.

Brian looked Peter in the eye. "Dad, not now."

"What's going on, Brian?" Junie reached behind her and put her hand on Sarah's back.

He touched her arm.

She recoiled.

"I told you that we had to talk." He looked at Peter, then said to Junie, "Not here. Let's go for a walk."

The pleading in Brian's eyes did not escape Junie. Her heart beat a mile a minute.

"Wait, I think I should be there, Brian." Peter's commanding voice had been replaced with one of caution.

"Dad." Brian shot him a harsh look.

"I have no idea what's going on, but Sarah is obviously afraid to walk up that hill, and I want to know why." She held Peter's gaze.

"Ruth, can you please take Sarah inside?"

Ruth reached for Sarah's hand. Sarah wouldn't budge. She looked up at Peter. Peter wiped his hand down his face. "I'm sorry, Sarah," he said.

"What did you do?" Junie yelled, wrapping her arms around Sarah.

Peter ignored her and knelt down before Sarah. "Sarah, I didn't mean to frighten you." He stood and looked at Brian. "I was only protecting your parents."

"What?" Junie flashed red toward Brian. "What's he talking about?"

Brian let out a breath, closed his eyes, and folded his arms across his chest. He opened them, blinking rapidly as they filled with tears.

"Brian?" Junie's tone softened.

"I think Sarah should go inside," he said quietly.

Junie looked from Peter to Brian, then back at her mother. She put her hands on Sarah's shoulders. "Why don't you go with Grandma? I'll be inside in a few minutes, okay?"

Sarah moved her finger up and down, beckoning her mother closer. She put her mouth up to Junie's ear. Her warm whisper was magnificent and horrible at once. Junie shivered. She stood and looked at Brian and Peter.

"What does she mean, *can I tell*?" Junie's hands shook. "So help me, if you hurt my daughter, I will kill you. Both of you." She pushed Sarah behind her again.

"June!" Ruth exclaimed.

"Stay out of this," she said to Ruth. "What does she mean?" Junie yelled. She turned back to Sarah. "Yes, you can tell. You can always tell Mommy anything." She crouched, steeling herself for the worst.

Sarah stared up at Peter. Junie followed her gaze, watched Peter nod. She bent down so her ear was flush with Sarah's mouth and listened.

"Papa Peter said not to tell," Sarah whispered.

Junie lowered herself to the grass. The world spun before her.

"I can explain," Peter said.

"Dad." Brian held his hand out to the side, warding him off. "Let her be."

Junie held on to Sarah like a vice.

"It's my fault," Peter confessed. "She found…something…something of Ellen's, when she was digging in my garden, and I told her not to mention it, that it might cause problems."

Junie still didn't understand. She gritted her teeth, pushing her words through them. "So help me, Peter. If you hurt her. If you touched her."

"Junie, please," Brian pleaded. "This isn't something we should discuss here." He nodded toward Sarah.

Ruth took Sarah by the hand and led her back to the house. Sarah looked over her shoulder at her parents, her eyes sad, wet with tears.

Chapter Fifty

Junie breathed deeply, pushing herself to her feet. Brian reached to support her and she pushed him away. Her voice failed her the first time she tried to speak. She looked at Peter, and bile rose in her throat. She swallowed it down, then pulled her shoulders back and readied herself for a conversation she did not want to have.

"Junie," Peter began. "She found Ellen's earring."

Junie held her hand up and shook her head. None of it made any sense. How would Ellen's earring cause problems for them? She wasn't ready to hear it, whatever it was. She stared at Peter's house, remembering the laughter she shared with Ellen, the fear when she finally realized that Ellen wasn't coming back. She thought of Peter in his office, ignoring his family, and Brian—golden boy Brian—angry and mean after Ellen's disappearance.

"If this has to do with Ellen, then I want to hear it up there." Junie couldn't believe the words that came from her mouth. She forced herself up the hill, leaving Brian and Peter to trail behind. She felt pulled to the garden by something bigger than all of them. Memories of Ellen came rushing back—not the sad, dismal memories of recent days, but the happier memories, of birthday parties and riding bikes.

She walked through the bushes and into the backyard. The unkempt garden lay before her, a wild and weed-filled mess. Junie stared at it, wondering what answers it held. She heard their footsteps approaching from behind and tensed the muscles in her legs, determined not to crumble under the weight of whatever confession Brian might give.

She thought of Brian, their love, their life. She loved him. She did. There was no doubt in her mind about that love. But the conundrum of their lives, and of Ellen's disappearance, had sent their relationship awry and even scared her. She thought of Sarah, sweet Sarah, whose innocence had somehow been stolen. Tears dripped down her cheeks.

She turned to face Brian, then had to look away. She had no idea what she'd be dealing with in the moments to come, and she wasn't sure she could trust her eyes not to betray her thoughts.

"Okay," she said in a thin voice. "Tell me everything. Please."

She listened to Brian suck in a long breath, then blow it out slowly. She stared down at her shoes, concentrating on a speck of dirt, the grass flattened around the garden—a path. She concentrated on anything to keep from hearing what Brian had to say. Maybe if she concentrated hard enough, it would go away. *Poof!* Like whatever it was had never even happened.

"I'm not sure how to start," Brian said.

She could feel him looking at Peter, drawing strength from him. She imagined Peter pulling himself up to his full height, putting his protective arms around his son. She knew it killed Peter that Brian wouldn't allow it, and she didn't care.

"Ellen—"

"Wait." Junie interrupted. "I'm not sure I'm ready. I need to hear about Sarah. What happened to Sarah?"

She waited. The silence was deafening.

"That was all me, Junie." Peter stood beside her. "I didn't want to cause any trouble between you and Brian, that's all. I didn't know I would frighten her so badly, and then, once I learned of what had happened, well, Brian and I don't talk very often, so by the time I heard, I didn't know what to do. I thought maybe she'd snap out of it." He reached for Junie's arm.

She went rigid beneath his touch. Her voice shook when she spoke. "What happened? I don't understand what you said to her, or what happened."

"She was digging in the garden, and she found an earring of Ellen's."

"The hoop." *Of course. Sarah had been fascinated with Kayla's earring because it had been identical to the one she'd found. Ellen's. Ellen. Oh God. Ellen.* Junie's eyes shot to the mangled garden. Her chest felt as though it might explode, constricting and throbbing in tandem.

"Yes, the hoop." He folded his hands together, then put them in his trouser pockets.

"But why would that cause problems for me and Brian?" She looked up at Peter, saw the tears welling in his eyes. She turned to Brian, who looked as if he might be sick. His face had become ashen; the sparkle in his eyes faded. He looked *empty*.

"June, there's something you need to know." Tears streamed down his cheeks. "Ellen—" He choked on his words.

Junie lifted her eyes to meet his. The fear and love she'd felt over the past few days coalesced, leaving her confused, unsure of her ability to trust her own instincts. She'd never seen Brian so fragile. Had she pushed him too far? She reached for his arm, then realized he might have done something awful and pulled her arm back to her side.

Peter went to him. Junie watched him wrap his arm around Brian. Brian didn't flinch. He didn't pull away or make a negative remark.

Who are these people? The scene was so foreign that she had to struggle to concentrate, to remain in control. For so long she'd wanted nothing more than for Brian and his father to unite; she'd imagined the scene only moments earlier.

"It's okay, son," Peter said.

Junie waited, a lump blocking words from escaping her throat and tears falling down her cheeks. It felt like forever, waiting to hear what he had to say, but she knew only moments had passed.

"That day in the woods. You were there," Brian said.

Junie shook her head. *No? Yes?*

"I heard you when you were running out. I turned and saw you. I know you saw me," he said.

Junie's body trembled. "N-no. I don't—"

Brian's voice escalated. "Yes. You saw me standing on Lovers' Rock."

Brian flashed before her, the rock held high above his head, his voice pealing through the forest like a spear. "Get outta here, squirt!"

Junie's head shook from side to side. "No. I didn't see anything. I don't remember."

"It's okay, Junie," Peter consoled her.

"No, no. I don't know what you're saying. I don't remember."

"She showed up. She was supposed to be at the library, but she came to the woods. She was always doing that. Right, Dad?" He turned to Peter, his eyes begging for support.

Peter looked down. "She had a mind of her own."

"She came to the creek, and she saw me." Brian swiped at his tears. "She saw me. You have no idea what it was like, living in my father's shadow." Brian moved away from Peter's side, pacing next to the garden. "Always having to be perfect, get the best grades, be the best at everything. Ellen, she didn't have to be anything but *cute little Ellen*. She had no pressure. There were no friggin' expectations." He glared at Peter. "Were there, Dad?"

"Brian." Junie's voice came out as a whisper. Her heart ached for him. How could she not have known how much resentment he carried for his father? It all made sense now, the desire to move away, not join his father's practice. The way he avoided Peter at all costs.

"No, don't Brian me. You're about to hate me," he said, and crossed his arms over his chest. Sobs racked his body. He covered his face with his hand.

Junie went to his side. He swatted her away. "No. You have to hear this. God, you have to hear this."

He glared at his father, his face a mask of pain.

"She came into the woods, and she saw me there. I told her to go away. I wanted to just be alone, just...I was smoking pot." He glared at Peter. "That's right, perfect Brian, golden boy Brian was toking it up, smoking pot, killing my brain cells just to stay sane. But she wouldn't go. She said she'd tell. She said she'd make sure Dad knew." Brian's chest rose and fell with each heavy breath.

Junie shook her head. "What did you do?"

"She stood by the creek, laughing. She laughed at me."

"Brian?" His image flashed before Junie. *The rock.* "The rock. Oh God, you killed her. Didn't you?"

"No, he didn't," Peter answered.

Junie spun to face him, her jaw slackened.

"Brian didn't kill Ellen. He threw a rock at her. She slipped, hit her head, and went into convulsions." Peter recited it robotically, as if he were stating facts in a case. "She had a seizure. She fell under the water. It was too deep, too far from where he was on top of the rock. Brian couldn't do anything to save her. He couldn't save her. He couldn't—" He broke down in sobs and leaned against the house. He lifted his fist and hit the bricks on the side of the house with the side of his fist.

"It's my fault. You heard him; he blames me. I killed Ellen."

Junie's mind raced. She wondered what Ellen was thinking during her final moments. Was she panicked, scared, angry at her brother? Did she scream for her mother or father, or did she not have time to register the severity of what was happening? Junie's chest tightened with a sickening terror. She couldn't believe what she was hearing, and yet it all began to make sense. The pieces of her memory puzzle shifted slowly into place. She had seen Brian. She ran back to Katie's, thinking he never saw her. She told Katie she'd seen him throw something at Ellen. The secret. Katie had held the secret for all these years, tortured by it. *Oh God, what have I done?* It made perfect sense, except...

"Where is she?" Junie asked.

Brian and Peter looked at each other, their faces contorted with grief.

"Where is Ellen? Oh God, what did you do? Where is she?" She stood in the garden, weeds around her ankles, staring down her husband and father-in-law.

"We buried her," Peter said quietly. "We had to. The authorities never would have believed it was an accident. You saw the Brian most everyone saw, but when it comes to the law, things are different when you're an attorney's kid. No matter how good of a kid he was, he'd be made an example that no one is above the law. We kept it quiet. This…this would have landed him in jail. His chance at a normal life would have been over. I couldn't lose both my daughter and my son."

Junie was stuck on *Buried her*. "Where? Oh God." She paced. "Does Susan know? Does my mom know? Did my dad know?"

"My mom knew. She found out. That's why she left."

"She left because of her affair with my father," Junie spat.

"Affair?" Brian asked.

"It wasn't an affair. It was a friendship, and no, she didn't leave because of that." Peter flushed.

"But you let my mother think she did." Anger burned within her veins. "How could you do that?"

"Your father knew."

"What?"

"He knew. He saw me that night in the garden. I broke down and confessed to him."

Junie shot her eyes to the garden. *The garden. Oh my God.*

"Your father knew. He told me what to do, what to use, for—"

Nausea rose in Junie's throat. *My father?* "Did you know that my father knew what happened?" she asked Brian.

"I had no idea that he knew, but it makes sense. He never wanted you to marry me."

"You knew that he didn't want me to marry you?" Junie looked at Brian through new eyes. He'd never said a word to her. Why? "You never said anything, and why wouldn't my father have told me?"

Brian shrugged. "Why make it harder for you? I knew how hurt you were, going against your father's wishes. Why make it worse than it had to be?"

"Your father knew how much you loved Brian, and he knew Brian hadn't hurt Ellen," Peter said. "He couldn't hurt Ellen. Your father loved him. He just couldn't accept what had happened. He knew Brian didn't do it; he knew it was the truth. But he…he understood why we did what we did, and he helped us to understand what we needed to do for her—"

"Daddy?" Junie whispered.

"Junie, about a month before he died, we talked. He told me he forgave Brian long ago and that Brian was an excellent father and husband. Your father, he was a brilliant man. He knew Brian would never hurt anyone on purpose."

"You threw the rock," she accused Brian.

"I did. Not at her. I threw it at the big tree. You know, the one that the roots go over the rocks?"

She thought of the tree shading the creek and then of the roses she'd found on the rocks.

"I hit the tree. I swear to you, Junie. I would never have thrown a rock at Ellen. I loved her. I was jealous, but she was—" Brian's shoulders arced forward. Strangled sobs came from deep within his chest. He gasped for a breath, wiping at the tears that streamed down his cheeks. "She was my squirt, my sister," he cried. "I loved her. I loved her!"

"The roses at the creek?"

"I put them there," Brian said quietly. "I didn't visit Dad," he admitted. Brian wiped his tears. "I miss her. Damn it, Junie. I miss my sister. I love her. I…it…"

Junie reached for him, then dropped her arms to her sides. She desperately wanted to run to him, hold him tight, take away his pain. She ached with love for him, and at the same time, anger, maybe even teetering on hatred—for his lies, for the loss of Ellen's life. Her mind was twisting, her stomach burning. She had to hear the rest. No more lies. She had to be strong enough to bear the truth. Junie took a step back, away from Brian. Her hand moved to cover her mouth. She dropped it, then crossed her arms over her chest.

"Your meetings? You're not working on a case together, are you?" She watched their eyes meet.

Brian shook his head. "He couldn't take it anymore. Dad wanted to tell you, for Sarah's sake, but I wanted to talk to you first. I thought at Deep Creek we'd have time to talk."

Junie's heart ached. All these years, all the lies. No wonder Brian didn't want to talk about Ellen. How could he? She couldn't be near Brian or Peter any longer, but she had to know. "Where is she?" She knew the answer.

Peter nodded toward the garden.

"Oh God. Sarah's digging."

"I'm sorry." Peter paced. A bead of sweat glistened on his brow. He put his hands in his pockets, then pulled them out. "She found the earring Ellen was wearing when she died. I panicked." Peter threw his hands up, then brought them down and covered his face. Through tears, he confessed, "I was too harsh. I took her by the shoulders. Jesus, I must have scared the shit out of her." He pleaded with Junie. "I'm so sorry. I shook her. I shook her," he repeated, as if he couldn't believe he'd done it. "I put the fear of God into her. I didn't mean to." He paced. "Maybe I did. I don't know. I just knew I had to shut her up. If anyone found out—"

Junie slapped him across the cheek, sobbing, unable to erase the image of Peter shaking Sarah, scolding her, terrifying her. "How dare you," she seethed, and then turned her back to him.

"I never would have said anything to her had I known where it would lead or the damage that it would do." Peter walked in front of Junie, swiping at the tears in his eyes. "June, I screwed up. What I did to Sarah, the fear I incited. My God, I'm a monster. You're right. I told her that her father could go to jail, that it would ruin her family." He sobbed, clenching and unclenching his fists. "She was so frightened. No wonder she stopped talking. How can you ever forgive me?" He turned to Brian. "I thought we'd lose him, too. I thought he'd—we'd go to jail."

"You used my daughter to protect yourself. That's unforgiveable. What type of person are you?"

"Junie—" Brian interrupted.

Junie held her hand up to quiet him. She knelt, placing her hand beneath the weeds and closed her eyes. He'd scared Sarah into submission. He'd caused her regression. Junie rocked forward and back, trying to keep the hatred that burned inside her at bay. He'd ruined Sarah's life. Brian had stolen Ellen's life. *Ellen*. A strange sense of relief washed through her. Junie wasn't losing her mind. Ellen hadn't been sold as a sex slave. She wasn't taken by a stranger and tortured. She was dead. Ellen was dead—and now she had to save Sarah.

Chapter Fifty-One

Junie hung up the phone, ready to face her daughter. Thank goodness Theresa had taken her emergency phone call. Junie explained that Peter had told Sarah not to tell her or Brian about Ellen's earring that she'd found in the garden because it would really upset her and Brian. She didn't go into details about what had happened to Ellen. She couldn't see any good coming from the sharing of that knowledge—she could barely deal with it herself—and she worried about legal ramifications. Would Theresa have to reveal what she was told? Junie wasn't sure, and she didn't want to find out. She needed to focus on the process of healing for Sarah.

Theresa thought that Sarah was experiencing selective mutism with regressive side effects. In essence, the secret she held was too big for her to deal with, so she stopped speaking and reverted to a younger state, a state where much less was expected of her. Theresa indicated that it could take weeks, months, or even years to bring Sarah's mental state back to normal. She also indicated that, depending on Sarah's perception of the safety of her environment, her desire to speak and control herself as a typical four-year-old could also return in the blink of an eye. In other words, she had no idea of timing, but thankfully, it appeared that Sarah's regression and silence were self-imposed.

"What are you going to do now?" Ruth asked.

Junie watched Brian and Peter in the yard, where they remained after Junie had gone inside. She was furious with Peter for dragging Sarah into the whole mess. Peter had let his garden go after Sarah found the earring. He didn't want Sarah wandering up and digging up anything else. Junie wondered what else there could be. Shoes? Clothing? Bones? Bile rose in her throat.

Brian and Peter embraced. Junie couldn't watch. The betrayal ran too deep.

She turned away.

"I don't know. Can I stay here? For now, I mean."

"What about Bliss, Sarah's school?"

"Shane can handle it, and it's not far. I can go in a few times each week." She looked at Sarah, curled on the couch in the living room. "Besides, I think Sarah deserves a bit of a break. Theresa said to keep her life as normal as possible, so maybe you're right, but I can't go home, not yet. Maybe just a week or two?"

Ruth nodded. "This is a lot to digest. Do you want to see my therapist?"

"Maybe."

Junie sat next to Sarah and brushed her curls from her forehead. Her daughter had been through so much. How could she not have put two and two together?

"Sweetie?"

Sarah did not answer.

"You didn't do anything wrong." Sarah didn't know about what had happened to Ellen, and if Junie could help it, she would never know the truth. "Daddy just gets sad about Aunt Ellen being gone, and Papa Pete didn't want to upset him. Remember when you found the earring?"

Sarah blinked up at her through thick, wet lashes.

"Do you remember who Aunt Ellen was?" Junie hoped that the question didn't send Sarah further into her silence.

Sarah nodded.

Just to be sure, Junie reiterated. "She was Daddy's sister. She went away when she was younger. Daddy hasn't seen her in a very long time." Junie remembered the previous year, when Sarah had heard her on the phone telling Shane that Sarah had done something that reminded her of Brian's sister. Sarah had been relentless in her pursuit of who Daddy's sister was, and finally, Junie had given in and satisfied her four-year-old curiosity with two sentences: *Aunt Ellen was Daddy's sister. She went away, and he hasn't seen her for a very long time.* "That was Aunt Ellen's earring, and Papa Pete was worried that seeing it might make Daddy sad. That's why he told you that you mustn't tell us about it." Her stomach ached for the pain and confusion Sarah must have felt over the past several months. "I'm sorry that he scared you." Anger rose within her. Her cheeks flushed. She took a deep breath to calm herself down. She didn't want to upset Sarah any more than she already had. She used her index finger to draw Sarah's chin upward and looked into her eyes. "Baby, I can't change what Papa Pete said to you, but you need to know that you didn't do anything wrong and that nothing you could say or do to me or to Daddy would ever make us love you less. Nothing you could ever say or do would make us too angry to talk through things with you." Junie pulled Sarah close, feeling her chest hitch with little-girl tears.

Junie's heart sank. At least they thought they had the answer. Now they could start the healing process for Sarah.

She drew Sarah back and looked into her eyes.

Sarah popped her thumb into her mouth.

"Papa Pete is sorry, you know. He loves you very much." *Even if Mommy is pissed at him.*

Chapter Fifty-Two

Brian stayed at his father's house that night for the first time in almost thirty years. Junie allowed him to Skype Sarah at bedtime, although Junie had to leave the room. She couldn't stomach seeing him. As she tucked Sarah into bed, she watched the light in Peter's den go on, then immediately go out. Sadness enveloped her, weighing her down like a dark cloud dampens a sunny day.

She crawled into bed, wondering how in the hell they could ever get past the lies that had erupted. She stared at the ceiling, trying to convince herself that Brian was a killer, but she could not reconcile such thoughts to the Brian she knew and loved. Maybe he wasn't a killer, but shouldn't she blame him for Ellen's death? Her mind went around and around. Wasn't he at fault? Maybe, she decided. He threw the rock, causing her to slip and have the seizure that led to her death. He was a kid, she silently argued with herself. Fourteen years old! He hit the tree with the rock, not Ellen. He wasn't trying to hurt or kill her, just scare her. She was sure that Brian and Peter could defend their actions better than any other attorney in the United States, and the thought made her heart ache. What if they couldn't? Should Brian and Peter go to jail? What if they were lying? What if he really hit Ellen in the head and killed her? Thinking like her lawyer husband, she realized that the police, or at least the search dogs, would have found blood somewhere along the way.

Junie buried her face in the pillow and screamed.

She felt mildly better, then cried herself to sleep.

Junie didn't call Theresa again or her mother's therapist. She feared the ramifications of doing so—would they report Brian and Peter to the police? How would it affect Ruth? Sarah? Susan? Her days were consumed with wanting to be free of their lies. *Why?* she asked herself. *Why did this have to happen? Why did I have to pursue my memories?*

She purposely didn't seek Ruth's advice, though she knew her mother was always there, willing to lend an ear and talk things over. Junie didn't want her advice. She wanted her decision to be her own, but she didn't trust herself enough to make a decision.

How on earth would she navigate this new landscape of her life? Should she ignore what she now knew happened? Go on like the event never occurred?

Pretend Ellen wasn't buried in the garden on the hill? She could no sooner do that than pretend that her father hadn't had an affair. Knowledge was painful. Period.

Junie let Brian's calls go to voice mail. He'd gone back home and back to work. She wasn't ready to face him yet, or even think about talking to him. Messages worked for now.

"You know," Ruth said over breakfast, "the longer you put this off, the worse it will be, and not just for you, but you have a little girl to deal with, too."

Junie glared at her mother. How could she even entertain the thought of Junie talking to, or forgiving, Brian? Was that what she wanted, or did she want Junie to act as if the whole thing never happened?

"I know what you're thinking, June, and no, I don't think you should pretend it didn't happen."

"You really do know what I'm thinking. That's a little freaky."

"Not really. I've been your mother for a very long time. I just think you can't ignore the situation."

Junie jumped to her feet and paced in the small kitchen. She pressed her fingers to her temple. "Don't you think I know that, Mom?" She looked out the window at the landscaping truck parked at the bottom of Peter's driveway. Bile rose in her throat and she turned away.

"You need to talk to someone. My therapist? Your own? Someone, June. You can't handle this on your own."

Junie sat down across from Ruth. "Daddy knew. He

knew what happened."

Ruth nodded.

"Did you know? Did he tell you?"

"No, June, he didn't tell me. Peter called me last night and explained everything. Your father was a complex man. He would have protected my feelings, and yours."

"Right, like he protected yours when he had the affair?" Junie regretted her words the seconds they flew from her lips. She watched her mother pull her shoulders back. "I'm sorry, Mom, I didn't mean that."

"Yes, you did. It's okay. I get it. I understand where you're coming from. It doesn't mean that your words don't hurt, but they're fair."

Junie dropped her face into her hands. "Geez, Mom, how can you stand me? I'm such a bitch."

Ruth reached for her hand. "Honey, you're not a bitch. What you said is true. Daddy didn't protect my feelings when he was…there for Susan. But this—" She waved her hand toward Peter's house. "This situation is very different."

Junie didn't want her mother's advice, but she realized at that moment that she needed to hear what her mother had to say. She was not adept at handling these types of situations. Obviously, she thought, because she repressed the memories of them. She was caught in Brian and Peter's web of deceit and could feel the spiders crawling after her. She could not ignore, outrun, or repress this situation. She had to deal with it head on. She took a deep breath and listened to her mother describe the value of lies.

"Relationships are fragile things, Junie. Just because you are a mother, daughter, or spouse does not mean that you must always be honest."

Junie opened her mouth to argue, but Ruth spoke louder.

"I know. I taught you the value of honesty above all else, but there are certain times in life when the truth does not serve anyone very well."

"That's called a lie of convenience, Mom." Junie crossed her arms.

"No, that's not what I'm talking about. Deceit for your own benefit is not right. Your father's lies about Susan were wrong. They were damn wrong. He manipulated our marriage during that time, allowing himself to be with her, taking time from you, from our family—those lies that he told were lies of convenience. They were not acceptable, but as I said before, relationships are not always neat and tidy, and that...issue was what it was. Those lies that your father told, they were completely different from the secrets and lies that Peter and Brian held for all these years, and they were different from your father not telling me about what had happened to Ellen."

"Why? That makes no sense." Junie fumed.

Ruth spread her hands flat on the table, closed her eyes, inhaled deeply, then set her hands in her lap. She spoke in an even, unemotional tone. "Those lies, Junie, were lies for the protection of others. Let's look at Brian and Peter. Brian was just fourteen. A boy. A kid, and a very confused kid, but still, a sweet kid. I have known

Brian since he was knee high. That boy was not a killer. I do believe that he didn't throw that rock with the intention of hitting Ellen. Now, he might have scared her so badly that she slipped and fell, hit her head, had a seizure. Whatever happened, happened, but there's no way that I believe that he killed her in the actual sense of the word."

"But—"

"June Marie, hear me out, please."

Junie clenched her jaw and listened.

"Peter was, is, a prominent attorney. Did he cover it up to save himself? I don't think so. He's too good at what he does. He'd have won the case, but he's right, Brian's life would have been changed forever. He would have the mark on his record, even if it would have been sealed because of his youth. It would have been there, and people talk, so chances are, Brian would not have become the attorney that he is had they gone public."

"So what? So Ellen deserves to be hidden in a garden to save Brian's potential career? That's just awful. It's not how you brought me up."

Ruth looked down. "No, it's not. You're right about that, which is why this is so hard to explain." She lifted her eyes, met Junie's angry stare. "No matter how this would have ended up, their entire family would have been hurt. This would have followed them all publicly—not just privately—forever. And, Junie, you know that nice little life you've spent the last few years building for yourself and your daughter? Think about everywhere you go, everywhere Sarah goes, people whispering, pointing—you know it would be on the news. With Peter's reputation, it might even make national news. Then what? You spend your life hiding from Brian's mistake? Hiding from Ellen's slippery sneakers? You think Sarah has a lot to deal with now? Try throwing this on that little girl of yours."

She was right. Junie could feel it in her bones, a dull ache, a battle of right and wrong, and still, she couldn't figure out the right thing to do.

"Your father lied to protect me and you from having to be in this situation, I think. If he'd believed that Brian was at fault, your father wouldn't have kept the secret. He was not that kind of man."

Junie lifted her eyebrows.

"He would never cover up a murder. You know that." Ruth took a deep breath, then continued. "Peter lied to protect his family—and himself, no doubt, but his family first. He was thinking of Brian, and Susan, whom he lost anyway. Brian was too young to know better."

"He was not," Junie spat. "He was fourteen!"

"Yes, with a controlling father who determined his every move. I don't know about you, but at fourteen, I would not have gone up against Peter Olson. No way. Brian did what he was advised to do, strongly advised."

Tears slipped down Junie's cheeks. "He lied to me, Mom. For all these years, he lied to me." She wiped her tears with the back of her hand.

Ruth nodded. "Yes, he did. Junie, would you have married him if you'd known?"

Junie shook her head, blinking away her tears.

"Are you sure?" Ruth asked gently.

"I don't know," she said. Junie pulled her shoulders back and met her mother's eyes. "I don't think I would have."

"Okay, maybe not, but I think you would have. I think you were so in love with him that you'd have looked me in the eye and said, *Mom, he was a kid. It was an accident.* In fact, I can almost hear you say it. And you know what?"

Junie lifted her eyebrows in question.

"I would have supported you, because I know he's not a killer, and because there's nothing in this world that I want more than for you to be happy. Brian isn't a threat to you. He's not a threat to Sarah. He's someone who made a mistake and the outcome was much larger, and more gruesome, than most of our mistakes. He's someone who followed his father's guidance even if it was a bad call. But he's not a killer. A liar? Yes, but so was your father, and no matter how you turn it, I don't think that makes him unlovable."

Her mother's words hit her like ice in her veins. Junie shivered.

"Some lies," Ruth said, "can be put into perspective. You don't have to agree with them, and you don't have to forgive them, but some lies can be tucked away and lived with."

Chapter Fifty-Three

Days stretched into weeks, weeks into months, and months into almost a full year. Brian and Junie remained apart. Junie enrolled Sarah in a morning drop-in preschool program ten minutes from Ruth's house, and she and Shane worked out a schedule that suited both of them. Shane stood by Junie, though he was steadfast in his belief that she should consider reconciling with Brian. He reminded her of the connection that they shared and Brian's ever-present support. *That kind of love doesn't go away because he lied to you about the death of his sister. He's tortured himself for all these years. His father forced him into an untenable situation. Junie, he didn't ask to cover up Ellen's death, and he didn't ask to be Peter's golden boy, but he did ask to be your husband, and he did ask to have a child with you.*

Ruth entered the kitchen dressed in a purple suit and donning a giant red hat.

"Mom, you look ridiculous."

Ruth glowed. "I love it. It's been so long since I have done anything even remotely fun. When Mary Margaret suggested that we create the Getty Girls' Red Hat Society for all of us *older* women in our town, it seemed like it might be fun to try it."

"And what happened last month when you two went to that other Red Hat Society meeting in the next town over? Did they somehow rope you in, and now you're a cult follower? Hi, I'm Ruth Nailon, and I'm a widow? Like AA?" Junie listened to her own cattiness. What was going on with her? Was she jealous that her mother could move on and she seemed stuck in the mess of her own crazy life? Junie smoothed the red frosting onto the first layer of the cake she was making and waited for it to set before placing the second, smaller layer on top.

"You're such a fool. I'd hardly call this a cult, and the support is what I need. Many of the Red Hat women have been through the same thing I'm going through, June. I need this."

Junie mulled that over. Her mother deserved support, and maybe Junie was having a hard time understanding it because she'd missed out on those supportive relationships throughout the years. Whether she was jealous over her mother's ability to move forward or her ability to form long-lasting female friendships, jealousy was an ugly cohort. She needed to rein in her misplaced emotions. "I wish there was a support group for people in my position—Wives of Accidental Murderers with Selfish Fathers."

Ruth touched her arm. "I'm sorry, honey. I know how hard this year has been—for all of us." She peered over Junie's shoulder. "Whatcha building?"

"Red Hat cake." She winked. "I figured that if you were going to do this, you might as well do it right. This is for your...gathering of red hat goddesses. I can't have my mother showing up empty-handed every month." She set the second layer on the first, and the image of the hat became apparent.

"That's lovely!" Ruth said.

The top layer slid to the side. Junie caught it with her spatula. "Yeah, except it doesn't quite stay atop very well."

"Well, like life, things aren't always so—"

"Neat and tidy," Junie said in tune with her mother.

They chuckled.

"You can say that again." Junie settled the top layer into the center of the base, plastering it in place with the thick frosting. She squeezed the pastry bag, dipping and lifting, creating little elaborate icing flowers to hold the layer in place.

"Sometimes you just need to figure out the best way to accept what you've been given and make it work for you."

She set the pastry bag down next to the cake and looked at her mother. Gratitude swelled in her heart.

"Mom, in case I forget to tell you, you mean the world to me."

"Oh, Junie, please."

"Seriously. You teach me something every day. I know I will never be the same mom that you are, but I can strive to be, and I do strive to be, even if I fall short."

Ruth took her daughter's hand in her own and said, "You are a marvelous daughter, mother, and yes, even wife. We all do the best we can, June. That's all we can do in this lifetime."

When Brian Skyped to say good night to Sarah that evening, Shane's reminders drew Junie to him: *He didn't ask to be Peter's golden boy, but he did ask to be your husband, and he did ask to have a child with you.*

Brian's face was drawn, and for the first time since she learned about his lies, Junie found herself worrying about him—was he eating right, was he sleeping enough?

"How is she?" he asked.

Brian saw Sarah every weekend, but still Junie gushed over Sarah's progress. Her accidents had stopped completely, and she was becoming more communicative, even if that particular progress was slow. They'd continued to see Theresa on a weekly basis—for Sarah, not Junie, and it was helping her. Theresa didn't know what Brian had done, or where Ellen was buried, but she knew that Sarah had found Ellen's earring and her grandfather's admonishment was what sent her spiraling into regression and silence. Theresa was giving Junie guidelines on communication, how she should react to Sarah when Junie fears she's going in the wrong direction, and Junie was thankful for that guidance. Mostly she was thankful for the little changes she'd begun to see with Sarah—a nod here, a whispered, *No*, there. Theresa was slowly bringing Sarah out of her shell. Now that they understood where the issue began, Theresa was able to work with Sarah on rebuilding trust in all of her relationships.

The one thing Junie couldn't deny was that her daughter missed her father, and Junie wondered if Sarah might progress more quickly in her own home, with both parents present, but she wasn't ready to take that final leap.

"Junie, I'm sorry for everything. I miss you, and I miss Sarah."

"We miss you, too," she said, and realized that she'd meant it. She did miss Brian. The pain of Ellen's tragedy was slowly subsiding. Junie was able to see more clearly with the hurt pushed aside. She recognized her part in their relationship's disintegration. "I owe you an apology," she said. "You were right about Sarah. She did have emotional…baggage that she was dealing with, and I negated you. I'm really sorry." She was sorry, and the thought of how she disregarded Brian had been weighing on her all afternoon. She felt better having said her peace.

"Then come home." Brian had the same request every week. He never wavered in his professed love for Junie and Sarah.

It sounded so easy. Pack up their stuff, get in the car, and in an hour and a half, they'd be home. "I'm afraid to. How do I know what else you've lied to me about?"

"Junie." He stared directly into her eyes. "I have never lied to you about anything other than Ellen's disappearance and the issues that surrounded it. I adore you. You and Sarah are my world."

Junie flushed.

"Junie, listen to me, please. I thought you remembered everything, and I was going to bring it up when we first started dating, but then I realized that you didn't remember, and I didn't want to remind you. I know that was selfish, but I loved you. I do love you. I thought if I brought it back up, you'd never marry me." He looked down. "I'll be sorry for that for the rest of my life."

He was selfish, but so was she. She wished she never remembered and things could go back to the way they were, but that, too, she realized was not how real life worked.

"I wanted to tell you so many times, but each time you brought up Ellen, I was scared." He took a deep breath. "I didn't want to lose you. I see now that that was wrong. I should have laid it all out right on the table before we got married and probably before we got serious."

"No way. You were afraid you'd go to jail."

"No, I wasn't. I never was. I knew it was an accident. I didn't cause her seizure. She slipped and hit her head. I tried to get to her, but by the time I did, it was too late. I didn't know what to do, so I did the only thing I could. I called my dad."

Junie didn't want to hear the story again. She knew what happened next. Instead, she asked the question that had loomed in her mind for months. "What will you do now? Will you bury her?" She lowered her voice. "I mean for real?"

Brian shook his head. "No. It's too painful for my parents. Ellen loved roses, and she's been there forever at this point. We've already had a memorial."

"You're afraid of being caught."

"No, I'm not. I'd scream it from the rooftops if it would bring you home. But what good would it do? It's not going to bring you home. Think about it, Junie. My dad's already lost my mom and Ellen. My mom dealt with this years ago, and making it public would only bring her under scrutiny."

Junie shook her head. "I love you, but I don't know what the right thing to do is. Hell, I don't even know if I'd have married you if I'd known."

Brian sighed. "I know." His lips curved into a small smile. "Can I take you out Friday night? You know, it's all on the table now. No more lies. See if you like me. We can start over, well, kind of, anyway. No promises of a future, just two people seeing what might be."

Junie thought about his offer. She didn't want Sarah to grow up without a father, and she did love Brian. She just had to move past the past. She shook her head, not knowing if she ever could.

"Yes, I'd like that, but to be honest, I can't move

forward until this whole thing is dealt with properly. I don't want to live my life, or have Sarah live hers, in fear, wondering if anyone outside our family will ever find out."

"What are you saying?"

Junie didn't even know she needed what she was about to ask for until that very moment. Now she knew, and she could never move forward without this step. "You and your father need to come clean. You need to go to the police."

The silence stretched between them.

"My father—"

Junie didn't want to argue; she was past that. This is what she needed, and if they couldn't do it, then she'd never be able to move on with any sort of relationship with Brian, and she wasn't sure she'd let Sarah, either.

"I don't care what this does to his career, or yours. This is about doing the right thing, showing Sarah that you are not ashamed. She might not know what happened, but who's to say she never will? Do you want to live the rest of your life in fear? What if Sarah finds out one day? Then what?"

Brian remained silent.

"Brian, set the example you want her to follow. Fatherhood trumps fear."

Chapter Fifty-Four

Friday afternoon moved at a snail's pace. Junie flitted from one room to the next, nervous as a schoolgirl. Brian and Peter had both agreed to go to the police—a step in the right direction.

"Why don't you go out for a bit and get rid of that nervous energy of yours?" Ruth suggested.

"Where would I go?"

"Let's all go to the creek. Let's say goodbye to those bad memories and have our own little goodbye for Ellen. My therapist thought it might do you some good to find closure about Ellen. The creek was my idea."

Junie put her hand on her hip. "You discuss me with your therapist?"

"Of course. Oh, not the part about what really happened to Ellen, just that Sarah was going through a traumatic time and so are you. I'm your mother. I have a right to get my life back on track, too." Ruth headed for the stairs, then stopped and turned back toward Junie. "Junie, you do know that even when Sarah is an adult, your worries won't stop, right? I mean, look at me. You're an adult mother yourself, and I still have a need to help you in any way I can."

Junie felt her eyes well, something that had become an all-too-familiar event. "I know, Mom. Thank you." She watched her mother disappear up the stairs.

Ruth came back down with Sarah in tow.

"Want to go to the creek, sweetie?"

The ringlets on Sarah's head didn't bob. Her voice was like a long-missed sweet breeze on a hot summer's day. "Yes," she said.

Her voice, that one tiny word, brought a smile to Junie's lips.

Sarah used her finger to call her mother to her side. Junie was used to this. While Sarah had become more responsive, she preferred to whisper much of what she had to say. Junie bent to listen.

"Yes," Junie said, shooting a confused, anxious look at her mother. Junie tried to keep the worry out of her voice. "She wants to go see Papa Peter first."

"Well, then, Papa Peter's it is." Ruth nodded.

Walking up the driveway toward Peter's house brought the moment of impact rushing back to Junie. The hurt of his confession, the anger of what he'd done to Sarah. Junie concentrated on the blacktop beneath her, telling herself to be strong for Sarah. She could do this. It was a conversation, that's all, and if she and Brian had any chance at all, she needed to mend this particular fence.

They found Peter in the backyard, kneeling in the once again perfectly manicured rose garden. Trowel in hand. The knees of his jeans sat upon fresh mulch. Beside him lay a small yellow rosebush, the roots wrapped in burlap.

His face had tired in the short time since Junie had last seen him. Worry lines ran across his forehead, and his eyelids hung low over puffy, fatigued eyes. He caught Junie's gaze, held it.

Junie thrust her hands into the pocket of her jeans and looked away. She had no idea what to say, or how to mend this broken fence.

Unflappable Ruth came to her rescue, like always. "Our girl here wanted to see you." She gave Sarah a nudge forward.

Sarah looked at the garden, then back at Peter. Junie hadn't explained that Ellen was buried in the garden. She'd decided that there were certain burdens that small children didn't need to bear, and she'd wished, during recent weeks, that she'd been a small child and spared from the knowledge, too. Sarah had been led to believe that the earring alone would have made her mother and father miss Ellen so much that the sadness would have been a bit too much for them. Junie had clung to that explanation like a life preserver, trying to believe it herself.

Sarah knelt at the edge of the garden, her pink leggings bright against the green grass, bringing Easter to Junie's mind. She watched her daughter reach for

Peter's hand. Her pulse quickened with anticipation. *Please don't make this more difficult for her,* June prayed. She hadn't told Peter what she'd said to Sarah, and she didn't think she could handle clarifying anything to mar that explanation.

"I'm sorry I dug up the earring," Sarah whispered.

Peter glanced at Junie, then back to Sarah. He placed his large hand on Sarah's cheek, then inched closer to her. "You didn't do anything wrong, Sarah. Papa Peter overreacted. It was me who was sad, and I'm sorry. I never should have asked you to keep a secret, and I will never do it again." He kept his eyes trained on her.

Junie let out the breath she'd been holding captive. Junie knew that Peter wasn't faking the honesty in his eyes; no one could. She reached for Ruth's hand, thankful that her daughter was making her peace.

"Okay," Sarah said; then she dropped Peter's hand and stood. "We're going to say goodbye to Ellen at the creek. Do you want to come? Can we bring some roses?"

Junie's jaw dropped open. Who was this small child? Recognition moved hesitantly forward within her. A few quick breaths escaped her, the edges of her lips twitching into a smile, then fading quickly into a worried line again. Theresa had said that everyone's healing process was different, and that it might take days, months, or even years before they saw any marked changes in Sarah. *She must have more of Mom's strength than mine,* Junie thought.

Ruth squeezed her hand, caught her eye.

The three adults let out a simultaneous laugh. She was back! Sarah was back.

The weight of the past lifted as they drove to the park. Every now and again Sarah whispered a word, "Mommy. Tree. Park," as if she were testing her voice. Junie listened, unable to speak without tears filling her eyes. Her baby girl had returned. She held her mother's hand, using it to root herself in reality. *This is real*, she told herself. *My Sarah is coming back*.

They crossed the lawn toward the woods. Her father's warning echoed in her head. *Only derelicts hang out back there*. Junie bit her lower lip. She could do this, for herself, for Ellen, and even for Brian. *Brian*. Damn, they should have waited for him to arrive. It was okay, she decided. She could always come back with him later, if they were so inclined. Even though Brian had gone there alone to leave flowers on the rock, Junie still worried that coming back, with his family to bear witness, a clear and present acknowledgment to further solidify the truth that befell Ellen, might be too painful for him. That worry lingered in her mind like a beacon, alerting her to her changing tone toward him. She liked the feeling.

Sarah skipped ahead. Junie walked beside Ruth, with Peter behind them.

"Can you believe it? Our girl is back," Ruth said conspiratorially.

"I'm afraid to believe it, so we'd better not talk

about it." Junie felt Peter's hand on her shoulder. She spun around.

Peter's eyes held hers. "I'm truly sorry, with all of my heart and with every inch of my soul." He put his hand over his heart. "I never meant to hurt her, Junie. I hope you can forgive me."

Junie rolled her lips into her mouth to keep from sobbing. She nodded, letting Peter guide her into an embrace.

They stood by the water's edge, Junie holding Ruth's hand, Peter's head bowed, hands clasped before him. The leaves swayed in the breeze, filling the air with a gentle, swooshing rhythm. Sarah walked beneath the long branches, along the rocks, toward the unforgiven tree.

Junie gasped. "Sarah, honey—"

Ruth squeezed her hand. "Let her be."

Junie bit her lip, sure she'd put a hole right through it. *Okay*, she thought. *I can do this*. "Be careful," she called to Sarah.

Sarah turned quickly, flashing a bright smile. Junie's breath caught in her throat. *Ellen*. "Mom," she managed, just before falling to her knees. The memory came tumbling back in fits and spurts, like an old movie reel.

Ellen taunting Brian. "I'm telling!"

Brian standing on Lovers' Rock, telling her to shut up.

Ellen pointed at him. "Dad's gonna kill you!"

Brian lifted a rock.

No, no! Junie's mind called out.

His arm drew back, as if in slow motion. Junie flashed to Ellen, whose arms flew up. "No!" she screamed.

Brian's arm pushed forward. The rock flew from his hands. Junie's chest would explode. She had to help Ellen. She saw herself moving toward her.

A deep *thunk* stopped her in her tracks. The rock hit the tree, then shot at Ellen with such force that she lost her balance.

No! Junie silently screamed.

Ellen fell into the water. Her legs kicked up. She was under the water, her arms shot to the sides.

Brian scrambled down from the rock.

Junie's legs were paralyzed. She watched Brian sprint to Ellen, stumbling over a large root and finally reaching the water. Ellen had floated downstream, her arms out to her sides, her eyes closed, her body unmoving.

"June? Junie?"

Ruth's voice broke through the memory. Junie fought to remain with Ellen. She wasn't ready to leave. She could change the outcome. She could save Ellen—scream before Brian threw the rock.

"Call 911," Ruth shrieked.

Junie lay in a fog. *Don't call 911,* she said in her mind. *We can save her. We can revive her,* she thought, thinking of Ellen. She felt her fingers move as she came to. She reached for her mother's arm, grabbing hold so tight that she could feel her bone. Junie scanned the water's edge, frantically searching for Sarah. She caught sight of her sitting by the water, unaware of the unfolding drama. Junie gasped for breath.

"Should I call?" Peter knelt beside her. "Junie? Are you okay?"

Junie blinked away the fog in her mind. "I saw it. I remember," she said. "That day. The day." Junie sat on the ground, her knee aching from the impact of the fall, her heart racing. She looked up at Peter, renewed strength seeping into her limbs. She'd recalled it. She'd actually recalled the moment that Ellen died. Her heart ached, but the relief of the truth pushed that ache aside. "Brian didn't hit her with the rock. He didn't do it. It hit the tree." She reached for her mother's hand. "He wasn't lying. I was there. I saw it. The rock hit the tree."

Her chest heaved up and down with each panting breath. She'd seen Ellen's final moments. It pained and relieved her. What did Ellen think at the moment when her foot slipped on the wet rock and she tumbled backward, the cool water hitting her back? As she closed her eyes for what would be the final time, did her world go black instantly, or did she have time to wish for something more? Did she hurt, or was there really a light to guide her from her pain? Junie would never know, and that hurt almost as much as losing her best friend did. When the dam broke and her sobs pushed forth, they carried a release so great she felt as if she could see clearly for the first time in years. Memories streamed back—her run back to Katie's house. The pact they'd made—not to tell anyone what she'd seen. *Katie.*

Oh my God. She had to see her. She'd held on to the secret for so long, to protect whom? Junie? Brian? Did it matter? No, she decided, it didn't. For whatever reason, Katie had held their pact as sacred, and Junie owed her her life, or more accurately, her husband's life.

Chapter Fifty-Five

When Katie opened the door, Junie flushed with embarrassment. She hadn't taken her seriously, and she'd treated her badly. She fumbled with her keys until Katie reached for her. Junie fell into her arms. "I'm so sorry for being such a witch. I owe you so much."

Katie swatted the air. "It's okay," she said, but Junie heard a hesitation in her voice.

"I'm sorry. I...Can we talk?"

They talked for what felt like hours but must have been only minutes. Junie explained, through tears that she could not control, what she'd recalled and how she'd repressed the memories. Katie listened, nodding at times, and finally, thankfully, she reached for Junie's hand. Junie realized that Katie never put Brian throwing the rock together with Ellen's disappearance, and she was relieved.

"It's okay, sweetie," she said. "I believed you when

you said you didn't remember. I was angry, but that was just my nutty brain thinking this was all some kind of glorified sign. I mean, I know that we weren't that close back then, but that pact." She averted her eyes. "I thought it meant something more than it did."

"Why did you protect the pact for so long?" Junie asked, feeling like a cad. She should have been a better friend.

"I don't know. I thought it was bigger than us, that I was keeping something treasured that would tie us together maybe." She lifted her eyebrows. "It's stupid. I should have said something. I wasn't lucky like you, I *did* remember." Her words were not spiteful, simply honest. "I knew that if we told the police that Brian had thrown a rock at Ellen they'd think he was behind her disappearance, or at least they'd investigate him." She blushed. "I had a major crush on him. You know that, right?"

Katie had no idea to what degree she really had protected Brian. "My mom told me."

"I just didn't want him to get in trouble. Did you figure out what happened to Ellen after all?"

Junie wrapped her lie in the truth. "No, but at least there are no more secrets."

Chapter Fifty-Six

Junie awoke from her catnap on the couch to find Sarah staring at her. Her heart sank. Her eyes dropped to Sarah's crotch out of habit. Dry. Thank God.

"Hi, honey. Sorry. Mommy must have dozed off."

Sarah handed her a drawing just as Ruth entered the room.

"Hey, sleepyhead. I think your emotional bucket ran dry and you crashed into sleep. It's good for you. You needed it."

"Sorry, Mom." Junie sat up and dropped her eyes to the drawing. Three stick figures: one with long yellow hair, one with short brown hair, and a child, Sarah, with yellow curls drawn as swirly lines around her face. Off to each side was another person, a woman, drawn with a triangle skirt and dark hair, and a tall dark-haired man. *Mom, Peter.*

"This is beautiful," she said.

"It's our family," Sarah said.

"Yes, yes it is," Junie said.

The doorbell rang at exactly seven o'clock. Sarah ran down the stairs. "Daddy!"

Junie's heart skipped a beat. She'd just hung up from speaking with Shane and getting the lowdown on the upcoming week's schedule. Shane hadn't complained about her part-time schedule, but she'd be glad when she could return to a daily routine. She missed having dough beneath her fingernails, and somehow, baking at her mother's wasn't the same. She even missed her indecisive customers.

She filled a glass with water, watching her hands shake. She smoothed the new blouse she'd bought and hoped her new jeans and heels didn't look like she'd tried too hard.

"You gonna be okay?" Ruth smoothed a wayward lock of hair on Junie's shoulder.

Junie wrapped her hands around the glass to steady them. "Yeah, I think I am, actually." She set the glass down and faced her mother. "He is lovable, Mom, and so was Daddy."

The fifteen steps from the kitchen to the foyer took forever. Junie bit her lower lip, then released it. She didn't know what to do with her hands, but she didn't have to think about it for long. Brian met her in the hallway and reached for them.

"You look beautiful." His eyes ran over her body, sending a shudder of desire through her.

She smiled, unable to find her voice.

"Ready?" he asked.

She nodded.

"Dinner and a movie?" he asked.

"Yes." For the first time in a year, Junie didn't fill with anger when she looked at Brian. Hope swelled in her heart. Brian and Peter were working with their attorneys and dealing with the police. Brian had put his life and his career on the line for his daughter. *Baby steps,* Junie thought. *Baby steps.*

The End

Please enjoy a preview of HAVE NO SHAME

Have No Shame

Where civil rights and forbidden love collide.

Melissa Foster

"A gripping and poignant novel dealing with a subject once taboo in American society."
— *Hagerstown Magazine*

Chapter One

It was the end of winter 1967, my father was preparin' the fields for plantin', the Vietnam War was in full swing, and spring was peekin' its pretty head around the corner. The cypress trees stood tall and bare, like sentinels watchin' over the St. Francis River. The bugs arrived early, thick and hungry, circlin' my head like it was a big juicy vein as I walked across the rocks toward the water.

My legs pled with me to jump from rock to rock, like I used to do with my older sister, Maggie, who's now away at college. I hummed my new favorite song, *Penny Lane,* and continued walkin' instead of jumpin' because that's what's expected of me. I could just hear Daddy admonishin' me, "You're eighteen now, a grown up. Grown ups don't jump across rocks." Even if no one's watchin' me at the moment, I wouldn't want to disappoint Daddy. If Maggie were here, she'd jump. She might even get me to jump. But alone? No way.

The river usually smelled of sulfur and fish, with an underlyin' hint of desperation, but today it smelled like somethin' else all together. The rancid smell hit me like an invisible billow of smog. I covered my mouth and turned away, walkin' a little faster. I tried to get around the stench, thinkin' it was a dead animal carcass hidin' beneath the rocks. I couldn't outrun the smell, and before I knew it I was crouched five feet above the river on an outcroppin' of rocks, and my hummin' was replaced by retchin' and dry heavin' as the stench infiltrated my throat. I peered over the edge and fear singed my nerves like thousands of needles pokin' me all at once. Floatin' beneath me was the bloated and badly beaten body of a colored man. A scream escaped my lips. I stumbled backward and fell to my knees. My entire body began to shake. I covered my mouth to keep from throwin' up. I knew I should turn away, run, get help, but I could not go back the way I'd come. I was paralyzed with fear, and yet, I was strangely drawn to the bloated and ghastly figure.

I stood back up, then stumbled in my gray midi-skirt and saddle shoes as I made my way over the rocks and toward the riverbank. The silt-laden river was still beneath the floatin' body. A branch stretched across the river like a boney finger, snaggin' the bruised and beaten body by the torn trousers that clung to its waist. His bare chest and arms were so bloated that it looked as if they might pop. Tremblin' and gaspin' for breath, I lowered myself to the ground, warm tears streamin' down my cheeks.

While fear sucked my breath away, an underlyin' curiosity poked its way through to my consciousness. I covered my eyes then, tellin' myself to look away. The reality that I was seein' a dead man settled into my bones like ice. Shivers rattled my body. Whose father, brother, uncle, or friend was this man? I opened my eyes again and looked at him. *It's a him*, I told myself. I didn't want to see him as just an anonymous, dead colored man. He was someone, and he mattered. My heart pounded against my ribcage with an insistence—I needed to know who he was. I'd never seen a dead man before, and even though I could barely breathe, even though I could feel his image imprintin' into my brain, I would not look away. I wanted to know who had beaten him, and why. I wanted to tell his family I was sorry for their loss.

An uncontrollable urgency brought me to my feet and drew me closer, on rubber legs, to where I could see what was left of his face. A gruesome mass of flesh protruded from his mouth. His tongue had bloated and completely filled the openin', like a flesh-sock had been stuffed in the hole, stretchin' his lips until they tore and the raw pulp poked out. Chunks of skin were torn or bitten away from his eyes.

I don't know how long I stood there, my legs quakin', unable to speak or turn back the way I had come. I don't know how I got home that night, or what I said to anyone along the way. What I do know is that hearin' of a colored man's death was bad enough—I'd heard the rumors of whites beatin' colored men to death before—but actually seein' the man who had died, and witnessin' the awful remains of the beatin', now that terrified me to my core. A feelin' of shame bubbled within me. For the first time ever, I was embarrassed to be white, because in Forrest Town, Arkansas, you could be fairly certain it was my people who were the cause of his death. And as a young southern woman, I knew that the expectation was for me to get married, have children, and perpetuate the hate that had been bred in our lives. My children, they'd be born into the same hateful society. That realization brought me to my knees.

Chapter Two

It had been a few days since that awful night at the river, and I couldn't shake the image from my mind; the disfigured body lyin' in the water like yesterday's trash. At the time, I didn't recognize Byron Bingham. I only knew the middle-aged colored man from town gossip, as *that man whose wife was sleepin' with Billy Carlisle.* Daddy told me who he was after the police pulled him from the river. I know now that the purple, black, and red bruises that covered his skin were not caused from the beatin' alone, but rather by the seven days he'd spent dead in the river. I tried to talk to my boyfriend, Jimmy Lee, about the shame I'd carried ever since findin' that poor man's body, but Jimmy Lee believed he probably deserved whatever he got, so I swallowed the words. I wanted to share, but the feelin's still burned inside me like a growin' fire I couldn't control. It didn't help that some folks looked at me like I'd done somethin' bad by findin' Mr. Bingham. Even with those sneers reelin' around me, I couldn't help but want to see his family. I wanted to be part of their world, to bear witness to what was left behind in the wake of his terrible death, and to somehow connect with them, help them through the pain. Were they okay? How could they be?

I walked all the way to Division Street, the large two-story homes with shiny Buicks and Chevy Impalas out front fell away behind me. A rusty, red and white Ford Ranch Wagon turned down Division Street. There I stood, lookin' down the street that divided the colored side of town from the white side. Even the trees seemed to sag and sway, appearin' less vital than those in town. A chill ran up my back. *Don't go near those colored streets,* Daddy had warned me. *Those people will rape you faster than you can say chicken scratch.* I dried my sweaty palms on my pencil skirt as I craned my head, though I had no real idea what I was lookin' for. The desolate street stretched out before me, like the road itself felt the loss of Mr. Bingham. Small, wooden houses lined the dirt road like secondhand clothes, used and tattered. How had I never before noticed the loneliness of Division Street? Two young children were sittin' near the front porch of a small, clapboard house, just a few houses away from where I stood. My heart ached to move forward, crouch down right beside them, and see what they were doin'. Two women, who looked to be about my mama's age, stood in the gravel driveway. One held a big bowl of somethin'—beans, maybe? She lifted pieces of whatever it was, broke them, then put them back in the bowl. I wondered what it might be like to help them in the kitchen, bake somethin' delicious, and watch those little childrens' eyes light up at a perfect corn muffin. The short, plump woman had a dark wrap around her hair. The other one, a tiny flick of a woman with a stylish press and curl hairdo, looked in my direction. Our eyes met, then she shifted her head from side to side, as if she were afraid someone might jump out and yell at her for lookin' at me. I felt my cheeks tighten as a tentative smile spread across my lips. My fingertips lifted at my sides in a slight wave. She turned away quickly and crossed her arms. The air between me and those women who I wanted to know, thickened.

I felt stupid standin' there, wantin' to go down and talk to them, to see what the children were playin'. I wondered, did they know Mr. Bingham? Had his death impacted their lives? I wanted to apologize for what had happened, even though I had no idea how or why it had. I realized that the colored side of town had been almost invisible to me, save for understandin' that I was forbidden to go there. Those families had also been invisible to me. My cheeks burned as my feelin's of stupidity turned to shame.

A child's cackle split the silence. His laughter was infectious. I couldn't remember the last time I'd heard uninhibited giggles like that. It made me smile. I bit my lower lip, feelin' caught between what I'd been taught and the pull of my heart.

A Buick ambled by, slowin' as it passed behind me. I startled, rememberin' *my place*, as Daddy called it.

Daddy'd keep me right by his side if he could. He didn't like me to be around anyone he didn't know, said he couldn't take care of me if he didn't know where I was. I turned and headed back toward town, like I'd just stopped for a moment durin' a walk. The elderly white man drivin' the shiny, black car squinted at me, furrowed his brow, and then drove on.

I wondered what my daddy might think if he saw me gazin' down Division Street, where his farmhands lived. Daddy's farmhands, black men of all ages, were strong and responsible, and they worked in our fields and gardens with such vigorous commitment that it was as though the food and cotton were for their own personal use. Some of those dedicated men had worked for Daddy for years; others were new to the farm. I realized, surprisin'ly, that I'd never spoken to any one of them.

A long block later, I heard Jimmy Lee's old, red pick-up truck comin' up the road behind me. The town was so small, that I could hear it from a mile away with its loud, rumblin' engine. I wondered if someone had spotted me starin' down Division Street and told him to come collect me. He stopped the truck beside me and flung open the door, flashin' his big baby-blues beneath his wavy, brown hair. Jimmy Lee was growin' his hair out from his Elvis cut to somethin' more akin to Ringo Starr, and it was stuck in that in-between stage of lookin' like a mop. I liked anything that had to do with Ringo, so he was even more appealin' to me with his hair fallin' in his face.

"Alison, c'mon."

"Hey," I said, as I climbed onto the vinyl bench seat. He reached over and put his arm around me, pullin' me closer to him. I snuggled right into the strength of him. It was hard to believe we'd been datin' for two years. We'd met after church one Sunday mornin'. I used to wonder if Mama or Daddy had set it up that way, like a blind date, but there's no proof of that. Jimmy Lee's daddy, Jack Carlisle, was talkin' to my mama and daddy at the time, so we just started talkin' too. Jimmy Lee was the older, handsome guy that every girl had her eye on, and I was the lucky one he chose as his own. I'd been datin' Jimmy Lee since I was sixteen. He was handsome, I had to give him that, but ever since findin' Mr. Bingham, some of the things he'd done and said made my skin crawl. Others thought he was the perfect suitor for me. I wondered if that, along with my daddy's approval, was enough to make me swallow these new, uncomfortable feelin's that wrapped themselves like tentacles around every nerve in my body, and marry him.

I twisted the ring on my finger; Jimmy Lee's grandmother's engagement ring. In eight short weeks we'd be married and I'd no longer be Alison Tillman. I'd become Mrs. James Lee Carlisle. My heart ached with the thought.

The afternoon moved swiftly into a lazy and cool evenin'. I was still thinkin' about the women I'd seen on

Division Street when we stopped at the store for a few six-packs of beer. Jimmy Lee's favorite past time. Like so many other evenin's, we met up with my brother Jake and Jimmy Lee's best friend, Corky Talms, in the alley behind the General Store. I think everyone in town knew we hung out here, but no one ever bothered us. The alley was so narrow that there was only a foot or two of road between the right side of Jimmy Lee's truck and a stack of empty, cardboard delivery boxes, boastin' familiar names like Schlitz, Tab, and Fanta, lined up along the brick wall beside the back door of the store. On the other side of his truck, just inches from the driver's side door, a dumpster stood open, waftin' the stench of stale food into the air. Just beyond that was a small strip of grass, where Jake and Corky now sat. And behind them were the deep, dark woods that separated the nicer part of town from the poor.

I sat on the hood of Jimmy Lee's truck, and watched him take another swig of his beer. His square jaw tilted back, exposin' his powerful neck and broad chest. The familiar desire to kiss him rose within me as I watched his Adam's apple bounce up and down with each gulp.

Jimmy Lee smacked his lips as he lowered the beer bottle to rest on his Levi's. His eyes were as blue as the sea, and they jetted around the group. I recognized that hungry look. Jimmy Lee had to behave when he was away at college, for fear of his uncle pullin' his tuition, which I knew he could afford without much trouble. Jack Carlisle was a farmer and owned 350 acres, but his brother Billy owned the only furniture store in Forrest

Town, Arkansas, and was one of the wealthiest men in town. Jimmy Lee might have been king of Central High, but now he was a small fish in a big pond at Mississippi State. The bullish tactics that had worked in Forrest Town would likely get him hurt in Mississippi, and Billy Carlisle wasn't about to be humiliated by his nephew. Jimmy Lee was set to become the manager in his uncle's store, if he behaved and actually graduated. I was pretty sure that he'd behave while he was away at college and make it to graduation, but I rued those long weekends when he returned home, itchin' for trouble.

"Jimmy Lee, why don't we take a walk?" I suggested, though I didn't much feel like takin' a walk with Jimmy Lee. I never knew who we'd see or how he'd react.

He wrapped his arm around my shoulders and pulled me close. "How's my pretty little wife-to-be?" He kissed my cheek and offered me a sip of his beer, which I declined, too nervous to drink. I felt safe within his arms, but those colored boys were out there, and my nerves were tremblin' just thinkin' about what Jimmy Lee might do. I took my hands and placed them on his cheeks, forcin' his eyes to meet mine. Love lingered in his eyes, clear and bright, and I hoped it was enough of a pull to keep him from seekin' out trouble. Jimmy Lee was known for chasin' down colored boys when he thought they were up to no good, and I was realizin' that maybe he just liked doin' it. Maybe they weren't always up to no good. Ever since findin' Mr. Bingham's body, I noticed, and was more sensitive to, the ugliness of his actions.

I took inventory of the others. My brother Jake sat

on the ground fiddlin' with his shoelace. His golden hair, the pale-blond color of dried cornhusks, just like mine, though much thicker, was combed away from his high forehead, revealin' his too-young-for-a-nineteen-year-old, baby face. Jake seemed content to just sit on the grass and drink beer. He had spent the last year tryin' to measure up to our older sister's impeccable grades. While Jake remained in town after high school, attendin' Central Community College, Maggie, with her stellar grades and bigger-than-life personality, begged and pleaded until she convinced our father to send her to Marymount Manhattan College.

I wished more than ever that Maggie were home just then. We'd take a walk to the river like we used to, just the two of us, climb up to the loft in the barn, and giggle until Mama called us inside. We'd do anything other than sittin' around watchin' Jimmy Lee blow smoke rings and think about startin' trouble.

Corky cleared his throat, callin' my thoughts away from my sister. He looked up at me, thick tufts of dark hair bobbin' like springs atop his head as he nodded. I bristled at the schemin' look in his brown eyes. He smirked in that cocky way that was so familiar that it was almost borin'. With muscles that threatened to burst through every t-shirt he owned, one would think he'd be as abrasive as sandpaper, but he was the quiet type—'til somethin' or someone shook his reins. He came from a typical Forrest Town farm family. His father was a farmer, like mine, but unlike Daddy, who saw some value in education, Corky's father believed his son's sole purpose was to work the farm. Everyone in town knew that when Corky's daddy grew too old to farm, he would take over. Corky accepted his lot in life with a sense of proud entitlement. He saw no need for schoolin' when a job was so readily provided for him. I swear Corky was more machine than man. He worked from dawn 'til dusk on the farm, and still had the energy to show up here smellin' like DDT, or hay, or lumber, or whatever they happen to be plantin' or harvestin' at the time, and stir up trouble with Jimmy Lee.

Corky took a long pull of his beer, eyein' Jimmy Lee with a conspiratorial grin.

I tugged Jimmy Lee's arm again, hopin' he'd choose a walk with me over trouble with Corky, but I knew I was no match for a willin' participant in his devious shenanigans. Jimmy Lee shrugged me off and locked eyes with Corky. Tucked in the alley behind the General Store, trouble could be found fifty feet in any direction. I bent forward and peered around the side of the old, wooden buildin'. At ten o'clock at night, the streets were dark, but not too dark to notice the colored boys across the street walkin' at a fast pace with their heads down, hands shoved deep in their pockets. I recognized one of the boys from Daddy's farm. *Please don't let Jimmy Lee see them.* It was a futile hope, but I hoped just the same.

Jimmy Lee stretched. I craned my neck to look up at my handsome giant. Maggie called me Pixie. Although she and Jake both got Daddy's genes when it came to height, I stopped growin' at thirteen years old. While bein' five foot two has minor advantages, like bein' called a sweet nickname by my sister, I often felt like, and was treated as if, I were younger than my age.

Jimmy Lee set his beer down on the ground and wiped his hands on his jeans. "What're those cotton pickers doin' in town this late?" He smirked, shootin' a nod at Corky.

"Jimmy Lee, don't," I pleaded, feelin' kinda sick at the notion that he might go after those boys.

"Don't? Whaddaya mean, don't? This is what we do." He looked at Corky and nodded.

"It's just..." I turned away, then gathered the courage to say what was naggin' to be said. "It's just that, after findin' Mr. Bingham's body...it's just not right, Jimmy Lee. Leave those boys alone."

Jimmy Lee narrowed his eyes, put his arms on either side of me, and leaned into me. He kissed my forehead and ran his finger along my chin. "You let me worry about keepin' the streets safe, and I'll let you worry about—" he laughed. "Heck, worry about somethin' else, I don't know."

Corky tossed his empty bottle into the grass and was on his feet, pumpin' his fists. My heartbeat sped up.

"Jimmy Lee, please, just let 'em be," I begged. When he didn't react, I tried another tactic and batted my eyelashes, pulled him close, and whispered in his ear, "Let's go somewhere, just you and me." I hated myself for usin' my body as a negotiation point.

Jimmy Lee pulled away and I saw a momentary flash of consideration pass in his eyes. Then Corky slapped him on the back and that flash of consideration was gone, replaced with a darkness, a narrowin' of his eyes that spoke too loudly of hate.

"Let's get 'em," Corky said. The sleeves of his white t-shirt strained across his massive biceps. The five inches Jimmy Lee had on him seemed to disappear given the sheer volume of space Corky's body took up. He was as thick and strong as a bull.

I jumped off the hood of the truck. "Jimmy Lee, you leave those boys alone." I was surprised by my own vehemence. This was the stuff he did all the time, it wasn't new. I was used to him scarin' and beatin' on the colored boys in our area. It was somethin' that just *was.* But at that moment, all I could see in my mind was poor Byron Bingham.

Jimmy Lee looked at me for one beat too long. I thought I had him, that he'd give in and choose me over the fight. One second later, he turned to Jake and clapped his hands. "Let's go, Jake. We've got some manners to teach those boys."

"Don't, Jake," I begged. "Please, leave them alone!"

Jake looked nervously from me to Jimmy Lee. I knew he was decidin' if it was safer to side with me, which would lead to instant ridicule by Jimmy Lee, but would keep him out of a fight, or side with Jimmy Lee, which would not only put him in Jimmy Lee's favor, but also make his actions on par with our father's beliefs. He'd happily fight for a few bonus points with Daddy to balance out his poor grades.

My hands trembled at the thought of those innocent boys bein' hurt. "Jake, please," I pleaded. "Don't. Jimmy Lee—"

They were off, all three of them, stalkin' their prey,

movin' swiftly out from behind the General Store and down the center of the empty street. Their eyes trained on the two boys. Jimmy Lee walked at a fast clip, clenchin' and unclenchin' his fists, his shoulders rounded forward like a bull readyin' to charge.

I ran behind him, kickin' dirt up beneath my feet, beggin' him to stop. I screamed and pleaded until my throat was raw and my voice a tiny, frayed thread. The colored boys ran swift as deer, down an alley and toward the fields that ran parallel to Division Street, stealin' quick, fear-filled glances over their shoulders—glances that cried out in desperation and left me feelin' helpless and even culpable of what was yet to come.

Jimmy Lee, Jake, and Corky closed in on them like a sudden storm in the middle of the field. The grass swallowed their feet as they surrounded the boys like farmers herdin' their flock.

"Get that son of a bitch!" Jimmy Lee commanded, pointin' to the smaller of the two boys, Daddy's farmhand. The whites of his eyes shone bright as lightnin' against his charcoal skin.

Corky hooted and hollered into the night, "Yeeha! Let's play, boys!"

Bile rose in my throat at the thought of what I knew Jimmy Lee would do to them, and I couldn't help but wonder if he might take it as far as killin' those boys—if even by accident. I stood in the field, shakin' and cryin', then fell to my knees thirty feet from where they were, beggin' Jimmy Lee not to hurt them. Images of Mr. Bingham's bloated and beaten body, his tongue swollen beyond recognition, seared like fire into my mind.

Jimmy Lee moved in on the tremblin' boy. I was riveted to the coldness in his eyes. "No!" I screamed into the darkness. Jimmy Lee threw a glance my way, a scowl on his face. The smack of Jimmy Lee's fist against the boy's face brought me to my feet. When the boy cried out, agony filled my veins. I stumbled and ran as fast and hard as I could, and didn't stop until I was safely around the side of the General Store, hidden from the shame of what they were doin', hidden from the eyes that might find me in the night. There was no hidin' from the guilt, shame, and disgust that followed me like a shadow. I sank to my knees and cried for those boys, for Mr. Bingham, and for the loss of my love for Jimmy Lee.

(End of Sneak Peek)
To continue reading, be sure to pick up
HAVE NO SHAME

Every paperback and digital copy of HAVE NO SHAME provides readers with two full versions of the book and an option to read with or without the dialect in the narration

Acknowledgments

My deepest gratitude goes out to my readers, friends, family, bloggers, and social media fans and friends, who have inspired, supported, and encouraged me during my writing journey. Special thanks to Esther Iseman, PhD, who was kind enough to provide resources regarding repressed memories and walk me through several scenarios to flesh out Junie's life; Nicole Cook, an amazing baker and treasured friend, who helped me to create Junie's Life Sucks Bars and other delicious recipes; Kathleen Shoop, Patricia Fordyce, Hilde Alter, and Kian Vencill, who read early versions and helped me to bring my characters to life.

Big hugs to my editors, Kristen Weber and Penina Lopez, and my proofreaders, Jenna Bagnini, Juliette Hill, and Marlene Engel. Without each of you, my books would not be as well received. I'm not an easy person to work with when it comes to refining covers, and I am indebted to Natasha Brown for nudging and tweaking my cover with the patience of a saint. Thank you, Rachelle Ayala, for always making time to format (and reformat many times) my books. Your generosity does not go unnoticed.

The original title of this book was *Petals in the Wind*, and I'd like to thank Heather Taylor Severin, who entered to win a contest on my Facebook fan page to come up with a new title. Thank you, Heather. *Where Petals Fall* is perfect.

To my husband and children, once again, you amaze me with your patience and understanding of my crazy schedule. I adore you all.

Melissa Foster is an award-winning, International bestselling author. Her books have been recommended by USA Today's book blog, Hagerstown Magazine, The Patriot, and several other print venues. She is the founder of the Women's Nest, a social and support community for women, and the World Literary Café. When she's not writing, Melissa helps authors navigate the publishing industry through her author training programs on Fostering Success. Melissa hosts Aspiring Authors contests for children, and has painted and donated several murals to The Hospital for Sick Children in Washington, DC.

Visit Melissa on her website, or chat with her on The Women's Nest or social media. Melissa enjoys discussing her books with book clubs and reader groups, and welcomes an invitation to your event.

Melissa's books are available on Amazon, Barnes & Noble, and most online retailers.

www.MelissaFoster.com